THE SHAMAN BOY

PRAISE FOR THE SHAMAN BOY

'Caroline Pitcher writes very well indeed and I am astonished by her inventiveness and the richness of imagery and ideas. It's a feast of a book.'

– Berlie Doherty

'Packed with sights, sounds, smells and tastes, this is a story to savour with flavours that will linger.'

– Elizabeth Kay, author of *The Divide*

'Wonderful, absorbing . . . Caroline Pitcher has a sensitive and vital imagination – and she's a fantastic storyteller.'

– Leslie Wilson

'A compelling and uplifting read . . . The characters leap from the page . . . the plot is skilful and compelling.'

– Elizabeth Lindsay

Caroline Pitcher

THE SHAMAN BOY

EGMONT

For Richard, Lauren and Max, with all my love

EGMONT
We bring stories to life

This edition published 2007
by Egmont UK Limited
239 Kensington High Street
London W8 6SA

Text copyright © 2007 Caroline Pitcher
Cover copyright © 2007 David Wyatt
Music for 'Luka's Song' © 2006 Max Johnson

The moral rights of the author and cover illustrator have been asserted

ISBN 978 1 4052 0851 2

1 3 5 7 9 10 8 6 4 2

www.egmont.co.uk
www.carolinepitcher.co.uk

A CIP catalogue record for this title is available from
the British Library

Typeset by Avon DataSet Ltd, Bidford on Avon, Warwickshire
Printed and bound in Great Britain by the CPI Group

NOTE FROM THE AUTHOR

When a man with hair of frost and a cloak of
earth colours first strode into my imagination, he
was followed. There was a snow leopard, a golden
eagle, swallows, a pack of wolves, an otter, a hare,
a vulture, an owl and many other creatures from
the natural world. And there was Luka.
This is Luka's story. Travel with him.
Share his fears and joys, and the magic
that can either save him or put him
in extreme danger.

CONTENTS

Part Three: Summer

PART ONE: WINTER

A man walks in the mountains. His hair is white as frost.
At his shoulder flies an owl, and a hare runs at his feet.
Seven wolves wait at a distance.

The man is a shaman from the past.
He swings down the bundle of twigs from his back. With
a pinch of tinder and a piece of iron, he makes a fire
and his face shines gold.

He looks around him. There is one creature missing.
So the man with the hair of frost puts his fingers in his
mouth and whistles.

Down from the mountains bounds a snow leopard. Her
fur is dappled with clouds. She settles by the fire and
wraps her long tail around herself.

A boy will come looking for this cloud cat. The boy will
become a shaman too.

But the shaman boy is reckless.

1

INTO THE BLANKET CHEST

Luka was awake all night long, but not because it was so cold.

The owl was hooting out in the bare fruit trees, but that wasn't why.

He made himself stay awake.

At last he heard what he was waiting for.

It came padding out of the trees, through the hole in the wall into the snowy yard and snuffled at the door, *chuff* . . . *chuff*. It had come for him.

Luka's sight was slipping away. He was almost blind and could only see shadows. His parents were gone. He did not want to spend his life alone in the dark, not yet, and he did not want to listen to that whispering and name-calling, '*Idiot. Saphead. Moonraker. My mother knows who you really are.*'

Luka had nothing left to lose. So he was going to follow his dream.

He lay huddled in his blankets by the fire. He heard his brother Jez get up and leave for the bakery. The door closed, and at once Luka struggled out of his nest of blankets and felt his way up the staircase. He had to be careful because Jez had hacked out some of the wood to burn on their fire this terrible winter. Upstairs, the floorboards were rotten, with dynasties of mice living underneath. Luka wriggled across on his tummy, until he could put out his hand and touch the blanket chest.

Jez told him that their great-grandfather had made the chest from an oak tree, carving acorns with little impy faces and oak leaves all around the lid. Luka liked to trace the faces with his fingers and feel their pointed noses and grins. The blanket chest was the perfect place to hide. Luka lifted the lid and climbed inside. There was only just enough room because it was full of scratchy blankets they had been given in the war.

Luka let the lid fall shut, and there he crouched, listening.

He heard the dog sniffing around the chest. He heard the bus, slow as a woodlouse in the snow, changing gear on the hill, coming to take him to the orphanage for another long day. The engine coughed and died away. Peter the bus driver coughed too, because he smoked too many cigarettes. Luka hated that smell on the bus in the mornings.

There was a knock on the door, a *Come on, hurry up!* knock. The dog barked. Luka held his breath. Another knock. Another bark. The engine coughed and the bus chugged away. Luka let his breath go, *Phew!* With his lips against the scratchy blankets, he said, 'I'm very sorry, Imogen, but I can't come to the orphanage today. I am going to make everything change.' And Luka shook with excitement at what he was going to do.

He climbed out of the blanket chest. He crawled downstairs and felt all around his nest of blankets for his boots. He pulled them on. They were still soaking from yesterday's snow and they clung to his ankles like wet hands, so that Luka wished he had left them nearer the fire last night. Cold air rushed past his face and he knew that the dog was wagging her tail, because she thought they were both going out somewhere.

'Out of the way, dog, or I'll fall over you.' He dragged the chair to the back door and stumbled up on to it. He felt for the bolts. The top bolt was stiff. The bottom one was easy, but he had to tug hard at the door because the wood had warped with damp. One last great tug, and the door sprang open. The dazzling white world rushed straight in at him, as if the snow was made of sequins.

'Stop it, world,' said Luka. He screwed up his eyes and concentrated, trying to see the marks on the ground. *Yes. There they were. A trail of dark roses in the snow.*

Luka stuck out his right arm with his hand held straight. He turned his hand over and placed the palm in a dark rose. It was the wrong way up. He got up off the step, went down into the yard and turned back towards the doorstep. With his fingertips, he traced the cold indent of a round pad in the paw print. He touched it with his palm. He traced four strong toes, but found no place for his thumb.

'It has paws three times as big as my hands,' he cried.

He stood up and went inside for his gloves, the lunch Jez had packed for him to take to the orphanage, and the honey-coloured drum. He stuffed them down into his backpack and pulled it over his shoulders. The dog tried to come with him, but Luka heaved the door shut against her. Squinting hard at the ground, he crawled on all fours following the trail of paw prints through the snow, all the way round the yard and back again, and out through the hole in the wall.

In the kitchen the dog whined and scratched at the door. She had smelled tasty hare earlier, but now there was another sharper smell. It smelled of danger and beast. In the night she had heard howling from way back in her wild dog memory, but it was not the howling of dogs. The hair round her neck rose into a stiff ruff from fear.

2

THE CINNAMON HOUSE

Jez trudged through the snowy streets. Over the years, war had destroyed most of the village and left ruins, like the children's toppled towers of bricks at the orphanage. Jez never understood who was fighting, or why. Their little land in Eastern Europe was thick with soldiers from other countries and it had changed names so many times, no one could remember what it was called in the first place.

A tall hare crossed his path. It sat at the side of the street, looking at him.

'Get away, hare,' shouted Jez. 'You're lucky I haven't got a gun with me.'

The hare twitched its black-tipped ears and loped away behind a tumble of stones. Jez hurried on, glancing to either side of him. You never knew if there was a sniper behind a door, or in the shell of a house, until you heard the whine of his rifle, or the cry of his victim. There was always an enemy, even if you did not know who it was. This enemy lit matches in people's gas canisters so that they roared into flames. This enemy hid up in the church tower and fired when the bells tolled. This enemy stole chickens and sheep, ripped cabbages out of the fields, dug up potatoes, plunged the village into darkness and put poison in the wells and the water pipes. This enemy caused the screaming that woke Jez and Luka early, making them bury their heads under their pillows because they could not bear the sound.

Yet the chestnut tree was still there. Jez stopped underneath it, and gazed up into the web of branches, fringed with frozen white. He could see buds shiny as little hooves. Every autumn his father had lifted him up to reach the chestnuts. *Split open the spiny green case, and find the glossy nut hiding in velvet. Soak it in vinegar, load it on string and let battle begin!* Jez had been the school conker champion three years running.

Jez sighed, shook his father's smiling face right out of his head.

At the end of the broken street was the bakery. It was a tall house with a cat-slide roof and a blue door, and it leaned out from a corner, as if it wondered whether to fall down like its ruined friends. Jez's blind little brother Luka loved to come here to make bread stars and fish, kneading and punching the soft, stretchy dough. Dimitri the baker would put them in the oven for breakfast. Sometimes Dimitri asked Luka to make him a bread swallow, because it was his favourite bird. Then Luka would play with Syrup the ginger cat and her six kittens with their tiny cushioned paws.

Jez heaved open the big blue door, and breathed in the warm smell. So many buns, and apples stuffed with honey and raisins had been baked there for so many years that even the stones in the wall were steeped in the warm, spicy cinnamon sweetness and the tiles in the roof were full of it.

After the grey snow light in the street, the bakery was pitch black. A white shape crouched by the ovens, looking like a dragon with a furnace of flickering flames near its head. The dragon stood up and shouted, 'Morning, Jez.' It was Dimitri, his apron tied tightly across his stomach and his baker's hat pulled down to his black caterpillar eyebrows.

'Morning, Dimitri,' grunted Jez. He washed his hands in icy water. A tray of plaited loaves waited to be baked. Jez brushed them with milk and began to sprinkle them with poppy seeds.

The street door swung open and a blast of icy air roared into the bakery. Big Katrin stamped her red boots on the mat, *one, two!* and slammed the door shut. She pulled off her blue scarf and shook out her hair. Snow flew on to the stone floor and winked as it melted. She reached inside her fur coat and slapped a folded newspaper down on the table. She looked at Dimitri and she looked at Jez.

'Fix us some tea, Katrin,' said Dimitri. 'Tea upstairs and coffee downstairs. That's the way it's always been and that's the way it is.' Katrin clomped upstairs.

That's the way it is, mouthed Jez. They said the same things every day, and he liked that. He liked the routine. When he had finished sprinkling poppy seeds on the bread he slid the tray into the oven and closed the door.

'There's a Just For Us loaf for breakfast,' said Dimitri. He slapped his round stomach. It sounded like someone bursting a paper bag. Down the stairs clopped Katrin, bearing the brown teapot on a tray like a crown on a cushion for a king. The three of them sat with their hands wrapped round the warm mugs, and the Just for Us loaf dripping with melted cheese in the middle of the table. The tea soothed Jez's stomach.

'How is your little brother today?' asked Dimitri.

Jez sighed. 'He's reckless. He scares me, Dimitri. His eyesight is far worse, but he will never admit it.'

'It must have been the shock of losing your mother and father,' said Dimitri. 'You know Katrin and I will do whatever we can for you both.'

Big Katrin nodded, then dipped her head as she remembered who had stopped her that morning. Three strangers. Two men and a woman, her face shadowed by a hood trimmed with white ermine, who bent close to Katrin and said, 'We have been told to collect up the orphans.' The hairs on the back of Big Katrin's neck rose.

'We will pay well for them,' said the woman. 'But where are they?'

Buying children? Katrin had raised her arm and pointed down the road out of the village.

'You mean they have already been taken?' said the woman. Katrin nodded fiercely.

The strangers hesitated, exchanging glances. They turned and set off down the road. Only when they were out of sight did Katrin hurry on her way, thinking, *How long before they come back from their wild goose chase?*

Now Big Katrin sighed. She picked up the

newspaper. She unfolded it and smoothed it out on the table. She looked at Dimitri, and she looked at Jez. On the front page was a photograph.

'It's just a snowdrift,' said Jez. 'So what's special about that?'

Dimitri popped his spectacles on the end of his nose and looked again.

'It's not just a snowdrift, Jez. It's a wild beast on the loose. Haven't you heard about it? It took a sheep and dragged it up into a tree. It ate some and left the rest for later.'

'Rubbish,' said Jez. 'It's a hungry fox, or someone nicking food to feed their children. They just want to put something in the newspaper that isn't war. *And* the paper's four days old.'

Dimitri stabbed his floury finger at a faint shadow in a corner of the photograph.

'That's a beast,' he insisted.

'That's a snowdrift, Dimitri,' guffawed Jez.

'Maybe it is. Maybe it isn't. You be careful, Jez. And look after that little brother of yours.'

'Oh, he'll be at the orphanage by now,' said Jez. 'He really likes Imogen who works there. He'll be safe with her.'

'Good, because there's badness on the move,'

warned Dimitri. 'That Vaskalia woman was here yesterday, spying on the bakery. Katrin thinks she was looking for Luka.'

'I haven't seen Vaskalia since that time at school,' said Jez.

'What time at school? Tell me.'

'It happened years ago. Before the fighting when the school was still open. Vaskalia's son, Simlin, was as secretive and spiteful as a stinging nettle. He had a mark like a scorpion on his forehead . . . he called me names. In class he stuck pins in my back. Once he climbed up to the rafters and poured sour milk on me. After Dad had – had gone, he began to whisper behind his hand, just loud enough for everyone to hear. About Luka. Called him "a muggins, a moron, a white-eyed idiot".'

'What a snake. Luka was so little then. What happened?'

'I slapped Simlin. Hard. It made a red mark like a poppy on his milksop cheek. I felt much better at first. He wasn't going to call *my* brother names.'

'I don't blame you, Jez,' said Dimitri, 'but I bet that wasn't the end of the story.'

'It certainly wasn't,' said Jez. 'Next morning, the kids shouted, "Here comes Simlin's mother, the doll woman with her evil eye!" I tried to hurry past, but she grabbed my wrist and threatened me with werewolves and walking corpses if I did not say *sorry* to her son. She spat lime green on my foot. For three days, my wrist had a bracelet of blood round it and I had a blister on my toe as big as an orange mushroom.'

'Oh, Jez,' groaned Dimitri. 'Nobody should get on the wrong side of Vaskalia. Least of all you and Luka. Such bad things happened in the past.'

'What things?'

'Vaskalia wanted to marry your father.'

Jez saw Big Katrin nod and felt a twinge of fear because her face was so serious, her eyes so grave.

Dimitri went on, 'Vaskalia wanted your father for herself. But he went travelling and returned with your lovely mother. Vaskalia hated that. She's jealousy incarnate, Jez. And she knows a secret about your family. She hardly ever goes out of her five-sided house, so if she *is* up in the village . . . be careful, very careful.'

Jez stood up and said, 'Dimitri, *please*. You're scaring me. I'll look after Luka. I'll keep him safe from Vaskalia, and safe from this wild beast.'

3

THE ROPE BRIDGE

'*Why am I still crawling on all fours?*'

Luka stood up in the snow, blinking at the paw prints. The creature must be as big as the lion in the book his mother had read to him every night, years ago, before the dull boom of war, the dust-burst explosions and the crack of rifle fire began. It was a special book, with a cover as blue as gentian flowers, full of stories of griffins and dragons, and wild creatures dancing round a fire. There was a man in a beautiful cloak of colours. When the book was closed, the edges of its pages shone as steadfast gold like his mother's wedding ring.

Then people fell out of Luka's world. He did not know what had happened to his father. Jez would not talk about it. Soon after his father disappeared, Luka's sight began to fade. Worst of all, his mother pined. And then she was taken away from them.

Luka knew he was different. In his mind's eye he saw a picture of himself, standing behind glass, resting his palms against it. On the other side of the glass, Jez, Dimitri and Big Katrin, Imogen and the children from the orphanage read and baked, played and drew. They looked into each other's eyes and mirrored each other's frowns and smiles. Luka lived outside their world, so he was going to find the world of his dream. Last night the Cloud Cat had come looking for him, padding round his house in the dismal village, leaving its tracks to show him the way.

'Today it's all going to change!' cried Luka as he followed the trail, with his arms stuck out from his sides to help his balance. He giggled, thinking he was like a penguin.

He needed to be careful. Far beyond the village he knew there were mountains. To reach them he would have to go over the hills and he hoped that the Cloud Cat would not lead him to the Depths of Lumb.

At first Luka enjoyed the rhythm of his slow, heavy steps. The snow hushed everything. But soon, his eyes felt sore from the wind. He wanted to shut his eyelids and his lungs were beginning to burn with each breath. His chest heaved. His throat felt raw. The hush was closing in on him.

He could no longer see the Cloud Cat's paw prints. He stopped.

There was something standing at his side. He knew it was taller than he was.

'Are you frozen too?' Luka asked. It did not answer.

He held out his hand, slowly. It was a tree. *No.* It felt too smooth for a tree.

It was a post, covered in ice. There was a rope leading away from it. Luka put out his other hand. There was a post on that side too, and a rope. Luka peeled off first one glove, then the other and lay them down in the snow by the posts. Then he kneeled down.

'Logs. They're little logs with gaps in between.'

He stuck his fingers into a gap in the wood. He could waggle them at the other side. There was twisted rope binding the logs together. He gave the logs a little push. They swayed.

With a sinking heart, Luka realised where he was: the rope bridge. He could hear Jez's warning voice in his head: *Don't go over the rope bridge, Luka. If you fall into the Depths of Lumb you'll never come out the same.*

Luka blinked, peering at the bridge through the

fuzzy snow. There! Halfway across the snow was all scuffed up. The Cloud Cat had come this way.

As soon as he set foot on the bridge, it began to shake. Luka grasped the rope with both hands to steady himself. The bridge creaked and swayed. He gripped the rope tighter. In his mind he saw Imogen's strong plait of hair and wished he was holding on to that instead, because his hands told him that this rope was thin and frayed and the wind was blasting down the gorge. Luka stopped, but told himself, 'No, keep going, keep going and get to the other side before the rope breaks.'

His foot felt ground again, a narrow path leading downwards. A vicious wind skimmed the snow and blasted it along, hiding any tracks there may have been.

There was a rustling sound down on the snow near him. What was it? Luka was too tired to care. All he wanted to do was lie down and go to sleep. Maybe just for a moment? No. If he went to sleep in this snow he would freeze to death. He passed his hand over his eyes. Hard little icicles hung from his hair. Ice crusted his nostrils. His lungs hurt. Tears froze on his cheeks, but he told himself, 'Everything will be fine once I find the Cloud Cat.'

The path began to go up, steeply. He felt bumps under the snow. Must be steps or big stones. Somehow he was on all fours again, crawling up, his hands and feet scrabbling for safe holds, his stomach shocked with cold, his eyes screwed shut against snow and tears.

No more stones. Luka tried to get his balance and stood up, wobbling. He opened his eyes but found that he was looking through two kaleidoscopes. Each eye was a circle of white splintered into prisms. Worse, he was hit from all sides by spiteful little winds, whining and stabbing at his face, and Luka thought he heard the whispering: *Idiot. Idiot!* He crouched down as if he was praying while the winds picked on him like a gang of bullies in a playground.

A sob hung in the air. It was *his* voice. 'Jez? JEZ!'

The winds changed direction. Luka knew then that it wasn't wind rushing at him, brushing his forehead and buffeting his cheek, but some thing that was alive. Wing beats. *Big* wing beats. Whatever it was, it had waited for him to be at his weakest.

'Don't, please!' he begged, battering the air to be rid of it. Useless. The thing was already out of his reach. He wrapped his arms around his head as it flew full at him.

Luka heard a cry, and knew that he was falling down to the darkest place.

4

EMPTINESS

In the darkening afternoon, Jez trudged home. He clutched a bag of warm scones and a pat of butter wrapped carefully in muslin by Big Katrin. He licked his lips as he thought of them. Luka would want to eat them with cherry jam.

The snow bowled through the ruined streets, covering the rubble and turning it into castles from a fairy tale. The winter had come months before and never left. The world was wrong. It had gone tilting away from light and warmth and it had forgotten to tilt back again.

Jez heard creaking. He glanced fearfully over his shoulder, but decided it was just a roof complaining under the heavy snow. He hurried on, then caught his breath and stopped short.

A bulky shape came swaying out of an alleyway. It lumbered down the street towards Jez. A man was stumbling by a donkey as it picked its way over the snowy cobblestones.

Jez hesitated. Should he turn and run? He saw that the man was nervous too, cowering against his donkey as if he wished he could disappear. The donkey was laden down with panniers. Sitting on its back was a young woman, wrapped up against the cold. *Refugees.*

The man's head was bound with scarves but Jez saw his frightened eyes. They were the shape of almonds. Jez knew then that the man was one of the mountain people.

Something about them touched Jez. He turned to watch them swaying down the road, and in spite of his wariness he called after them, 'I wish you a safe journey.'

The man did not turn round, but raised his hand in acknowledgement.

Jez thought of fire and warm scones and hurried on to his own house.

He unlocked the front door and burst in. 'Luka? I'm back! With scones and BUTTER.'

The dog slunk across the floor and lay at his feet. Her ears were set back, pulling the skin away from her eyes.

'What's the matter with you? Your eyes are bulging like humbugs. Luka? LUKA!'

Jez's voice hung in the empty rooms.

He ran upstairs. He looked around. He wrenched up the lid of the blanket chest, where he often found Luka hiding from everything. Luka wasn't there today.

Jez stomped downstairs. Someone had pulled back the bolts on the door into the yard. Jez wrenched it open and blinked out. Fresh snow covered the ground. He pulled the door shut, bolting it now, turned, treading on the dog's paw so that she yelped. Jez grumbled at her and stumbled his way out into the streets again, down the hill and across the ruined village to the orphanage. The dog ran behind him with her belly low to the ground.

The orphans lived in a crumbling building with dips in the roof and boarded-up windows. It had been the school, but when the fighting started people would not let their children out of their sight. The school closed down.

Now the building was surrounded with rubble and the front door was as full of holes as a colander. Men with guns had wanted someone who was hiding inside. They had peppered the door with bullet holes and shattered the small windowpanes faster than boys throwing stones.

Jez hurried inside, scanning the big room for

Luka. A little girl with curly black hair knelt on the floor, humming to herself as she built a castle with wooden bricks. She set a row of arches carefully along the top. Another girl sat still, watching her.

Jez saw the row of heavy iron cots in the corner. A child in nappies stood up in one of them, holding the bars as if he was in a cage. He watched Jez with huge eyes. Eva, who used to work at the school, hurried over to the child. Jez remembered Eva laughing as she played What's the Time, Mr Wolf? with them at school. She sang to the children too, in a voice as sweet as a bell. But soon after the fighting began, a bomb fell on her house and killed her son. The joy fled from her face and her eyes looked washed away with crying. She grew into an old woman who could not chase anyone.

The door at the opposite end of the room opened. In walked a tall girl, carrying a boy. This was Imogen. When she had first arrived in the village, Luka still had some sight left. He had described the pictures Imogen painted, her glossy plait of hair and her soft apricot skin. Jez had never stopped still for long enough to look at her until today. Her eyes were dark and full, and immediately made Jez feel clumsy.

The boy Imogen was carrying had no legs. He leaned forward and poked Jez in the ribs.

'You're looking for Luka, aren't you?' he squealed. 'Well, he didn't come today.'

This must be Aidan. Luka is right – his voice is fat.

Aidan narrowed his eyes as if he was sharing a big secret. He said, 'Luka is a bad boy. He can't see so he thinks we can't see him either. He plays that little drum and dances and pretends he's not here. He's very naughty.'

'He's no naughtier than you are, Aidan,' said Imogen. Her voice was low as a cello. She had curvy smooth eyebrows that made Jez think of the glossy wings of a swallow. She set Aidan down on a chair. He scowled up at her and stuck out his lower lip. Jez looked at the heavy plait of hair hanging down her back and remembered the bell rope in the old church.

'Maybe Luka has gone to meet you from work?' she said.

'Not without the dog,' growled Jez.

'He wants his independence before his sight goes completely.'

'Yeah. That doctor who came with the occupation army said it might be di-jenny-er . . .'

'Degenerative,' she said.

'I know what it's called,' snapped Jez. 'Luka's luckier than *this* lot of orphans. He's got me, he's got the dog and a house and food, and . . .'

'And soon he'll be quite blind. So he's testing the limits.'

'He's testing *my* limits,' grumbled Jez, but he thought, *maybe she's right. He's gone to the bakery on his own to meet me.* Jez made up a picture in his mind and concentrated on it: Luka sitting at the table in the bakery scoffing buns while Dimitri snored in his chair. Jez smiled as he remembered Dimitri picking up Luka and swinging him round, only to sit him down on Big Katrin's apple pie.

What I want every day now is comfort. Safety. Routine.

Jez sighed. He felt as if he was wearing a heavy belt. From the belt hung little metal effigies of everything he had lost: the bicycle he had been promised, a fishing rod, a set of carving tools, a football to kick around with his father, the cake for his fourteenth birthday which was the first birthday without his parents, the notes of a song his mother sang in the kitchen as she scored diamond patterns on big potatoes and put them round the sizzling meat, and two tiny metal people: his mother and father. The things he had lost hung like trophies of cold metal, weighing him down and stopping him breathing deeply enough.

He had never thought he might lose Luka, too.

5

THE MAN WITH THE HAIR OF FROST

Imogen said, 'I'll make you some tea and something to eat.'

Jez sat down awkwardly on a child's chair. His bony knees almost touched his chin. The children watched him. They had old, wary faces.

Imogen brought him a bowl full of hot porridge, with a pool of milk and a dollop of damson jam, and a glass of apple tea sweetened with honey.

Aidan lunged for Jez's bowl, chattering angrily like a squirrel. Imogen laughed and fetched him porridge too. Aidan put the bowl right up to his face and lapped noisily. Imogen turned to Jez and smiled and he felt himself blush. He suddenly wondered what he looked like and tried to smooth down his hair. It felt coarse, even a bit sticky.

He mumbled, 'Sorry. I get cross quickly, especially with Luka. And don't just tell me to hold my breath and count to ten.'

'Ten is too many, Jez. I get the children to count

to seven. They have to think of seven special things. Sometimes it's seven favourite stories. But I never ask them their seven favourite people, because their favourite people are often missing. They like counting seven good things to eat. They can all do that.'

She giggled softly, and Jez worried that she thought he was a clumsy peasant with no manners who ate his food much too fast.

'You're not from round here, are you? Your voice is different.'

Her smile faded. 'I'm from the south. I couldn't stay in my own town. One day all my family were taken, all my brothers and sisters, while I was at college. I found my home was just a heap of stones. So I work here, with these children. I make them a home instead.'

'They must drive you mad,' said Jez, glancing round at the blobs of porridge on Aidan's nose, the hare-eyed boy shaking the bars of his cot, and the little girls squabbling over the bricks.

'They get me through the day. I'm too busy to think much because I have to look after them,' she said. She spoke calmly. She thought about things before she spoke. *Not like me.*

He said, 'I – my parents have gone too.'

'There is always someone to help, Jez. You are not on your own.'

Jez felt tears welling in his eyes. *Quick, don't let her see.* He swallowed hard and said, 'What did Aidan mean about Luka playing a drum?'

Imogen went to a cupboard and fetched a small honey-coloured drum. She placed it on the table. It was made of wood with thin hide stretched tight across the circlet. Bears and wolves and deer with antlers ran around it, carved in the wood. Stick figures danced and waved their arms, and Jez saw the wigwam shape of a little fire with billows of smoke.

'There's a pair of drums,' said Imogen, 'but the other drum has gone missing. Luka plays them with his palms and fingers. It's like his heart beating. He closes his eyes. Sometimes he dances. He wears that fur coat from the dressing-up box. We have to guess which animal he is. He can really lose himself in things, can't he?'

'Yeah, well he's really lost himself this time,' sighed Jez, picking up the drum and turning it round in his hands. He thought of Luka's small, intent face, the skin so thin you could almost see through it. Round his eyes the skin was fragile as crocus petals, veined with mauve.

Imogen said, 'Does he ever tell you about his dream?'

Luka had *tried* to tell him, but Jez had ignored him. 'I haven't got time for dreams. I've got work and food to worry about.'

'He thinks so much of you, Jez,' said Imogen.

He glanced up. She had a pretty mouth, full, with pointed bows to the lips, like the mouth of the stone angel that used to perch on a high ledge in the village church. His face burned red with embarrassment.

'I painted Luka's dream,' she said. 'Look.'

She held up a picture of a group of figures around a fire.

'That's really good,' said Jez. 'I've never seen a man with skin so golden green . . . It's like an acorn before it's ripe.'

'Luka says it's golden green as a russet apple. The man's hair sparkles as white as frost. He wears a cloak. He's the master of wild creatures. He gathers them together, puts his fingers in his mouth and whistles. Like this . . .' and Imogen put two fingers in her mouth and whistled shrill as a steam train. All the children except Maria jumped and squealed and laughed.

'Down from the mountains bounds a big cat. It winds itself around the man's legs like mist. Luka calls it a Cloud Cat. It settles by the fire. It purrs so deeply when it breathes out that the whole earth hums. The Cloud Cat curls its long tail around its head like a scarf and goes to sleep. Luka says it thinks no one can see it if it covers its eyes with its tail.'

Imogen smiled and then bit her lip. 'I wonder if Luka has gone searching for this dream? It's so real to him. He knew exactly what this Cloud Cat looked like. I think it's a snow leopard. Wait, Jez.'

But Jez was already running out with the dog at his heels.

6

WAR TRUCK

Jez ran all the way to the bakery. Dimitri was in the yard, collecting logs for the morning.

'Dimitri, I can't find Luka,' gasped Jez.

'That's bad . . . he shouldn't be out, not with this wild beast on the prowl. And –' Dimitri stopped himself just in time. He had an awful feeling he already knew where Luka might be but he did not want to worry Jez even more. He said, 'I'll go and look for him.'

Tears welled in Jez's eyes. Dimitri would help, he always would.

'Thanks, Dimitri. If you search the village, I'll go towards the mountains. I bet he's crossed the Depths of Lumb, just because I told him not to.' Jez began to tremble, so to hide his fear he stammered '*Brrr*, it's so cold and damp. Don't forget to close the woodshed door. The last thing you want is wet wood,' and then he hurried home again.

The house was cold as an empty coffin. Jez

ran out into the yard.

'Luka? LUKA!' His voice ribboned away over the wall and up the hillside. No one answered.

He ran inside and rolled up a sleeping bag. He grabbed a rucksack and packed it with a torch, matches, a bundle of strong cord, a knife with a curved horn handle that had been his father's, apples and a lump of cheese. On top he put the scones and butter. He turned to go, and began to whistle a tune he'd heard often on the radio, a song about a blackbird singing in the night and then learning to fly.

The whistling died on his lips.

A pair of yellow eyes was watching him through the window. They blinked and vanished. Something fluttered past the window.

At his side, the dog whimpered. Jez made himself whistle again, like a kettle trying to boil. It helped a little.

Outside in the yard, the tracks were already mussed up and sprinkled with new snow. Jez saw a print from Luka's boot. There were long marks, too, the tracks of a hare, and there were larger, rounder prints. They all led towards the hole in the wall. Jez had to bend down to get through and the dog jumped through after him.

It was strange to walk up this hill without Luka touching his arm every few minutes to make sure he was still near. The world was silent. Jez saw just one light in the village below, bobbing through the streets like a glow-worm.

Dimitri. Maybe Imogen is right. I'm not on my own.

Jez and the dog went backwards and forwards, forwards and backwards in the snow, trying to follow Luka's footprints. The dog stopped suddenly with one ear pricked and the other flopped over like the flap of an envelope. There was something ahead, just for her, something moving. It had long, black-tipped ears. The dog chased after it, over the hilltop and out of sight.

'Dog. Get back here at once,' hollered Jez. He called and whistled and cursed her, but she would not come back.

Everything leaves me, even the dog.

Jez set off up the hillside towards the Depths of Lumb. He wore his father's coat and his mother's hat as if they were armour. He'd had to work hard to keep going without his parents. The world was such a vicious place. Stupid Luka did not realise what a dangerous thing he was doing.

A grey shape caught his eye. Its flight was slanted

and silent. A ghost. He dare not turn round to look at it. It flew ahead of him. It soared up to the top of the hill, and then back again, as if it wanted him to see it.

It swooped past again and landed in a tree ahead. It paused. Then came a loud SHRIEK. Jez almost jumped out of his skin. The grey shape shrieked again. Trembling, he made himself face it. Yellow eyes glared at him as if he was the only thing alive in the whole snowy world.

It was an owl.

'Get lost, owl,' shouted Jez and beat his hands together. Why couldn't it leave him alone? He tried to walk east, muttering and swearing away, but in spite of himself his legs changed direction. He tramped towards the owl, a big feathery bundle of hope in the emptiness.

The owl shrieked with triumph. Its voice boomed through the silent night like the foghorn of a liner in the ocean. It launched itself into the air and Jez followed.

Then began the worst snowstorm Jez had ever seen. It began quickly, a whirlwind of white flakes. There was nothing but snow between the earth and the sky and Jez felt as if he was spinning in the centre of a white top. The thicker it became, the darker it seemed. As Jez blinked up, the flakes looked like big pieces of soot. They stung his face with cold. They smothered him.

Jez lurched on, blinded by the blizzard, smack into something hard. It was a stone wall. Keeping his shoulder against it, he edged along, turned a corner and fell in through a doorway to shelter at last. There was snow on the floor, some wet hay and a little fireplace. There was a small, high window space with no glass. Jez sank down on to his knees. It must be a hut for goatherds.

Relief flooded through him like a hot drink. He struggled to his feet and pulled the door towards him, dragging it shut over thick snow. He would stay here until dawn.

When Jez woke, it was dark. He did not know whether it was night or morning. So much snow had fallen that it was pressed right up against the window space, and frozen hard as concrete. Not one chink of light or air could get through.

Jez threw himself at the door. He pounded it with his fists and shouted, but the door would not budge.

He was snowed in.

The sounds began. Sad, eerie sounds. Hungry

sounds. Near. *Wolves*. Coming nearer. They must have heard him shouting. He backed away from the door. The howling came closer until it was right outside the hut. It stopped. He heard sniffing and thought of sharp snouts, dripping red tongues and scimitar teeth.

Silence. Then another sound, worse than the howling.

Digging. They were digging him out, digging at the snow against the door.

Jez shook with fear. *I'm a piece of meat waiting in a deep freeze*. They were at the window now. The digging was steady, deliberate. A wolf could squeeze in through there. They would wriggle through, one at a time, to get him. How many were there?

Jez heard the whine of a rifle, far away. A flurry, and he knew the wolves were gone. He pushed at the snow in the blocked window. The digging wolves had dislodged it. Snow crumbled in the top right corner and Jez sobbed and scrabbled until he had pulled away enough snow to push his way through.

Outside in the emptiness he saw the snow scuffed with tracks. Yet the wolves were nowhere to be seen. The sky was sullen. Snow smoked the air. He felt as if he was struggling through cold ash from a volcano. Through it he glimpsed a tree, and on it sat the owl, waiting for him.

The further they went, the deeper lay the snow. Once Jez lost his balance and found himself waist-deep in a drift. Heaving himself out was exhausting. His footsteps became slower and heavier because his boots were soaking.

'Wait, owl,' he called. It had settled in a tree and stacked its wings, and now turned towards him a disgruntled face as if to say *I shouldn't be up in the daytime. I should be asleep with my head swivelled right away from sights like you.*

Jez scrabbled in his rucksack for one of Big Katrin's scones. It tasted rich and sweet. He chewed sultanas while his mind churned. He could drink the water from melted snow. He had food. He had matches for a fire.

Jez knew that if he could keep his hands busy, he would be all right. All his life he had whittled away at pieces of wood. He wanted to make beautiful things, as his great-grandfather had done. This was not the time or place to carve, but he could make himself some snowshoes. He scrambled to a birch tree and peeled off two wide strips of silvery bark. He bound them on to his boots, under his feet and round the heel with strong cord from the ball in his rucksack. He stood up and took careful steps. The snowshoes slid across the snow like silk.

Jez turned to look back at the village far below. The roofs that remained were gathered on the slopes like a flock of white birds and beyond them he could see the sea, ice grey and rilled with silver. He could see the road that led out of the village. That was the last place Jez had seen his mother, taken away in the back of a truck. Jez had watched helplessly with Luka clinging to his knees. His mother looked back at them, her face a pale star in the darkness of the truck. Even now, Jez felt as if someone was reaching inside his chest and wringing out his heart with both hands.

The snowlight up here was dazzling. It hurt his eyes. He peeled off bark from a branch, took his father's knife and cut a mask to shield his eyes from the glare. He made a hole in each side, threaded through some cord and tied it at the back of his head.

Jez was very proud of his snow specs. At least he would not suffer snow-blindness. Then he began to worry how long Luka could survive out in this wilderness. Soon the second night would fall.

Something heavy was inching its way across the snow. Jez flung himself to the ground, praying that the falling snow would turn him invisible. An armoured war truck with huge wheels covered in caterpillar treads inched past him. He heard voices and squinnied at helmets, bulbous and netted like the eyes of houseflies.

Jez lay motionless, long after the ground had stopped shuddering.

Night was here. The moon shone and turned the snow to liquid silver. The owl fluttered ahead as softly as a giant moth. It landed again and turned to glare at him. Jez heard water racing and saw a stream, the colour of mercury. It must be the source of the river. There were seven stepping-stones across the stream. They glowed pale as pearls. The owl was perched on the middle stone. It took off and led Jez over the stream and up to a mountain ledge.

'You've led me to the mountains by a different route, not over the Depths of Lumb,' breathed Jez. 'Thank you, owl.'

He sank down on the ledge. He craved sleep. He took out his sleeping bag and burrowed into it. In the distance was a dull boom of a landmine, and the crack and whine of a rifle shot. Jez felt as if these sounds had been with him all his life. In a waking dream, he saw his father's dear golden-skinned face as he crouched by the house wall, mouthing, *Stay there*.

At last, mercifully, that dream fled away.

What followed it was worse.

7

CHOIR OF WOLVES

Dimitri headed out of the village and down the road towards the sea. On the way he knocked on doors and asked people to look out for Luka. He trudged on until he came to a little wooden house with five sides. The roof sagged. Timbers stuck out of it like splinters. The windowpanes were cracked and thick with brown dirt, as if no human being had looked out of them for years, but Dimitri smelled wood smoke on the cold air. Vaskalia *was* there.

He rapped on the door, puffing breath into the darkness.

At once it creaked open.

Dimitri was a short man, but even he was taller than this woman wrapped in shawls and scarves. She wore mittens of matted black stuff with her fingers poking out. Around her scrawny wrists were copper bangles. Her eyes rolled at Dimitri. They looked different ways, so that he wondered if she could see behind him.

Her son Simlin hovered in the doorway behind her. Dimitri could see his pale face, his long hands and thin feet sticking out around her as if together they made some strange god image. Vaskalia's wideness hid her son's skinny body. Peering past her into the five-sided house, Dimitri could see a red eyeball of fire glowing in the middle of the floor. Shapes hung from the beams, fluttering in the wind from the open door. They might have been dried fish, or posies of herbs and flowers, or spare scarves. The earthen floor was littered with bones.

Dimitri cleared his throat and said, 'I'm looking for Luka. The boy who can't see properly.'

'I know perfectly well which boy you mean,' she snapped. 'I have seen him in all kinds of places. We can't help you.'

'You heartless hag!' cried Dimitri before he could stop himself. 'People would help you if your son went missing.'

'My son *wouldn't* go missing, baker man, because he never leaves my side. *You* are a fool to leave your bakery unattended. Who knows what evil might get in there?'

'What superstitious rubbish you talk, woman,' said Dimitri.

'Take care what you say to me, and take care out there,' she warned. 'The wolves have returned to the forest. You'd make a tidy tea for them, baker man.' She put her head on one side and whispered, 'Listen . . . listen to the wolves singing.'

The moment she spoke of wolves, Dimitri heard them. Far away. One wolf howled, then another, and another, each with a different note, howling in a mournful choir.

'A wolf choir sings of death, you know,' crooned Vaskalia. 'And *you* have forgotten your shotgun. It's a bad winter, baker man, but it's not as bad as the winters I knew as a child. I rode to school on a billy goat with my inkwell tucked in my armpit to stop it freezing. My childhood was full of real hardship.'

'And you think mine wasn't?' said Dimitri. 'But this winter is like no other. It's far harder. You know that.'

Vaskalia did not answer. From under her cocoon of shawls and scarves she took a little copper cup that glowed and held it out to him. A coy smile twitched her lips.

Dimitri hesitated, thinking that he was asking for trouble if he refused her hospitality. He raised the cup to his lips and knocked the liquid back.

Mmm . . . it was sweet and spicy, like nothing he had ever tasted before. It crept around his throat and chest like fingers of fire.

'That was a welcoming drink, from my very own recipe,' she crooned. 'I am *so* glad you liked it.' But then the flirt changed into a whirl of anger. 'Be off with you, fat man! If you are wise – which you are not – you'll be more careful about the way you speak to me tomorrow.'

'Don't worry, I'm going,' shouted Dimitri and he stormed away, muttering, 'Go boil up your cauldron, crone,' and wishing he had never talked to her at all.

He tramped on down the road, shining his torch ahead so that the beam bobbed on the snow like a will-o'-the-wisp. The inn was on a bend. The top storey had been blown off since Dimitri was last there. He could see light behind the windows and heard the murmur of voices as he turned the big ring handle of the door.

At once lights dimmed. Voices stopped. People had learned to dread the turning handle, the stranger at the door. Who would it be? Men with garlands of bullets around their necks, or someone bringing medicine for your child?

Dimitri peered into darkness. Bottles and glasses

glinted in the light from the fire, but there was no one to be seen.

'Friend,' he called. 'It's Dimitri from the bakery.' People rose from behind the tables. The lamps were turned up high again and lit their faces softly as if they were in an oil painting.

'Dimitri Founari!' cried the innkeeper. 'What brings you here on such a night?'

'I'm looking for the boy Luka. He's gone missing.'

'Is that the odd one? Jez's little brother?'

'That's him. Please, everyone, keep your eyes open. He might be sleeping in your barn, or he might have fallen down somewhere and broken his ankle.'

The innkeeper filled a glass for Dimitri. 'It's on the house,' he said, holding up his hand against the coins Dimitri offered. 'It's good to see you, even if it is trouble that brought you here. This bad winter has even turned my brandy to syrup. Please sit down, Dimitri.'

Dimitri did so, thankfully. He tipped back his glass and the warmth spread across his throat. He glanced round. There were faces he recognised but had not seen for months: George the shoemaker, Peter who drove the village bus, Ivan the blacksmith and that old doctor.

'That blind boy dinna come on me bus this morning, baker,' said Peter. 'I knocked and I knocked but no one answered.'

Before Dimitri could reply, a voice he did not recognise said, 'There's a wild beast on the loose. You men should hunt it down.'

'Our forest is full of wild beasts,' said the innkeeper as he polished a glass. 'They keep well out of the way because of the war.'

'You should do something about them,' growled the voice. It sounded like the toes of a boot swirling patterns in gravel. Dimitri had now had so many drinks that all he could see was three blurred figures sitting in the nook of the fireplace. Three hooded heads.

He said, 'We've always lived alongside the wild creatures. They don't bother us.'

'You should kill them before they kill you,' growled the voice. 'Think of the money you could make from their fur.'

Dimitri stood up. Twisted faces swam before him. The villagers' eyes were shining at the thought of a hunt. He sighed. There had been too much shooting and killing these last few years, but little food, money or comfort.

51

He saw a violin case on a table. He had not played his own fiddle for years. It lay up on a shelf at the bakery, covered in dust, because there were no weddings, parties or dancing days any more. There were only wakes, when everyone wailed and tore their hair with grief. And now Luka had disappeared. Dimitri wanted to weep because he loved Luka and Jez as if they were his own sons, and they had suffered so much already.

He opened the case, took out the fiddle and placed it on his shoulder. Taking the bow, he played music that was full of the sadness that had happened in the land. He did not play for long. He was beginning to feel unwell. His head hurt. He felt dizzy. He lurched off towards the door.

The hooded strangers leaned forward to watch him go.

8

GARLIC AND WET NELLIE

Dimitri wanted to keep on looking for Luka, but he felt too ill. His feet led him home. When he reached the bakery, he staggered straight upstairs to bed and fell asleep at once, still in his boots and greatcoat. He had wild, terrifying dreams of being chased by a spitting troll with a scarf around its head.

He woke up in a house that was hotter than he had ever known it. *Hot as hell*. Dimitri went slowly downstairs. He had a bad, bad feeling.

His baker's instinct sent him to look at the last of his yeast, the baker's miracle.

It had turned to brown sludge.

He went into his larder, lowered his face to the big white jug and sniffed. The milk smelled like dead fish. Dimitri felt his stomach heave. But the stone walls and floor kept the larder cool. How could the milk have turned so quickly?

What about the butter? Big Katrin used it to bake her cakes every third day, when the bread was finished. Dimitri fetched the three-legged stool. He climbed on to it, swaying with dizziness. The butter was slumped across the white marble slab. It began to drip down on to the floor and set into a greasy yellow pool.

'It's like candle wax,' groaned Dimitri. Teetering on the stool, he stuck his finger into the sludge and raised it to his lips.

'*Eugh*. It's rancid,' he spat.

The handle of the street door turned. Dimitri jumped down off the stool and crouched on the floor with his arms wrapped around his head. He heard her boots stamp on the mat, *one, two*. Dimitri turned his head beneath his arms and opened one eye. He could just see her standing in her coat. Her nose wrinkled. Dimitri stood up and watched her round the larder door. She untied her scarf and laid it carefully on the table.

Dimitri took a deep breath and trotted out of the larder.

'Oh. Hello, Katrin. The – er – yeast . . . milk . . . and butter . . .' He felt like a naughty little boy at school, telling tales to the teacher. He showed her the sludgy crumbs that would never raise the bread, and then the milk. She looked at him and she looked at the curdled milk. She sniffed. Then she opened a window, took the jug and poured the whole smelly lot on to the snow outside.

She headed for her butter. Dimitri ran after her and hopped up on to his stool so that his eyes were on a level with hers. Katrin's eyes reminded Dimitri of the dark brown sugar and cinnamon mix he sprinkled thickly on buns so that it melted into dark caramel.

Dimitri babbled away to her, all about the cottage with five sides and the dead fish and bones and leaves, and Simlin crouched by the fire.

'Katrin, she talked of spoiling and poison and she says she's seen Luka in all kinds of places . . .' Into his mind crowded old enemies, family feuds and ancient malice. He thought of lies, bad wishes, pins stuck into dolls' necks and curses hissed in corners.

Big Katrin looked at him for a long moment. She took a cloth and poured the rancid butter on to it, knotting the top. She wiped down the marble slab. She fished out the useless blob of yeast and wrapped it up in muslin.

Katrin cut thick slices of rich wet nellie. This was a village favourite, a pudding made from leftover bread, fruit and marzipan. She selected a ginger cake shaped like a bar of bronze, a golden cake studded with cherries, and a cake as thickly embroidered with nuts as the centre of a sunflower. From the back of a cupboard she pulled out folded cardboard and assembled a large box. She set her chosen cakes in the box and packed the gaps with the slices of wet nellie.

'What's all that lot for?' cried Dimitri. 'Where's your pride, Katrin?'

Katrin put on her scarf and tied it under her chin. All the while she gazed at Dimitri. He let himself have a little gaze back. Those eyes could turn a man into a blancmange.

'Wait, I'll come with you. I know exactly what to do.'

He ran into his larder and reached under the shelf where he kept a basket of vegetables. He rummaged until his hand closed round a bulb that felt as if it was wrapped in tissue paper. Garlic. A fat, juicy bulb made of pink and white cloves wrapped in their papery skins.

Dimitri waved it at Katrin. He hesitated. Then he opened his mouth wide, shoved the whole bulb in and bit it. *Garlic*. THAT was how to deal with curses, vampires and old magic. Dimitri spluttered and coughed. His eyes and nose streamed until he had to turn away from Katrin and spit the whole chewed bulb on to the floor.

Katrin looked at him. She waved her hand in front of her nose and pulled a face. She handed him a small piece of wet nellie to dull the burning taste of garlic in his mouth.

Then she closed the cake box again, and waited for Dimitri to open the door.

9

THE DEPTHS

The thing knocked Luka down into the Depths of Lumb.

He tumbled over and over in a hailstorm of stones and rattling scree. Stopped. Struggled to sit up. His back ached. His body stung. He was so cold that his bones hurt and he could not get his breath properly. There was weight all round his face, cold weight. He stuck out his tongue and tasted snow. *Idiot. Idiot!*

Luka set his mind's eye on the Cloud Cat. It prowled far away, secretive in its leopard landscape of snow and rocks. It paused, its lithe body silent, tense, and leaped across a mountain chasm. The cat's grace and power lifted Luka's spirits. Strength flowed down his arms and legs as his mind's eye watched it swagger, the snake-like markings of its fur rippling over its powerful body. It turned to stare as if it was looking straight at him.

Luka began to dig with his hands. He pushed and

pushed with his right shoulder, digging and shoving although his arms were weak. With a creak, the snow on his right side split and crumpled and fell away Luka crawled out from the drift. He sat there, numb.

His mind had lost the Cloud Cat.

He heard a vibration as if Dimitri had plucked one of his fiddle strings. Something was stirring under the ground. The vibration grew louder until Luka had to clap his hands over his ears. The noise was like the roaring of those tanks that had bumped through the village, right below him, slithering up to the crust of the world. *What is it?*

Luka remembered what Imogen said whenever he was feeling bad: *The only way is up.* Summoning every tiny drop of his energy, Luka clawed his way upward, away from whatever was coming after him. Something tried to grab his ankle and pull him down. *But the only way is up.*

He had to keep climbing. Twice he slipped down again, not far, but enough to make him cry with frustration.

And then his eyelids turned blinding white. Daylight. The world had opened out to the sky again. He heard bleating. Something jumped away across the rocks, must be a mountain goat, up on the crags.

Luka's throat hurt as if he'd been shouting too much, but he thought exultantly, *Jez, I'm out of the Depths of Lumb.*

He sat up and pulled his backpack on to his knee, slipping the straps over his shoulders. He took out his drum. He tapped it gently. Where were his gloves? His hands hurt, yet his fingers began to tap a soft rhythm. The sound was soothing, rather like a lullaby, except that it didn't send him to sleep. It slowed his breathing down and made him feel calm. He set his mind on the Cloud Cat again. There it was, in the distance, leaping down the crags towards him on its powerful paws. He saw the eyes set like pieces of cold gold in its face, and watched its shoulder blades slide like pistons under its dappled coat.

Please come nearer. Please come to me.

The drumbeats stayed in the air around him. The Cloud Cat was just out of his reach. Concentrating on it drained Luka's strength. Try as he might, he could not coax it any closer.

As Luka sat playing his drum, a hungry rat scuttled towards the rope bridge and crawled on to the logs of the bridge opposite Luka and began to gnaw at the rope until it broke.

The bridge snaked away across the chasm with

the rat clinging on tight. The bridge dangled use-
lessly from the other side of the gorge. Now there
would be no way back for Luka, and no way across
for Jez.

The rat scrambled all the way to the top as if it
was boarding a boat, and scuttled away to a new life.

10

THE OLD MAGIC

Big Katrin strode through the village and out again. Her red boots squealed. She strode on until she stood before the little house with five sides. Black smoke belched from the stovepipe chimney in the centre of the roof. Katrin banged three times on the door and the whole house shook. Lumps of snow slid off the roof and plopped to the ground.

She banged on the door again. It creaked open. Katrin saw Simlin's pallid face. He stared straight at her without blinking. Big Katrin had always won staring competitions when she was a child, and she could still win. Soon Simlin cast his eyes down to his thin bare feet. Big Katrin heard springs twang and a dull thud as Vaskalia flopped off the bed and shuffled towards the door. Vaskalia peered round her son's waist. Her face was shrivelled with malice.

'How's your bread this morning, ogress?' she taunted.

Big Katrin ducked her head and strode in through the door. Something crunched under her scarlet boots. Katrin's nose wrinkled. The cottage smelled of old flesh, unwashed clothes and some other things that should not be in *anyone's* house. Katrin set her cake box, bundles of bad yeast and butter, down on the greasy table.

Vaskalia's eyes swivelled like the eyes of a chameleon. She shrieked, 'So you think *I* made the bakery red hot? You think *I* turned your butter and yeast so foul and rancid? Am I so powerful? Well, you're right. I did, I did.'

Big Katrin opened the box. Vaskalia began to dribble. She gloated, 'Hee hee. Cakey cake. I accept your offering, and your apology, and I shall not turn your yeast bad again.'

Katrin inclined her head graciously. Vaskalia and her son immediately crammed their mouths full of cake.

'But let it be a warning to you,' spluttered Vaskalia, 'never forget the old magic. The soldiers from across the sea bring new magic. They bring trinkets, pictures that move, needles to stick in sick people, boxes that steal your face away. When the soldiers leave, they take their magic with them, but the old magic is still here. It always will be. So you should keep that blind boy indoors.'

A lump of spit full of crumbs landed on Katrin's chin. Katrin took out her handkerchief and wiped her face carefully, thinking *There will be an orange spot there tomorrow*. Vaskalia's pointed tongue darted around her lips, flipping anything it found back into her mouth, so Katrin took a step back out of range.

'*And* they change everything, them from across the sea. They made this winter worse with their new magic, their big machines and trinkets. They should stay at home and make it bad *there*.'

Something hit the door. Vaskalia scuttled across the room and opened it.

At first Katrin thought the creature was a giant beetle, because it wore a carapace of long wings, but it had only two legs, not six. Those legs looked strong enough to pick up a child. It was a huge vulture, with a head that was bald except for feathers around the beak.

The vulture waddled up to Vaskalia, and dropped a bloodied rabbit at her feet. It turned its head towards Katrin and glared at her with eyes as unchanging as stones, then opened its wings and beat them so hard that gusts of icy air drove the flames in the fire flat.

Simlin was crouched in a corner. He did not like Bone Cracker. It knew more than birds should, and it ate everything down to the very last scrap.

Vaskalia said slyly, 'Why don't you ask my Bone Cracker if he's seen your blind boy?'

She scuttled towards a high shelf. Katrin saw dolls up there, swaddled in dirty bandages like mummies and stuck full of pins. Vaskalia tried to reach up and grope around for something, but Katrin was there first, found it, picked it up and held it just out of reach.

Vaskalia squealed with rage and jumped up and down, battering Katrin with her black-mittened fists. She sank her teeth into Katrin's arm, but Katrin shook her off as a terrier shakes a rat, and looked down at what lay cupped in her hands.

It was a ball made of glass, like the float for a sea fisherman's net. The glass was smeared with grease and soot. Katrin turned it over and caught her breath.

Inside it was Luka.

He was struggling with something inside the glass ball. His arms were beating. Then he stopped moving and curled up tight, hiding his face.

Vaskalia hissed, 'What do you see? Break your silence, ogress.'

Katrin would not. If she gave away any knowledge or secret about Luka, this woman would use it against him.

Vaskalia picked up the cleaver, still watching Katrin, trying to discover what she had seen in the ball. The cleaver blade glinted in the firelight. On the table was a flat stone, strewn with leaves, clusters of purple berries and curls of bark. Vaskalia began to chop, with a hand at each end of the cleaver. The purple berries bled on to the stone. A bone fell from the rafters above, and Vaskalia could not stop chopping so she chopped that too, slicing it into smaller and smaller shreds, as her eyes swivelled. The mixture smelled like bad cheese, but Vaskalia boasted, 'Every precious ingredient is from my garden. I have more than a hundred plants out there.'

She's making old magic. Why? What does she want with Luka?

At once Vaskalia knew Katrin's thought. She hissed, 'I'll tell you this, because I know you will stay silent. In Jez and Luka's family there waits a gift. It comes to one child in every few generations and it is in *this* one. That lanky scarecrow Jez has no gift for anything at all. Why should Luka be the one to get the gift? It should be *my* son's turn, *Simlin's* turn.'

Before Katrin's horrified eyes, Vaskalia whirled the cleaver above her head faster and faster, wailing, 'Luka's father should have married *me*. Think what a magnificent pair we would have made. Think what gifted children we would have brought howling into the world. Just look at the droolgob I got instead.'

Vaskalia hurled the cleaver, just missing Simlin, so that it stuck in the wall, quivering with a high note. She gnawed at her copper bangles, filled her cheeks with spittle and spat hard into the fire. The flames exploded and roared up emerald green.

Simlin whimpered in the corner. *Poor sallow creature*, thought Katrin. For the first time she noticed a red birthmark on his forehead. It was shaped like a scorpion, with its stinging tail twisted up over its back.

Vaskalia said, 'Luka does not know he has a gift. If he discovers his gift and uses it, just once, it will go from strength to strength. He will have it forever and all our lives will change. But *I* have something that belongs with that gift.'

What is it? Katrin put her head on one side. *And where is it?*

'Ha! You'll not trick me into telling you that,' crowed Vaskalia. 'It is hidden in the most secret place of all.'

Big Katrin glanced down at the glass ball cupped in her hands and raised her eyebrows.

'My family has used that seeing ball for hundreds of years,' gloated Vaskalia. 'We are not peasants like you common folk. *I* can see Luka wherever he is.'

She's lying, thought Katrin, and she set the ball gently back up on the shelf.

Vaskalia said slyly, 'You are taking such care with the seeing ball. I know you can see the blind boy in there. If the seeing ball is broken, whoever is in it will die.'

Big Katrin hurried back to the bakery. A notice hung on the door. It was written in thick pencil on a bit of brown cardboard from a box, fixed on by two nails:

NO BRED TWODAY BICOS OF BAD BAD
SIRKUMSTANSEES SORRY.

Katrin smelled coffee. Dimitri would have made a full pot of coffee to calm him down. Katrin needed some too, after her time with that woman.

Together they must plan how to find the brothers before Vaskalia did.

11

SHIFT

L uka stumbled on upwards through the snow. He felt as if he had journeyed for days and days in a pale wasteland.

Gunfire. One, two, three, four rifle shots, tearing through the air and Luka threw himself down and lay still, except for his lips, pleading, 'Please stay safe at home, Jez.'

The gunfire died away. Luka listened to the silence, but into his head crept those words from the Whisperer: *Idiot. Saphead. Moonraker. My mother knows all about you. She knows who you really are. Idiot.*

The whispering always made him feel as if he was shrinking, but now the shrinking feeling turned into anger. He would *not* have these names inside his head. He had known his sight would leave him since a summer's day when he stretched out his hand to free a yellow butterfly from a spider's web. It was only a leaf. Now he was almost blind but he was not an idiot. Why couldn't the Whisperer just shut up and stop picking on him?

Luka cried out loud, 'So your mother knows all about me, does she, Mr Whisperer? She knows who I really am, does she? Well, *I'll* show you who I really am. *I'll* show you what I can become. I'll show you all.'

He stood up and stamped his feet in the snow. He turned round and round like a spinning top, and fell down again, giggling helplessly. When the giggling stopped, Luka sat up straight. He felt calm and sure now. The anger had ebbed away. It left behind it determination, cold and hard as iron. He strode onwards until he felt safety around him, as if the lie of the land welcomed him.

Luka cleared his throat. He settled down to play the drum once more. He sat drumming softly, in time to the beat of his heart. This time he would not stop. His spirit lifted. Sweat broke out all over his face and body.

And suddenly the Cloud Cat was near him. Luka could reach out his hand and touch that luxuriant white fur. He stroked it. The fur was dense and dappled with dark rings, as if drops of melted snow had fallen from the trees and patterned the snow below. The cat was panting slightly and Luka felt its hot breath on his cheek. Luka gazed up at its round head with the small ears. On the back of each ear was a white spot in the centre of the dark fur. He watched its long powerful body and thick scarf tail, and realised that he was not seeing with his mind's eye now.

The Cloud Cat had come to him at last.

It made him want to get to his feet and dance! It made him want to leap into the light. His life was a cage, and the Cloud Cat had come to help him escape from it. Currents of warm energy ran between them. He cried out, 'Take me with you, Cloud Cat. Let me *be* you and see through your eyes. Please.'

Luka stopped drumming and sat quite still. The cat filled his mind. He smelled its hot, sour breath and saw its curved teeth. He heard a rattling sound from its throat. He looked into its gold nugget eyes and felt them drink him in until he forgot himself. The cat was all around him, left and right, front and back. Then it was as if Luka stepped off a mountainside into emptiness. He was lost, happily lost, and it didn't hurt at all. His heart stopped. He was drifting, shifting through things he thought he should have felt, but didn't.

The whole world stepped sideways.

Luka left his body. He shape shifted and was one with the Cloud Cat at last.

They were running along a twisting path; Luka felt strong shoulders rocking and round paws padding on snow. He heard deep, fast breathing somewhere near, and saw that it was getting lighter because they were climbing, away from the Depths, up rocks so steep that Luka felt upside down, but safe.

His breathing was quick and light. He watched a cloud of crystals drift as he breathed out. His shower of crystal breath fell on to the snow crust with a soft, rustling sound. So *that's* what that sound had been.

Luka could *see*. Close to him he saw dense fur, patterned with charcoal roses, and far away stretched ranges of blue sky and white-topped mountains. Below spread forests, laden with snow. Among the trees darted small animals, busy in their lives. In the rivers Luka saw the gleam of fishes and the bright-eyed faces of water animals with sleek brown bodies.

High up here on the mountainside, the wind tore around the peaks, singing its wild song. It brought him a cold salt smell from far away, and Luka saw the sea through long-sighted eyes, a sea of silver and violet, moving and staying still.

They sprang in a high arc, over a dark space, over torrents of foaming water, and landed to bound away again over rocks frozen white as pearls. There was no gunshot, no people, no fighting. Luka wanted to shout with the freedom. What came out was a loud yowl.

Padding along snow, on warm, fur-covered feet that did not break the snow crust, loping along rock as silver-blue and smooth as a frozen lake, into a friendly darkness. Dry. No cutting wind now.

Hot, rough tongue scrubbing his face clean. Lie down in this cave, very hungry, find a bag with food, eat, *chuff chuff.* Look up at dark blue roof, blue rock spangled with stars like a night sky. Purr with pleasure. So tired. So restful now. Out of danger. Safe. Content.

All around was deep darkness, not the creeping shadows of his poor sight. Darkness as comforting as velvet, blue velvet, for this cave was made out of sparkling blue rock. Luka had strength now. There was a rhythm, as if he was still tapping his drum. Luka listened. It must be the Cloud Cat's heart, and his, but there were *two* other beats, like a pair of tiny tabla, and a strong cat smell. Like lots of Syrups and her kittens, but fiercer.

And there was the scent of burning wood.

Luka heard the crackling and sparking of twigs. The walls of the cave glowed orange. Luka watched a shadow spread across the orange wall. It was the shadow of a cat, towering over him. It turned its face down and curled back its lips in a soft snarl over the shadow of a boy, curled up on the ledge, and nuzzled him.

Echoes travelled around the cave, in and out of the honeycomb and back again. Words. The words echoed and caught each other up, like dominoes. They were dream words, more like music than language, but they were words meant just for him.

'Luka. Reckless boy. You chose the most difficult shift first. The hare and the owl offered themselves as companions for your first change, but oh no. Luka wanted the Cloud Cat. Luka aimed high.'

'Because I wanted her most of all,' cried Luka.

'The Cloud Cat came down from the mountains to you. She cannot stay for long. Not this time. You have not thought what danger you have put her in. You must learn caution and patience if you

75

are to be a true shaman and wear the cloak . . .'

The great cat shadow stirred on the orange wall. It flowed across the cave and drew the boy shadow inside itself.

12

SPLINTERS AND BONES

Vaskalia had been busy all evening, sticking pins into her dolls. Her eyes rolled, each its own way, but every now and then they levelled, and she thrust the pin in deep. The new doll, a big one with her eyes dyed dark with a root from the garden and her feet and legs coloured scarlet for boots, had used up all the pins in the tin.

Vaskalia poured herself another drink from her big copper jug. The drink was the colour of purple nightshade from the black sloes steeping in the bottom. It made her eyes water and her lips smack and twang. She set to work on another doll, a smaller one with a round stomach. She wanted it to have a white baker's hat, but there was nothing white in her bits box. Furious, Vaskalia spat in the fat doll's face and stomped off to bed.

Simlin listened to the metal springs groan. Every night his mother took a long time to settle. He heard her rolling over and over, muttering to herself, 'Keep it hidden. Keep it safe . . .' while the bed jangled and twanged, but at last he heard her piggy snores and whistles. Out he crept, searching for scraps. Apple cores, plum stones, bits of gristle, shinbones, grease skimmed from the tabletop, anything would do, to feed the hunger that twisted in his belly. His mother ate the best of their food.

Simlin scrambled up the wall to the rafter. Hand over hand, he travelled along it like a speedy sloth. No titbits here . . . His hand felt a furry skull with a narrow pointed nose. His fingers traced the cold glass eyes set in the sunken face. Once it had been a dark fox, running across the hillside, its bushy tail behind it. There was a white fox skin, too, snowy and limp now. His mother draped the limp bodies around her neck if ever she went out. When Simlin was little their glass eyes and sharp faces terrified him. Now he just felt sorry for them. *Poor empty foxes, without their insides.*

He hung by his feet and examined his mother's dolls on the high shelf. He picked up the baker doll and sniffed it, hoping it would smell of bread. It didn't. Simlin had often sniffed with longing that sweet morning smell of fresh baking from the baker's tall house. What did it taste like?

He put the baker doll back and dropped lightly to the floor. He saw a small skeleton near the dry wood. He pounced upon it and gnawed it like a squirrel with a nut, but Bone Cracker had already picked away the last scrapings of flesh. He sighed and threw the skeleton down.

Glass ball . . . Simlin sprang on to the table and reached across to the shelf until his hand closed round the ball. His legs wobbled. He clutched the ball tight and got himself right again on his two long feet. Then he climbed down carefully and squatted by the fire, so that its light shone on the glass.

Stupid mother. She had forgotten how she got the glass ball. She had not told that big woman the real story. The ball did not belong to his mother's family at all. It had come to Simlin. When he was a baby Vaskalia kept him in a box. He grew bigger. He managed to open the lid. He started to crawl and then toddle. His mother kept ramming him back into the box and forcing down the lid. Simlin believed that all little boys lived in boxes.

When Vaskalia went to the marketplace and set out her stall of spells and potions, she kept Simlin underneath, packed into a wooden crate with onions and turnips from her garden. One morning he heard something come rumbling down the cobbled street. He struggled up from the middle of the vegetables and saw a ball rolling down the hill. It dropped into the gutter and rolled on like a pinball in a game. It was shiny and lovely and Simlin squealed with excitement.

The ball stopped. The gutter was dammed by fallen leaves from the ancient walnut tree which stood in the centre of the village, keeping the marketplace free from creepy crawlies and flying insects. The ball could roll no further. The sun glinted on the glass. Vaskalia heard her son mewling and scrabbling in his box and bent down ready to cuff him around his head, but he held out his hands to that ball glinting in the gutter.

Looking quickly from side to side and all around, Vaskalia scuttled across the cobblestones and grabbed the ball. She stuffed it up under her blouse like a third breast, and bound it to her body with scarves.

'Mine, mine!' gurgled Simlin. His mother fetched him a sharp smack on the ear. She packed up her stall into the onion box, scooping the vegetables, potions, pills and charms on top of him and stomped home fast, the box held on her hip with the bawling, snotty Simlin inside.

Simlin never got to play with the glass ball. It lived high up on the shelf. It kept trying to leave but his mother wedged her horrid dolls round so that it could not roll away. Every night she took it down and gazed into it, crooning. She would not let Simlin hold the ball but he did, secretly, when Bone Cracker was night hunting and his mother was asleep. Then he climbed around the five walls and gazed into the ball.

Once he saw a wolf with slavering jaws. Another time he saw a scorpion . . . but he did not tell his mother.

Simlin was beginning to suspect that she could not see the things in the ball.

Now he spat on the ball and rubbed it on his sleeve. He put his face right up close. His spittle cleared and he saw a little boy trapped inside. Asleep. Or dead.

Behind the little boy there was a shadow. As he watched, the shadow grew a clear outline. It was a big creature with a broad chest and shoulder bones like axe blades. Simlin's jaw dropped. That was the little boy from the orphanage, the one with the big swaggering brother who had slapped him at school years ago! Simlin liked to hang like a bat in the orphanage rafters and whisper names down at that boy: *Saphead, Moonraker,* and the favourite name, *Idiot.*

Simlin took a deep breath, picked up the ball and threw it down as hard as he could.

The seeing ball shattered. The pieces glittered like splinters of ice. Simlin dragged open the door and tottered outside. The daylight hurt his eyes. The snow was losing its crispness and his bare feet sank into mush as if he was in an icy swamp. He hid among some brambles and spied on the dark house from his prickly cage.

Splinters of glass glittered on the earth floor. As Simlin watched, they began to move. They drew closer and clustered tight again, fitting together again.

The seeing ball rolled out of the door, through the garden and away down the road towards the sea. Simlin jumped up and down with excitement. The glass ball was full of his power, not Mother's.

13

THE KITE WITH NO STRING

The dream of his father's dear face had left Jez. Now, on the cold ledge in the mountains, the owl fluttered, uncertain whether to land. It perched on his rucksack. Jez was smothered in another nightmare, as if a pillow was over his face. He heard a crack and looked up at a huge kite with a white face painted on it, hovering above him.

The kite had no string. It was a vulture with a white face. Something was dangling helplessly underneath it. Something small. Twist and moan as he might, Jez just could not wake himself up.

At last it was silence that woke him. He was on a ledge. Below him, a dark stream wound through the rocks like an adder. Across it were seven pale islands.

He could see clearly, because at last the snow had stopped falling.

Jez remembered that the owl had brought him here last night. He would never have found his way without it. *Where was it now?*

Jez picked his way along the ledge, and came to the mouth of a cave. The dark inside looked so thick, Jez felt he could plunge his hand right into it and feel its softness. It lured him in. It scared him, too. The cave was like a great gullet, waiting to swallow him up.

He stepped inside and gasped. The ceiling was vaulted like a cathedral. It glowed blue and it was sprinkled with stars. Stalactites hung like stone tears. There were smaller caves leading off from the big one, like a honeycomb nursery in a beehive. Each little blue cave sparkled.

On the cave floor were the embers of a fire. Jez caught the faint scent of burning wood, but that was overtaken by a stronger scent of something alive.

He heard fast, light breathing and stared into the darkness. In an instant, two gold stones lit up, shining at him. Out of the darkness formed the great shape of a white leopard, reclining on the ledge. Its eyes held him. They drew him into a world of wildness, without people, with nothing he knew in it.

Run, Run. The alarm clamoured in Jez's head, almost hurting him, *Run!*

But he couldn't move. He was locked into those

eyes, as if he had been hypnotised. The leopard lowered its round head. It nuzzled something by its side and turned its gaze back on Jez as if to say, *Look what I've got* . . . A small bundle formed itself in Jez's sight. Against the leopard lay the shape of a child, curled and still.

'Luka,' cried Jez and the word echoed in and out of the honeycomb caves, *Luka, Luka*.

Luka's face was pale as ashes in the fireplace early in the morning. It was Luka's shape, in Luka's clothes, but Jez knew that Luka himself was not in there. His body was like a coat he had taken off and left behind.

Jez longed to pick up the boy shape and hold it close to him. He stole glances at the leopard. It took his breath away. It was far bigger than any cat could ever be and its paws were huge and round with a bunch of short toes. The plump soles underneath the paws were furry. The paws looked as if they belonged to a giant toy, yet Jez knew they concealed sheaved claws as deadly as scimitars, and knew those soft lips might draw back to reveal teeth that could rip him to shreds.

The leopard did not bother to get up. It was so sure of itself. It watched him, never blinking. Lithe muscles rippled under its seamless skin. Jez heard its quick predator's breathing.

The gold nugget eyes drained Jez's fear. He stepped forward, first one foot then the other, bent his knees and slid his arms under the body of his brother. The leopard rumbled deep in its throat. The tip of its tail twitched. It held Jez in its gaze as he straightened up, lifting Luka's body, light as a bundle of twigs. Jez stepped backwards as if he were in the presence of an emperor. Still the crystalline eyes held his, locked tight.

Jez edged his way back out on to the ledge and stood with Luka in his arms, blinking. He heard a growl from inside the cave. A soft sound as the leopard dropped down to the floor. He heard it padding after him, out on to the ledge. He saw its pale otherworld eyes change in the daylight, its pupils shrinking to black slits in the golden centre.

A dog barked.

Shocked back into a familiar world, Jez glanced over the edge of the ledge. A dog was splashing across the stepping-stones of the stream. Behind her hung a mist of lean grey shapes. *Wolves.*

And further down the hillside was a black matchstick figure, head down, looking for tracks. It prowled steadily through the snow, a rifle slung across its back. This man would kill.

Jez felt something unfamiliar touch his face. Warmth. His eyes became weak and watery so that he had to close them. He turned to the east and opened his eyes but everything went black. He blinked quickly. The eclipse on his eyes cleared and he saw, floating above the earth just under a veil of cloud, a silvery yellow lantern, which broke cover. It surfaced and shone. *The sun.* The clouds raced away, leaving behind them a sky so vivid it made Jez gasp. He cradled his brother tight, thinking that his own body warmth would flow into Luka and bring him back to life, surely.

To the east the horizon was streaked with waves of pink and turquoise and lemon, as if glass had been painted with thin colours. Over to the west it was as intense blue as the gentian flowers that grew among the mountain rocks.

Jez felt a monumental shift as if the world was turning faster, to make up for lost time.

He heard a low growl. He had forgotten all about the leopard. He heard the quick *chuff chuff* of its breathing and smelled the strong cat smell of its fur. The leopard crouched, gathering its strength ready to leap. Jez saw how low its belly was to the ground, saw a muscle twitch beneath its skin and the tip of its great tail flick. And he saw the matchstick figure struggle to raise a gun to its shoulder.

'No!' screamed Jez.

The white leopard sprang. It leaped in perfect grace, with its tail streaming out behind it like a sail, and landed soundlessly on the rock above the ledge. It looked back at Jez and the limp form in his arms and Jez understood they were free to go. He set off along the ledge. The melting snow made the ground treacherous. He reached the river. Rills of melt water trickled through the frozen crust, dappling the ice with cloud patterns that reminded Jez of that leopard's fur. The stepping-stones gleamed white as pearls.

Water raced down the mountainside now, leaving dark rivulets in the snow. Jez careered along the edge of the forest. Snow flopped to the forest floor in great wet dollops. Jez stopped short, almost dropping his brother. He saw blood. It scarred the snow. His eye followed a trail of dark crimson drops to a clump of bloodied feathers. *The owl with the carriage lamp eyes* . . . Jez remembered that dream, and the disturbance in the trees, the kite, the sound of wide wings. A sob caught in his throat.

He set off again, lurching from side to side down the hillside, and heard 'Jez. Wait.'

A figure was battling through the snow towards them.

'Dimitri,' cried Jez.

'Let me see him,' whispered Dimitri. He laid his hand on Luka's forehead, then on his neck. He said nothing, but turned and stared up at the hillside.

'Look,' shouted Jez. The snow leopard was bounding away up the hillside, the dappled fur shifting across its back like rings of water in the sunlight. Behind it ran seven lean shapes and a little way after them loped a hare.

As the creatures ran together, Dimitri and Jez saw that the snowline had crept further up the mountain. Dimitri cried, 'Someone is up there, Jez,' and he put his hand up to his eyes to shade them from the sun. 'Look. Far in front of them . . .'

Jez watched the snow disappear before his eyes as if someone was wearing a cloak of white, striding away from them, with the cloak billowing out behind him, pulling away. Further and further the cloak of snow retreated.

In its place, where the snow cloak had smothered

the land, appeared the colours of the living earth: green and gold, purple and brown.

'The winter has left. We are forgiven,' said Dimitri.

Jez thought, *The Earth looks after itself. The rivers and forests and their creatures will survive in spite of our war.*

The leopard bounded out of sight. Jez felt Luka stir in his arms.

14

THE INVISIBLE WALL

Simlin chased the glass ball as it rolled down the road. His sides ached, but the ball would not wait for him. It did not want to be taken prisoner and kept up on a shelf, surrounded by the pinsticking dolls.

'Wait, glass ball, I look after you,' he cried.

The road was wet. Melt water was trickling down from the mountains, gurgling in the gutters and soaking the earth as the heavy snow dissolved in the sunshine.

'Garden!' gasped Simlin, loping on down the road. His mother would sleep until noon and her garden would flood. She would rage, but what could he do? *Serve her right.* He puffed on, past the inn missing its top storey. He had heard that the road went towards the sea. The sea must be that sheet of iron he could see from the top of the orphanage. If you went the other way, you met mountains. *What were mountains like when they were close up to you?*

Would they spit at you? What was a sea? Could you eat it?

'Never know-woh,' he wailed, because he could go no further. She had put an invisible wall across the road. Simlin hit the air with flat palms, then with his angry fists. He could not go past this wall. He could not break it down. His mother had built it with a spell to keep him close.

He turned and drove his shoulder hard against the wall. The wall pushed back and sent him spinning along the road, as if he was a top it had whipped. He battered that wall up and down. He ran to and fro, searching for a way through but every time the wall blocked his way.

Simlin spun, wailing, clutching his bruised shoulder. Mother's power was strong as stone. He spied a glint. There was the ball, wedged up against a fallen branch. *Quick.* He threw himself at it and peered close. There was nobody in there now.

Take it back home. It was Mother's voice. She had always told him what to do, every minute of the day. Simlin picked up the seeing ball and turned back, his heart heavy as lead inside his ribcage. His splayed bare feet were blue with cold. Filthy water swirled around his skinny ankles, slopping coldly on his skin and leaving a crust of dirt.

He talked aloud to himself as he slopped along.
An idea had hit his head, a mind-smack. 'Simlin, you
must get power. Then Mother will love you.'

15

THE SHADOW IN THE
WOOD STORE

'Katrin? Get the door open and the kettle *on.*'

The bolts slid, the door opened and Dimitri ushered Jez and his armful inside.

Jez lay Luka gently on the long trestle table. Dimitri built up the fires until the flames leaped high. Big Katrin clomped upstairs to put the kettle on, then clomped down again and bent over Luka, stroking his forehead. Katrin had worried in secret that the hooded strangers looking for orphans had taken Luka. Relieved, she listened to Dimitri's tale of seeing the brothers, the wolves, the retreating cloak of snow and the white leopard.

'No. Of course I didn't shoot it, Katrin,' he blustered, thinking, *I almost did!*

Katrin put her fingers on Luka's neck, feeling for his pulse. Her eyes were dark wells so full of sadness that Dimitri had to look away. The village must not lose another son. All they could do was wait. The kettle whistled and Katrin clomped back upstairs.

Jez leaned over Luka and whispered, 'I don't understand what happened, but all I wanted to do was to bring you back. And I have.'

'Why didn't that snow leopard attack you, Jez?' said Dimitri, 'and how did you know where to find them?'

Jez shook his head and held up his hands to stop Dimitri's questions. He felt light-headed. It was a good feeling. He had returned to people he loved and things he knew. Back to his routine. He picked up a piece of wood from the log basket and took out his knife.

The bakery door opened and in hurried Imogen.

'Thank goodness. How did you find him, Dimitri?' she said.

'Jez found him,' said Dimitri. 'He rescued him from the wild beast. Jez is a hero.'

'I know that,' she said, and Jez felt his face blush.

He said, 'I know it sounds strange, but I don't think Luka was in danger. The snow leopard was watching over him. Oh, I wish he'd wake up.'

'Shh . . . he'll recover now that he's safely back with us,' whispered Imogen.

Big Katrin clomped downstairs with the tray of

tea. The four of them cradled the cups in their hands and sat in silence, looking at each other, looking away, looking at Luka, looking at the fine flames in the fireplace. It was a precious silence.

Katrin's mind had been turning like a mill wheel, churning with ideas. Jez and Luka should move into the rooms above the bakery. It was warm. They would be safe. Dimitri could look after those boys (with her help) but he must think it was his own idea. Katrin drank her tea and went upstairs again. She opened drawers that smelled of lavender and pulled out eiderdowns, blankets and pillows, which had lain unused for years.

After a while Dimitri followed her to see why she wasn't preparing food.

He looked at the bedding spread everywhere, clapped his hands and laughed. He pounded down the stairs two at a time and danced across the floor towards Jez, shouting: 'Why don't you both move in here?'

'Eh?'

'You're more than welcome. It'll be like having two sons, but I get them ready made. I won't have to spend years changing nappies and being woken up in the night first!'

Big Katrin staggered downstairs with sheets and blankets. She let down the wooden racks that hung from the ceiling and spread the sheets and blankets over them to catch the warm cinnamon air.

'If you are getting two sons, then you should get yourself a wife, Dimitri,' said Imogen craftily. She and Jez stared at Katrin who concentrated on smoothing out a pillowcase.

'I could *easily* get myself a wife,' chuckled Dimitri. 'I've got a girlfriend in a little shack up the road, but her eyes make me feel funny and my lips turn green when she kisses me.'

At once he wished he'd kept quiet. Supposing Vaskalia found out that he had mocked her? He quickly changed the subject. 'We'll get back to normal tomorrow. We'll bake lots of bread, even if I have to use that powdered yeast. Needs must when the devil drives.'

He rubbed his hands together gleefully at the thought of tomorrow's baking. 'I'd better warm the ovens ready. It's thawing at last. The rivers will be full and the miller will be happy because his water wheel will turn and he can grind his flour. Maybe people will come back to the village now and we'll have lots of new customers.'

He took his wheelbarrow and went outside to the wood store. He gazed up and saw that the sky was sprinkled with stars. There was a white curve of moon. It was a clear sky now, free from snow clouds. *Spring will begin. My swallows will return and I shall see their smiling faces.*

Dimitri opened the door of his wood store. How good it smelled, of oak and walnut, cherry, apple and pear. Mmmm . . . only the best wood for *his* bakery. He sniffed deeply and wished he hadn't, because there was that other smell again . . . almost as if Syrup had been in there.

Dimitri loaded up the wheelbarrow with logs and pushed it inside.

The second he had gone, a shadow slipped out of the wood store. Keeping close to the wall, it stole into the street and ran off into the night.

It was a black panther, escaped long ago from a zoo in the bombed south. It had been roaming around the village all winter.

By the time Dimitri returned to lock up, the panther was gone far into the forest.

16

DANCING DAYS AHEAD

L uka lay still. He was listening to the sounds of the bakery. Only moments ago he had been somewhere else, listening to the Cloud Cat's breaths, to the clinking of the ice thawing, drop by drop, sounding like splintered glass. He had heard melt water drip from the snow as the long winter yielded at last.

Now he heard the kettle whistle, the rasping of Syrup's tongue as she washed her kittens, and the crackling of twigs on the fire. The kittens mewed, the dog whimpered in her sleep as she dreamed. He smelled cinnamon, and a cake baking, and the lavender that Big Katrin put in bedclothes. He felt warm and safe among people he loved.

Dimitri murmured, 'Come back to us, Luka. Wake up. Please.'

Luka had travelled such distances and had not the strength to answer, or even to open his eyes. He heard rustling. It was Jez rummaging in his backpack. Jez shouted, 'Wow, Luka ate all the sandwiches I made him, and all the apples. Good.'

'I fed them to the Cloud Cat.'

Dimitri and Jez looked at each other. They looked down at Luka. His face looked just the same, but he had spoken and he spoke again.

'She was so hungry. Syrup got greedy when she was full up of kittens, didn't she? And the Cloud Cat has cubs inside her body. I heard two heartbeats like drums. Now she can go back to her lonely places. She's very shy. How did you find me, Jez?'

'A grey owl led me to you,' said Jez. 'You must rest now. The story is over. We'll come to live here with Dimitri and everything will be safe and sound and back to normal.'

Luka knew it would never be safe or sound or back to normal again. He had always known that he was the odd one out, and now he had discovered why: there was a power inside him. A gift. He could shift his spirit into other creatures.

Luka wriggled with the joy of this secret. There were other places and beings for him, and if he could change like that, so could the everyday world. He felt Jez smiling down at him. He opened his eyes and Jez gasped. They were not Luka's eyes. Jez was looking into the gold eyes of the snow leopard, into their world of wildness.

He backed away from Luka, shaking his head. *He's changed. I'll have to watch him all the time. I'm going to need help looking after him now.*

'About time too, Katrin,' cried Dimitri as Katrin cut into the coffee cake she had baked. It was sweet and moist, with creamy icing, and a fairy ring of walnuts on the top. Dimitri ate three slices, before Katrin tapped him on the arm and pointed up at the tall cupboard.

Dimitri nodded. He fetched the three-legged stool. He climbed on and reached up to the back of the top shelf, coughing at the dust. He stepped down again carefully, with his fiddle and bow. He put the fiddle on his shoulder and tuned it, wincing at the squeakiness. When it began to sound sweet again, he played the music that had been locked away in his heart for so long. Plaintiff music. Music of winter and war. Love songs and laments for people who were lost to them forever. Music for the sea, the mountains and the forests.

Nobody spoke. Big Katrin listened, eyes closed. Jez stared into the fire, the music flooding his mind. Imogen thought of her family. The music said everything they wanted to say, but without words. The dog lay on her back in front of the fire, legs splayed, showing a round pink tummy. Syrup pinned down one kitten, washing it fiercely with her sandpaper tongue while the others licked the last bits of cake icing from the plate.

Now that Luka had returned and the thaw had begun, Dimitri was sure that the time to dance would come again. Not tonight, because everyone was too tired. Even so he could not resist playing a jig, light and quick and joyful:

Just Luka stood up. He stretched out his arms to them all and a wide smile spread across his face. Then he began to dance.

PART TWO: SPRING

PART TWO SINGLE

*High in the sky flies an eagle, watching the ground
with golden eyes.*

*The man with hair of frost walks in the mountains. He
wears a cloak that billows around him.*

*It is made of the colours of the earth: marigold-yellow,
rose-hip red and the green of new beech leaves.*

*His voice is everywhere. It echoes in the wind around
the mountaintops: 'Luka. You have chosen the right
creature this time. Do you love him enough?'*

THE SUNSHINE THIEF

The sunshine streamed through the skylight in the bakery roof. It woke Jez. Luka heard him counting, *Seven . . . fourteen . . . twenty-one . . .* At *forty-nine* BANG, Jez leaped out of bed and shivered for a delicious moment. At *sixty-three* CRASH, he flung open the door and warm air from the bakery billowed up the staircase and into the attic.

'Can we go to the river today?' asked Luka sleepily. He knew that one of his spirit shifts would happen near water. This time, he would think carefully first, and the man with the hair of frost would not think he was reckless.

'Yeah. We can go when the baking's finished,' muttered Jez. 'Now go back to sleep.'

Luka listened to Jez scramble into his clothes, charge out of the attic and hurl himself down the stairs.

The dog was sprawled across Luka's legs. Her paws twitched. In her sleep she was running with the wolf pack. Luka lay, listening to the river tumbling from the mountains. He heard the swallows' wings scissor as they flitted from the bakery roof to the woodshed. Downstairs, the trays packed with loaves slid into the ovens. The doors slammed shut. Big Katrin arrived for work and soon the kettle began to whistle.

Luka dozed. He drifted into dreams of his Cloud Cat. Luka and the Cloud Cat bounded through the mountains and he saw the world greedily through her eyes. He was woken briefly by the footsteps of Dimitri and Katrin out on the cobblestones, then slept again.

Luka's mother had eyes made of silver.

He saw her in his half-dreams, smiling down at him. He begged her to stay, but she shook her head and vanished.

Luka woke up, sweating.

Someone was at the bakery door. A hand brushed against the doorknocker.

That was all.

Downstairs, Jez sat at the table, thinking about eating another cinnamon bun. Luka was safe asleep in the attic, and his breakfast waited for him on a plate, two slices of Just For Us loaf with curls of yellow butter.

Dimitri and Big Katrin had gone to the miller's for

flour. The open door let in a long panel of sunshine. It lay across the flagstones, gleaming with the promise of fine days and the end of the fighting.

A shadow slid in through the door. It stole the sunshine.

It stole Jez's happiness, too. It left him with that horrible feeling he knew so well, that sense of dread, as if he wore a heavy belt hung with all the lost treasures of his childhood, childhood charms made of lead. They dragged Jez down. The only treasure he had left was his brother, Luka.

As Jez stared at the shadow on the floor, it withdrew.

He made himself stand and walk to the door.

Nobody was there.

But when he looked up the narrow street, he saw the shadow crawling away over the cobblestones.

Jez sat down again.

We're all right. It was just a shadow. We're safe here in the bakery with Dimitri and Katrin.

2

IN THE EAGLE'S EYE

'What's that noise?' asked Luka, sitting by the river. 'There's a throbbing noise, like an engine, and I just heard a dog yap.'

Luka's hearing was as sharp as a cat's. He heard the rhythm of the eagle's wing-beats as clearly as a drum-roll. He heard its yelp of triumph, too.

'Rubbish,' scoffed Jez. 'The sea is miles away and there's no yappy dog.'

'But I can hear an engine up in the sky.'

'All *I* can hear is you prattling!' said Jez. He sat up and yawned. He rubbed his eyes, and looked around. 'Ah. The sun has shifted that mist at last. I can see all the way up to the mountaintops.'

'What can you see?'

'Just a few goats running away up the rocks. Snow. And . . . wow.'

'*What?* Tell me.'

'There's a big gold bird up there in the sky above the mountains. It's an eagle. That was the yelping noise you heard, and the wingbeats like an engine. We saw a golden eagle when you were little, Luka. When you rode on the horse with Mum. Remember?'

A sharp pain twisted under Luka's ribs. He did not want to remember riding safe with his mother, sheltered by her arms. He did not want to remember listening to his mother's soft, low voice.

Jez reminisced, 'Yeah, you were on the horse, but I had to walk, and I got horrible blisters because my shoes were too small. Do you remember?'

'No. I don't. So tell me what the eagle looks like.'

'It's like a black angel edged in gold. Or . . . or a cloud with the sun behind it. It's got talons like meat hooks they hang lambs and pigs on. Dad said its beak and talons were like its knife and fork.'

Luka did not want to think about his father, either, but Jez went on, 'Dad said it looked as if it was wearing baggy feather trousers. It has golden eyes that can see for miles.'

'So it can see us all the way down here?'

'I suppose so.'

'Could it catch me, Jez?'

'A sparrow could carry *you* off. Know your place, small fry,' cried Jez, pushing Luka over on to the grass. 'Now, I'm going for a walk.'

Luka heard him galumph along the bank, his feet crushing the wet grass. He heard the dog panting after him, and he shouted, 'Be careful of landmines, Jez!'

He tensed his body, waiting for a *boom*. It didn't come.

The deep snow had melted and filled the river to the brim, sending it rushing towards the sea. Luka listened to it singing and to the wind rustling in the ash trees. The birds were rowdy, boasting and squabbling and fluttering at each other and over and over again, the cuckoo sang those two silly notes.

Luka heard the ground shake and grasses break when Jez tramped back. Along with the tramping came a burning, acrid smell.

'Eugh, Jez. You stink.'

Jez sniffed his sleeve and said, 'Wild garlic.'

The dog barked sharply, making them jump, and Jez shouted, 'Shut up, and lie down!'

Luka put out his hand to stroke her and felt the hairs on her back bristling.

'There's nothing to bark at on such a beautiful day,' he said and began to hum one of Dimitri's tunes to her.

The brothers sat with their faces raised to the sun,

wanting its warmth after the long winter. They closed their eyes in pleasure, loving the light beating on their eyelids.

So Jez did not see the thin figure that slipped between the trees. And Luka, humming his melody, did not hear the twigs snap as it hid to spy upon them.

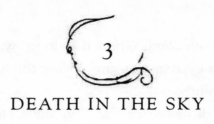

3

DEATH IN THE SKY

Jez opened his eyes and blinked at a spattering of yellow stars in the grass. They were celandine flowers, opening in the sunlight.

Luka said, 'Spring is very loud, isn't it? I don't know how people cope with seeing things as well as hearing them.' The energy of life thrummed through him. He felt as if he could put up his hand and snatch it out of the air.

Jez turned to stare at his little brother. He often said odd things, but he was getting even odder since he had wandered away into the snow and been lost. In this sunshine, Luka's face was as pale as ever. It was shaped like a slender heart framed with ragged black curls. His skin was translucent. The veins under his skin were violet, as if they were the veins on a crocus.

Yet Luka was *not* fragile. There was a strength shining from inside, as if someone else was with him, *in* him, making him stronger. Jez was afraid of that strength.

'Come on,' he said, getting to his feet.

'Where are we going?'

'Back to the village.' Jez grabbed Luka's arm, to start him on the way.

The eagle riding the wind current watched them move with his stern yellow eye. His talons twitched and he flexed his wide wings so that the gold-tipped feathers rippled. Below him on the snow flew his shadow, an angel of death without eyes. He must hunt. If his mate had to leave the nest to find food, their eggs would chill and the eaglets inside them would freeze to death.

A threat moved into his long vision. It was a large bird with a pale head, soaring above the forest. It was approaching *his* air space. It might find *his* nest.

The eagle forgot about those creatures on the riverbank. His whole being concentrated on the invader. He rose on the swell of air like a dark sail ripped from a boat's mast.

At the last moment the intruder saw him and turned back. The eagle sat on the wind, watching it flap its ponderous way back across the forest.

A croak distracted him. A crow. *It* hadn't seen him.

The eagle changed direction. He flew above the hapless crow and hovered, wing tips trembling gold.

He steadied himself, and fell clean as the blade of a guillotine, scooping the crow out of the sky and slicing with his hind claws.

Luka and Jez and the panting dog hurried on, unaware of the death in the sky above them, and the figure following behind them on the ground.

'Jez, slow down,' cried Luka. 'What's that twittering?'

Liquid song tumbled out of the sky as if someone was pouring silver from a jug.

'It's a skylark,' said Jez.

Luka stood, listening to the skylark, thinking that anything singing so joyfully might burst. He said, 'Imagine being up in the sky like that.'

'And imagine flying straight up from the ground like that,' shivered Jez, remembering those black planes that whizzed over the village when the occupation began. One had landed on the cliffs above the sea. It crouched like a great dung beetle and then roared straight up into the air until it had disappeared.

The brothers had stopped by a thicket of thorn bushes. It was an ancient hedge, run wild in the war because nobody had time to cut it. Buds as round as pearls clung to the rough black twigs between the thorns. Jez sniffed. *Mmmm.* The smell of flowers was almost too sweet. Jez just had to have them. He saw a crown of brilliant blue spears shining in the darkness. The colour was intense as if it was from another dimension. Jez struggled into the thicket, cursing, and snapped every bluebell stem his hand touched.

'What are you *doing* in there?' shouted Luka. 'Come on out.'

Jez did not hear him. In the middle of the closed thicket, the blue-green scent was heady. His toe caught in a root and he stumbled and swore at a cord twisted around his ankle. *Ivy*. It gripped his leg with strong little suckers as if it was an animal. He dragged the ivy cord away from his ankle and battled his way out of the thicket back into the luminous spring world.

'Hold out your hand,' said Jez and closed Luka's hand around a mass of flower stalks.

'*Mmmm*, lovely. They smell like heaven,' said Luka. 'But they're all slimy and sappy. I hope they look better than they feel. What are you going to do with them?'

'I'll take them to the orphanage for the children.'

Luka snorted with laughter. He knew that Jez wanted to give the bluebells to Imogen. He bent his face down to the flowers until his senses were drenched by their sweet scent. 'What kind of blue are these bells?' he asked.

'*Blue* blue. Violet. Bluer than blue . . . Hey, *I* can't describe it. What do you think I am? A poet?'

'No,' said Luka. 'Definitely not.'

The brothers set off again towards the village, while the eagle sailed down to his nest with the crow pinioned in his talons.

The thin figure followed the brothers, keeping out of sight.

It darted under the thorn bushes and out again. It picked up a fallen flower and held it to its face. Sniffed. Coughed and spluttered. Threw the flower down, whispering, '*Idiot.*'

4

THE END OF THE STORY

Jez strode through the village with Luka trotting close, bumping against him every now and then. The dog ran with them, froth gathering around her pink tongue.

In the long winter, snow had cast a spell over the war-battered village, turning it into a fairy-tale land of castles and towers. Now the snow had melted and given the secret away: this land was made of ruined houses. It was a dump. Broken chairs, smashed bottles and cups from crumbled kitchens lay among the stones, ready to cut the children who longed to play there.

The brothers disappeared round a corner. They were still being watched. Framed by a glassless window in a crumbling wall peered the face of their pursuer, Simlin. He blinked watery eyes in the sunlight.

The brothers and the panting dog arrived at the big door peppered with bullet holes.

Jez took the flowers from Luka's arms and dropped them in the porch.

As soon as the brothers walked into the orphanage, the children ran towards Luka. They grabbed his hands, stroked his hair, hugged him and planted noisy kisses on his cheek.

Imogen hurried towards them and Jez's heart missed a beat. She picked up Luka and swung him into the air.

'You look great. It's wonderful to see you up and about,' she cried. 'Jez, you've really nursed him well.' Jez's face burned with pleasure so he looked away, fast.

'But you need to fatten up a bit,' she said.

'*Me?* I'm just small and neat,' said Luka.

'You *do* look very funny,' squealed Aidan-who-had-to-be-carried-everywhere. 'I think you've shrunk. And your face is whiter than ever. But I forgot. You can't see yourself in a mirror, can you?' He lunged forward on his chair, grabbed Luka's hand and squealed, 'C'mon, then. We want to know exactly where you've been.'

Luka reached both hands up to Aidan's face and felt his bunched-up cheeks. Aidan was smiling, so maybe he was not scheming to do something nasty.

'I'll tell you all about it,' he said. 'Sit down, Aidan.'

'I can't do anything else without any legs,' crowed Aidan, as Imogen wedged cushions around him to keep him from falling.

Jez fetched a chair and set it down on the threadbare rug, guiding Luka to it. The children thundered across the groaning floorboards, climbed over each other and squabbled to sit nearest to Luka. They looked up at him expectantly. Jez watched their small, ancient faces. These children had already seen so much death and sorrow.

There was a cry from the other end of the room, *Me too.* Eva hurried over to the iron cot in the corner where a little boy was shaking the iron bars. His eyes were round as a hare's. He held up his arms. Eva lifted him out, murmuring, 'We won't forget you, Stefan.' He kicked at her until she set him down, then dashed towards the children on all fours and lay on his stomach, gazing up at Luka.

The last child to arrive was Maria, stone deaf now. Men from a valley to the east had set fire to the gas canister next to her house.

Luka perched on the chair, gripping the seat with both hands and swinging his thin legs. Now that the time had come to tell his story, all the feelings he had felt out in the snow returned: dread, joy, and fear.

'Come on, Luka. Get on with it,' ordered Aidan in his fat voice. '*Once upon a time* . . .'

'I wanted to go off into the snow,' said Luka. 'I was sick of darkness. Sick of banging into walls. I kept having dreams about somewhere else. So . . . I hid in my great-grandfather's old blanket chest until the bus had gone away again. I lifted the lid, crept downstairs, opened the door . . . and . . .'

'What was out there?' cried the children.

'He doesn't know because he's blind,' stated Aidan. 'Aren't you? Dead-eye-Luka.'

'So what if I am blind, Mr No Legs? Half-a-boy-Aidan.'

'Peppermint eyes. Boiled sweet eyes. Why did you go off on your own?'

'Because I wanted to. I wanted to find out if it was as exciting as my dream.'

'And was it?' shrilled Aidan, squirming in his cushions.

'Yes. It was fantastic.'

Jez saw his little brother's shining face and felt his heart sink.

Luka was sure of his story now. He said, 'I

124

crawled across the yard. Then I thought, that's silly, you're on all fours like the dog. So I stood up and walked on my two legs. Like this. For miles and miles. There was a swaying bridge and something tried to throw me down into the Depths of Lumb.' Luka hung his head. When he raised it again he said, 'I'm not telling you the whole story because some of you will be frightened.'

'Tell us, Luka, tell us!' screamed the children.

'I fell down a chasm, into the darkest place of all. I hated it. I struggled and struggled and in the end I got away.'

The story was too much for some of the children. Michael squirmed across the rug on his tummy and pulled himself up on to Eva's lap. Ellie wrapped her arms tight round herself and began to rock forwards and backwards, and Florin cradled his block of wood and whispered *bang bang dead*.

Luka's face flushed pink and he stood up in his excitement and shouted, 'I climbed and climbed.' He pawed the air to show how he did it. 'Just think how I felt.'

'Cold?' cried Lisa.

'Yes. I thought I might freeze into an icicle and have to stay there forever.'

'*Then* what happened?' bawled Aidan.

'I played –' Luka sucked in his breath. His face tightened. He could not go on.

'You haven't finished yet,' screeched Aidan, his face red and tight with envy. 'You have not told us what you found at the bottom of the Depths of Lumb. And *I* think you are so *bad* to go off by yourself!'

'I wasn't by myself,' said Luka, turning his face towards the angry squeal. 'Didn't you like the story, Aidan?'

'No. You haven't told us everything, have you?' he sneered. 'Coward!'

'AIDAN,' shouted Imogen but his face was pink with excitement now. He babbled, 'I'll tell *you* everything, Luka. The landmine that blew me up was called a Pineapple Mine, and it was made far away, in *another land*. It was supposed to blow up tanks but it blew my legs off instead, and threw lots of splinter bits all over the place *and* killed my parents. So there, Luka, so *there*!'

Luka felt the hot blood of embarrassment rushing up to his face. Why did Aidan always find the bit of memory that hurt?

Aidan perched on his pile of cushions. His arms were folded. His lip was curled in disdain. His empty trouser legs dangled beneath his body. He announced, 'You never went down to the darkest place, Luka, because you're scared of ghosts, aren't you? My mother and father are ghosties and so are yours. Where's your dad? Where's your mum?'

Sadness rose up in Luka's chest. He swallowed hard.

Aidan shrieked, 'And you're frightened of them, aren't you, Luka? You're *frightened*.'

There was a sickening crunch as the ceiling split open and plaster and rubble rained down from above.

Aidan disappeared.

Silence.

Then Imogen said, her voice shaking, 'Walk to the side of the room. All of you.' The children did as they were told, too shocked to cry. They lined up and Imogen cried, 'Someone's missing!'

'*I'm* missing,' said Luka calmly, still on his chair, 'because I can't see where I am supposed to go.'

'And *I* am still on my cushions,' said Aidan. 'Eva? Imogen? Get me now. My head hurts and my mouth is full of rubble.'

'You look like a statue on a plinth, Aidan,' teased Eva as she parted his hair and found a cut.

Jez stood by Luka and tried not to laugh.

127

'Do I look funny, then?' asked Luka.

'I'm afraid so. Like a grubby little snowman.'

Luka tried to smile. The falling ceiling had given him a shock . . . but there was worse. He heard the whispering again, '*Idiot. Saphead. Moonraker. Idiot.*'

'There's still somebody missing,' cried Imogen. 'There should be thirteen, with Luka. Where is the other one?'

In the centre of the room hung a dusty cloud. There stood a little figure, drenched in fallen plaster. *Maria*. Imogen hurried to her and brushed the dust away from her eyes and mouth with her hand. She knelt in front of her and signed with her hands, 'Are you all right?' Maria blinked and nodded.

'Eugh.' Aidan began to spit, hard, to rid his mouth of dust. Soon they were all at it.

Jez stared up at the gape in the ceiling. 'The rafters must have shifted. Perhaps the bomb that got Eva's house shook everything up. Destabilised it.'

The orphans nodded at Jez's big word. It made them feel better.

'Every day I think the floor will cave in, or that the old electrics will burn down the building,' wailed Imogen. 'And now this! I must keep them safe. What shall I do?'

Jez looked down at her distraught face and his heart lurched. Usually she was calm and clear as a drink of water.

He said, 'It's what shall *we* do, Imogen. They're not just your responsibility. They're everybody's. I'll find wood to cover up the hole, and –'

'Why has the roof waited all this time to fall down?' interrupted Aidan. 'Perhaps there's a big fat king rat living up there.'

'Shh, Aidan,' scolded Imogen. 'You'll frighten the little ones.'

Aidan chortled with glee. 'Luka? Finish the story.'

Luka felt sorry for Aidan but he could not tell him or anybody what happened at the end of his story. It was dangerous knowledge.

He had a secret gift.

It filled him with excitement and terror.

5

THROUGH THE HOLE IN THE ROOF

Simlin waited, still as a sleeping bat, long after the ceiling collapsed. If they heard a single sound, they would look up and discover him.

He heard the brothers bickering. The big one wanted to leave. The blind boy was trying to find something. Simlin heard a cupboard door open, heard him rooting around inside, making everything fall out on to the floor. *'Idiot,'* whispered Simlin.

At last he heard them call *Goodbye*. Simlin took a deep breath and spun, fast as an acrobat in a circus. He hooked his long feet over the rafter and hung there, swaying gently.

Now that the big hole had happened he could see even better. *These* children were all together round a table, except one boy who crouched by the door with a piece of wood, making *bang bang dead* noises.

The women sliced apples into crescent moons. They fetched drinks. Simlin could see steam rising from the mugs. Someone laughed, even though the ceiling had come down.

The fat squealing boy was being carried, cuddled up, all close to the pretty woman with the long plait of hair. A sob rose in Simlin's thin chest. *Ugly half-boy with the big bulging eyes gets cuddled.*

He swallowed hard, and stifled the sob, but a whimper sneaked out. *Careful.* He squeezed his eyes tight shut and waited, but nobody had heard him. They were too busy with each other to notice *him.*

Simlin had often been here. He climbed up the outside of the orphanage as if his feet were sticky like a fly's feet. It had been easy to pull some loose tiles off the roof and squeeze in, wriggle across the rafters, and work away, gouging out that spy-hole in the ceiling, and today the spy-hole had made itself even bigger.

This was Simlin's favourite thing: spying, especially spying on the people down there. Mother never noticed he was out. Spitting, too. He had learned that from Mother.

He heard the pretty woman call, 'Let's go for a walk and look at the spring. We can find some flowers. Open the door, please, Florin. Florin, *please* stop shooting us.'

The Eva woman carried Lazy-Boy-No-Legs to the door.

'There are flowers all over the floor of the porch already,' squealed Lazy-Boy-No-Legs. 'Blue ones. All limp and squishy.'

Simlin heard all their feet trotting, the door shut, the rafters tremble. Then silence. *Alone.*

Simlin gripped the rafter tightly and lurched forwards, arms out as if he was on a trapeze. He dangled there, swinging backwards and forwards, gazing down into the orphanage.

A shaft of sunlight came in high from a window. Simlin saw specks of dust turning in the sunlight, all gold. He gazed into the room wistfully. No Mother smells down *there*. No thick soot, bits of gristle or skeletons on the floor. Look at all their chairs and cots, and little cups and plates. Look at the toys, the wooden building bricks, the tricycle and the soft bears.

If Mother got the blind boy, Simlin might live with the pretty women and the toys . . .

He swung his body up and wriggled back, quick as a lizard, across the rafters. Two little birds flew twittering around his head. They had made a nest for their babies, all lined with soft down. Four white speckled eggs. *Grab*. Simlin put the eggs in his pocket to eat later. Out on the roof he stretched up and gazed around him at the world dressed in spring.

That blind boy would never see all this.

6

BAD WISHES

Luka sat on a chair in the yard, enjoying the afternoon sunshine. Jez was at the orphanage talking to Imogen. Dimitri was gingerly checking through his new sacks of flour. He had heard of a baker in the city blown up by a bomb hidden in his flour. That baker made bread for the military, but you could never be too careful.

Luka turned the drum round in his hands and felt the creatures carved into its wood. Smooth skin was stretched tightly across the drum. He tapped it. The sound from this drum in the cupboard was deeper than the note from its sister, the one that had drummed the elusive Cloud Cat to him. He could not remember where that drum was now.

Something landed on his hand. He stopped drumming and searched around but couldn't find anything. There. It happened again, light on his face. It bounced away like a tiny ball. Another one. Now a few together, like raindrops, but not wet.

It stopped again. Luka heard Dimitri come bustling outside, and the sound of a tin prised open. He smelled paint. The baker burst into song and made him jump.

'I don't remember the last time I heard you singing, Dimitri,' he said.

Dimitri laughed. 'I can't even remember the words. Listen to the swallows, whizzing in and out of the wood store. They make much better music than me. I love them. But their nests are in a real mess after last winter. They've started mud-plastering.'

'So *that's* it,' said Luka. 'The swallows are dropping mud on me.'

'And I don't blame them,' teased Jez from the doorway. 'Hey, Luka, Katrin wants you. In you go.' Luka took his drum and disappeared inside.

'Oh no . . . what's this?' said Dimitri. He tore off a bunch of wizened flowers from the doorknocker. 'It's a bad wish posy. Hexwort . . . Witch's thimbles . . . Belladonna . . . Vaskalia has been here.'

He threw the posy down and ground it under his boot, twisting his heel until it was just yellow powder. Taking up his brush he began to work blue paint all over the door, while streams of sweat ran down his dark face.

Jez stared down at the yellow powder that had been Vaskalia's gift of hate. It changed everything and settled a sombre cloud over the bakery. Jez wanted that mood dispersed and banished, so he took a deep breath and said, 'That is going to be the best door in the village, Dimitri. I just wish I could fix the orphanage that easily. Poor children.'

'Why don't you get Imogen to bring them for breakfast tomorrow?' said Dimitri.

'What, *all* of them?'

'Yes, *all* of them. I'll ask Katrin to make sugar buns.'

The next morning, Dimitri left Jez to tidy up after baking and gave his door the last coat of blue paint. He stood back to admire it. 'Blue as hyacinths,' he said contentedly.

Luka came down late and set his drum on the table, giving it a loving pat. Big Katrin began to cook his breakfast. Luka listened to the butter spit-spatter in the pan and two eggs crack on the edge of the bowl. He heard the pinch of salt, half a turn from the pepper grinder, and the whisk beating the eggs in the bowl. The bowl tipped, the beaten eggs slid into the hot butter and made it sizzle.

The loaf sighed as Katrin's knife sliced though it. The fresh smell made Luka's mouth water. He heard the spreading of soft butter and the twist of the jam pot lid, releasing the scent of blackberry jam.

Syrup the cat landed on his knee. Luka felt bendy-soft needles pricking his leg when a couple of her kittens hauled themselves up after her. A rough tongue licked his hand. Luka stroked the cat and kittens, with first one hand, then another, paddling faster and faster. He felt the tiny shivers of the kittens' purr and Syrup's deep vibration, right through her body. Luka chuckled as he imagined the Cloud Cat bounding on to his knee. *She* would flatten him and take his skin off with her great rough tongue.

Cloud Cat. Luka smiled as he recalled his time with her. That long winter had smothered so much. Now the world was spinning on its way once more, and the energy was in Luka's veins, too, waiting for his next change – whatever that might be.

Big Katrin placed the plate of eggs and toast on the table. Luka ate, slowly. He was still in his dream world after he had finished eating. Katrin put a towel around his shoulders and began snipping away at his hair, something she had meant to do for days.

Luka sat dreaming until he heard the children arrive.

It was Aidan who did it. Luka heard him squealing '*Sticky, sticky.*' All the other children tiptoed past the shining blue door on the way to their special breakfast, but Aidan lunged forward from Eva's arms, pressed both hands hard on the wet paint of the door, squealing.

Dimitri said, through gritted teeth, 'Luckily for you, Aidan, I've got a bottle of turpentine out in my wood store. Now I'm going to have to paint the door all over again.'

He stomped out. 'Don't be rude, Aidan,' snapped Eva and Luka guessed Aidan was pulling faces at the baker's angry back. He heard Katrin sweep up his curls and the dustpan clatter by the door to empty later. Katrin sliced up a plait of bread and handed each child a hunk to dip into the bowl of honey. Except for Aidan.

'Give me some bread, Big Katrin,' yelled Aidan.

'Not with your hands covered in paint,' said Imogen.

'I hate you,' he spat.

'Just behave yourself. Hold out your hands,' said Dimitri. Luka smelled turpentine and heard Dimitri wiping Aidan's hands while he squealed curses.

'There,' said Dimitri. 'Now show them to Katrin, and if she thinks they are clean enough, you can eat.'

Luka sensed Aidan's rage, but Katrin must have thought the hands were clean enough, for Aidan was positioned at the table, high on a sack of flour, to scoff bread and sweet runny honey. Katrin had baked plump buns and topped them with sugar icing which dribbled down their sides. She had made two buns each, always wanting to spoil the children, always anxious that those three hooded figures might come back for them.

Luka ate both his sugar buns, even after his scrambled eggs on toast.

'What's the matter, Imogen? Aren't you hungry?' asked Jez and she turned to him with wide brown eyes that made his toes curl inside his boots.

'I just don't know how I'm going to keep on looking after the children,' she said. 'There's hardly any money for food. But thank you for mending the hole in the ceiling.'

Dimitri tore off the end of the loaf. He said, 'The warlords should compensate us for all the damage they've done.' He plunged his bread into the honey. 'They've forgotten about us. They expect us to help ourselves.'

Aidan piped up, 'But how *can* we help ourselves, Mr Baker? We have no mothers and fathers. We have no money. Maria can't hear. Luka can't see. Some of us are missing bits of brain, and some of us haven't even got legs.'

'There must be some way of earning more money,' spluttered Dimitri with his mouth so full that Aidan squealed, 'Mr Baker, there is honey dribbling all down your chin. *Deesgusting*. Have you always been a baker?'

'Not always,' said Dimitri. 'For a few years I was a seaman, working on boats and travelling across the seas. I liked that for a while. The further you stand from the mountains, the more clearly you see them.' He wiped away the honey with the back of his hand and said, 'I've some savings hidden away. But the children need so much.'

'I want to buy proper beds and throw away those rusty old cots,' said Imogen. 'We need a wheelchair for Aidan, a hearing aid for Maria, and Ellie, you need a new dress. You all need shoes . . . books . . . paper and things for colouring . . . but how can we get them?'

'You're good with your hands, Jez. There are always other ways to try. You could carve things to sell,' suggested Luka.

'I suppose I could carve wood,' mused Jez. 'But there's something at the back of my mind. Something I've seen somewhere that I could carve . . . Luka, when you ran away, which way did you go?'

Luka sighed. 'Out of the back door, across the yard and up the hillside.'

'And then?'

'Jez, I can't see. You followed me, so why can't *you* remember the way?'

'*You* have forgotten that the world was covered in snow. Everywhere looked the same.'

'Did it?'

'Are you trying to make me angry? What happened in the Depths of Lumb?'

Luka turned his face away. He stared towards the oven range and would not say anything.

Dimitri said, 'Don't nag him like that, Jez.'

Jez remembered what Imogen had told him: *When you feel that rage rushing over you, name seven special things.* He thought, 'She likes flowers. So here goes: bluebells, celandine, forget-me-not, buttercup, stitchwort . . .'

But this time it did not calm Jez down. He did not want to finish his breakfast. That feeling of dread had returned to his stomach. Something momentous had happened to Luka. *What?* And would it happen again?

7

A BASKET OF CHERRIES

All the children except Aidan and Luka fell asleep, face down in the crumbs.

Aidan was perched high like a king on his flour sack, Luka sat daydreaming.

'Nothing is right in this land,' said Eva. 'Have you heard about the old clock in the city? The one with figures that whirr round at midnight? It's stuck. There's just Death carrying his scythe, and Disease, and people fighting.' She shivered.

'There's more to life than that,' said Dimitri. He stood up and stretched.

Imogen whispered, 'Wake up' in Lisa's ear. Lisa stirred and smiled, and then Imogen gently shook Maria's shoulder. The little girl jumped and gave a wailing cry, without opening her eyes.

'I don't *want* to go,' announced Aidan.

'Katrin and I will walk back with you,' said Dimitri. He scooped Aidan out of his throne of sacks and hugged him, chuckling, 'Little troublemaker!'

'Forgive me?' squealed Aidan.

'*This* time,' growled Dimitri.

When they'd gone, Luka made a cradle of his arms on the table and rested his head lightly on his drum.

'Why don't you go and have a sleep?' said Jez.

'I think I will,' said Luka and felt his way to the stairs.

Jez began cleaning up. He wiped the top of the range, scooping crumbs and flour into his hand.

He paused at a noise on the doorstep. A shadow slid over it on to the flagstones.

The dog growled. She slunk towards the door, and stopped, one paw raised, eyes fixed on the squat figure in the doorway.

'Don't tell me that lazy good-for-nothing baker is out again?' crowed Vaskalia.

Dark foxes lay around her shoulders. They had pointed snouts and glass eyes. Their fur was mangy. Vaskalia had scarves wrapped around her head too, but she had left a slit for her gobstopper eyes.

'Why don't you call off your dog?' she whined.

Jez snapped his fingers and the dog slunk back to him.

'I have come all this way, bearing gifts for the poor

blind boy. I have brought him a basketful of cherries. I know he likes them. Take them, scarecrow.'

She thrust the basket at Jez. It was covered with a filthy patterned cloth, yet a sweet smell wafted up and Jez licked his lips.

'Aren't you going to ask me inside?' said Vaskalia.

'We've no bread left. And it's not *my* bakery.' Jez willed Dimitri to hurry back.

Vaskalia cupped a hand to her mouth as if she was sharing a secret with him, and said, 'Dimitri would expect you to ask me in. He is one of my admirers. He longs to ask for my hand in marriage, but he cannot find the courage.'

Jez wanted to laugh, but he was scared and it came out as a spluttering raspberry. Her eyes wheeled round him, looking in different directions. She was weighing him up, thought Jez, and that worm of warning began to wriggle in his stomach. *Dread* . . .

She said slyly, 'Do you know who *I* saw?'

Jez looked away down the street, but he could not move.

She was watching his face. She said, '*I* saw your mother.'

'*Where?*'

'I saw her in the city. In a window. Past the market. Near the castle. Down a little winding way, at the top of a tall timbered house.'

'My mother is gone. And *you* don't know her,' cried Jez.

'Oh, but I do, I do. I knew her long ago. And it *was* your mother. *I* saw her hand. Do you remember it?'

Of course Jez remembered his mother's hand. It was one of his first memories.

It had been his fault. When he was small, Jez was lured to the range by little steam clouds and a delicious fruity smell. His mother turned, just in time to see him reaching for the jam pan. She grabbed it out of his reach, sending crimson jam splashing on to her hand. Little Jez was frightened by her screams and joined in, wailing. His mother smiled and shushed him and plunged her hand into cold water. After that, whenever he traced the scar and tried to kiss the red scald, she assured him it was better.

Jez hated this woman for saying she had seen his mother, *hated* her. His mother was gone.

'Well, well. Look what the cat's brought in. It's Vaskal*eea*,' growled Dimitri, returning at last with Big

146

Katrin. 'What are you doing so far from home? Those bad spirits will be coming down the chimney while you're out.'

'My son is at home. He will keep my cottage safe,' she twittered. She rolled one of her eyes back towards Jez.

Dimitri snapped, 'Today's bread has all gone, madam.'

'It's not bread I want,' she said, fluttering her crusty eyelashes at Dimitri. 'I am here with gifts for the blind boy. I have brought my very best, reddest cherries. All for him!'

Again she thrust the basket at Jez. He backed away, shaking his head, and instead Big Katrin took it. Vaskalia's face puckered with rage. There was no way she could get past Big Katrin, so she announced haughtily, 'I have urgent business at home,' and stepped out into the street again. As she turned her foot touched against the dustpan full of Luka's wild curls. She gave Jez a questioning glance and went on her way.

Big Katrin fetched her wooden spoon with the long handle. She gingerly raised the filthy cloth that covered the basket and frowned. It was spring, far too early in the year for cherries, but there they were, plump and shiny as beetle backs, and dredged with stuck sugar. Katrin put her head down to the basket and sniffed.

With her face this close, she saw a little movement in the middle.

Quick as a wink, Katrin jerked back her head and threw the cloth over again.

What to do? This hoard of poison would never burn. She glanced over at the hillside and found what she was looking for in the wood store. She squeezed through the hole in the wall and began to dig. Burial was the only way.

After a few minutes, Katrin rested on the spade and looked around her. She gasped when she noticed tiny yellow flowers growing below the back window of the bakery. They hadn't been there yesterday.

Groundsel. It grew on witch's pee. Big Katrin pictured Vaskalia squatting on Dimitri's land to pee streams of wickedness, like a lynx marking its territory, and her stomach heaved.

May was a bad month for old magic, but it had met its match in Big Katrin. She buried the basket and shovelled the earth heavily back on top. Nothing could wriggle its way out of *there*. Tonight she would salt the earth all around to cleanse it. In a day or two she would plant a thorn bush and forget-me-nots close to the bakery to protect Dimitri and the brothers.

And she mustn't forget to clean up that disgusting blob of orange spittle on the doorstep.

Vaskalia waited, out of sight. She watched Katrin begin to dig and crept back towards the bakery door. Pinching her thumb and forefinger together, she took some of Luka's hair from the dustpan. She tucked the dark curls under the dead foxes, and scuttled away through the village with her head down and her shadow crawling behind her. She did not want to be seen. Some villagers shouted things at her, and if they were feeling really brave, they threw cabbages. She hated these people. It was *her* village, she was born in the pentangle house on the edge of it and she would never ever leave.

Nor would she give up her claim on that blind boy.

On the road out towards the sea, Vaskalia saw the smoke belching from her house. She stomped through the garden, opened the door and screeched, 'Stop burning all that wood, milksop. A small fire is all we need to stop them coming down the chimney.'

Simlin scurried into the corner, sending a dish clattering. He flung his arms up in front of his face. Would she notice the pan he'd used to cook the little speckled eggs he had taken from the orphanage roof? He'd scoured it hard with a piece of pumice stone.

Vaskalia had other things on her mind. Her dolls stared down at her hand in the fingerless mitten as it closed round the seeing ball and lifted it up to her rolling eyes.

'Nothing, nothing,' she whined. 'Where has he gone?' She whirled round at Simlin. 'And why have I got you instead, you prince of disappointment.'

Simlin's birthmark flamed livid orange. Mother said his birthmark was a creature called a scorpion with a stinging tail. She said it lived on hot rocks and horrible ugly children. The birthmark tickled Simlin when he was frightened of Mother, and when he felt angry at her. *Not going to tell you I have been out and seen the blind boy. Not going to tell you I see him in ball sometimes. Simlin's own secret.*

He heard the *groan-ping* of the bedsprings as she bounced on to her bed, and the shuffle of the curtains as she tugged them around herself. Simlin heard her hiding something under her pillow. He longed for her to fall asleep. It was hard to tell when she slept, because the little house with five sides was always full of sounds. The fire in the middle of the floor hissed like a dragon as it crawled over dank green logs. There was shifting and whistling from up on the beams where Bone Cracker the vulture shifted from foot to scaly foot. It stretched its big wings and flapped them as if it was shaking out a coat.

Simlin heard sagging, boinging and clattering, as his mother rolled around on her fat mattress. He heard her gnawing at the copper bangles round her wrist. Spitting, then green explosions bursting in the fire. Snorts and snuffles as she slept.

Simlin thought of the children in the orphanage with their steaming drinks, crescents of apple and their laughter. He curled up by the fire with his arms wrapped round his knees and sucked his thumb. He drifted thankfully away into sleep.

At some time in the night he was woken by a scraping noise. Something large was being dragged across the floor, stirring the earth. It made his throat tickle. Mother was chuntering orders, *'Put it here. Underneath . . .'* Simlin hid his face on his knees.

A little while after that he heard hooves trotting away from the five-sided house. Simlin slept again, fitfully.

8

INTO THIN AIR

Luka crept down from the attic and sat on the stair by the bakery door. He listened to that woman talking about his mother. Her voice was like a saw, grating backwards and forwards. It twisted in the emptiness under his ribs. It hurt him. His mother had been taken away. She did not *want* to go, so she must hurt, too.

Luka could not bear it.

He had to find out if that woman spoke the truth.

Early next morning, Luka slipped out of bed. Jez was asleep. Even Dimitri was still wheezing like a bellows in his bedroom underneath the attic.

It was just before dawn, the time when people have not intruded on the world. Nothing is fixed. It is a time of overlap.

It was the right time to change, and he knew what change it must be.

Luka felt his way downstairs. His stomach

rumbled, but he knew not to eat breakfast on such a day. He must be clear-headed and ready.

He turned the key in the back door as softly as he could. Nobody must witness what was about to happen.

Luka found the chair and placed it in the yard. He fetched his drum from the table. He perched on the chair. As he began to tap his drum with his fingertips, the swallows started to twitter and warble. Luka thought about making those tiny noises in his own throat.

He heard them swoop. What was it like to fly? Dimitri had described the swallows to Luka because they were his favourite birds. He said they looked as if they were smiling. Luka could picture the streamer tail, and the sleek feathered body, blue as midnight on the back and pale as rosy dawn underneath.

Luka stood up, spread his arms and curved them behind him like wings.

What would the world look like through a swallow's eyes? Dimitri said their eyes were round and dewy in their red faces, and ringed with yellow. Their eyes were large for such small creatures, so their sight was good.

Luka would look through those eyes, and use the

gift to search for his mother.

He sat down again. He picked up his drum and began to tap a rhythm, slow and soft but insistent, matching the rhythm of his pulse. On and on he played, drumming himself into a trance. The rhythm matched his heartbeat. Calm flowed through his mind and body.

He put down the drum and waited.

He felt a rush of air as the birds swooped past him. One swallow came again and again. Its wing touched his cheek. He knew it was a leader, guiding other birds across oceans and strange lands to be here in time for spring. A miracle bird.

Luka put his mind around it, and right into it, just as his mind had flooded into the Cloud Cat. He forgot about his breathing, forgot about his hungry stomach, forgot about the bakery, the orphanage, his mother, even Jez.

And then Luka was cast out. There was no air and no light, no sound or breath. There was nothing, and he struggled to get out of the emptiness.

I'm lost. Am I dying?

Luka's body sat on the chair in the baker's yard, like an empty costume, whilst his spirit vanished into thin air. *Sky Shifter.*

Luka was free. He soared with the swallow. The invisible flicker of life that was truly Luka merged with the bird, flying with it, seeing what it saw. They flew high, where the air was thin and translucent with sunlight, and the earth shimmered below.

Luka remembered a blanket that his mother had made. It was a patchwork of coloured cloths. He loved to run his hand across the blanket and feel each different cloth, the rough hessian, soft velvet and wool, workaday cotton and light silk. His mother had sewn them together with green thread, in stitches that arched like bridges. Luka liked to trace the viaduct of stitches with his fingers.

Once Jez had draped the blanket around his shoulders, like a rich, coloured cloak.

From up here, the earth looked like that patchwork cloak. There was the sombre green of a forest whose trees had shed its snow, the new green of woodlands and orchards, hedgerows washed with the pink of blossom and buds, and a field full of shining grass blurred with scarlet poppies. The colours were fresh and distinct. The sun was closer in springtime. Its clear light glanced across the land.

Somewhere beyond this is my mother.

They flew over the village. That tall house leaning

out as if it would topple over was the bakery. Luka saw his skylight in the cat-slide roof. A sandy blob paced up and down the street, sniffing and looking for him.

There was the orphanage. In the roof was a gaping hole.

They flew above a little five-sided house shaped like a pentangle. From the chimney twisted a spiral of acrid black smoke. *Who lives there?*

A squadron of geese beat past, in the shape of a great arrowhead across the sky, honking frantically. Luka saw their strong straight necks and smelled their hot feathery bodies as the swallow swooped out of their way and flew higher still. The geese beat away, taking their exulting clamour with them.

A skylark approached from underneath. It battled on upwards, singing so strongly that its throat trembled with defiance and left a silver ribbon of song unravelling in the air below. Luka wanted to catch the song and keep it forever.

He thought, *It's an omen. It means I'll find my mother, safe and sound.*

Far below, a man and horse were ploughing. The turning earth was glossy brown. It dried in the sunshine, pink as the feathers on a chaffinch's breast.

Across the sky sailed white clouds like clipper boats. The sky stretched wide open from horizon to horizon. How could anything be so *vast*?

Behind them rose the mountains, ancient beings with white hair and blue-green limbs. In Luka's memory, Dimitri's voice murmured *The further you stand from the mountains, the more clearly you see them.*

From up here the world looked as if it was at peace. There was no gunfire, no bloodshed and no fear. Up here, Luka understood that he had been given the power to help more than just himself.

Luka and the swallow danced in the sky, dipping and soaring among the clouds. Sky dancers. They were the only ones who knew the steps.

9

MIND LIKE A WATER WHEEL

Jez had been awake for much of the night,
thinking about his mother. She was always just to
the side of his mind. Now his mind churned like the
miller's water wheel. He saw his mother's anguished
face in the back of that truck as it drove away down
that road, all those years ago.

Her eyes would not leave him. His mother's eyes
were pale and light, neither blue nor green nor
hazel. Jez's father said they were the colour of the
leaves of an olive tree, but Luka believed they were
made of silver.

All through the fighting, people had vanished for
no reason. Jez did not want to think about where his
mother might have been taken, or what might have
been done to her. He was sure that he would never
see her again, and so he tried not to let his mind
wander, but now Vaskalia had stirred up that debris.

He buried his face in the pillow and cried himself
to sleep.

When he woke, his head ached. A blade of sun cut through the skylight and pointed down to Luka's bed. It was empty. Luka must be awake already.

Jez raced downstairs. Dimitri and Big Katrin were sitting at the table, teapot and cups before them.

'Why didn't you wake me?' cried Jez.

'Slow down, Jez,' said Dimitri, smiling. 'We decided that you needed a lie-in.' He grinned at Jez's early morning hair. It was sticking up, tufty as a scarecrow's. Dimitri reached out to ruffle it.

'Does it look funny?' mumbled Jez. 'Katrin . . . would you cut it sometime, please?' She nodded and poured him a cup of tea.

'And I need a shave,' he said, passing his hand across his prickly chin. 'Have you got an old razor, Dimitri?'

'Yes and you shall have it.' Dimitri yawned, stretching his strong little arms above his head and Jez thought, *It's all right for* him. *His chest is like a barrel and his arms are packed with muscles.*

He said, 'Is Luka outside, then?'

Dimitri shrugged. 'Isn't he still upstairs?'

Jez tore into the yard. He found his brother sitting on the little chair, his eyelids closed. He whispered, 'Luka? LUKA!' He tapped his shoulder.

160

Luka did not move. Panic flooded through Jez.

'Dimitri, Katrin,' he shouted. 'I can't wake him up.'

Dimitri hurried out. He peered into Luka's face and said, 'Let him rest,' hoping he sounded reassuring. They carried Luka up to his bed. Katrin put her hand on his forehead and thought how cold he was. She took hold of his wrist. His pulse was still beating, although it was slow.

'What'll we do?' whispered Jez, clawing his fingers through his hair.

'We'll leave him to recover,' said Dimitri. 'What happened to him out in the snow took more out of him than we thought. Letting him rest is all we *can* do. Get on with our work and leave him in peace.'

Big Katrin glared at him.

Dimitri shuffled from foot to foot. 'Don't look at me like that, Katrin. Of course we will keep watch. He's vulnerable. And I know someone who would take advantage of that. So, Jez, either you or I must always be in the bakery.'

In spite of his anxiety, Jez grinned. He said, 'I think Big Katrin is quite capable of dealing with Vaskalia.'

10

SEEING THINGS

Simlin crouched at the window of the five-sided house. He twitched the curtain with his nose and watched his mother stomping around her garden.

Mother looked up at the sky. She put her mittened hand to shade her eyes. What was she staring at? Something little up there. Something flying. It looked like one of those birds that flew to hot places for the winter.

Mother moved out of sight. At once, Simlin scooted across the cottage to the doll shelf. That blind boy was back in the seeing ball again. He was sitting on a chair. He wasn't moving. Something *else* was moving. It was curved, like a bow. It swooped up into the sky as if it was a crescent of dark moon.

Simlin's mouth hung open as he watched it. *Lovely, lovely. Oh.* Simlin realised that the crescent was a bird. It had a fork with two prongs for a tail.

The blind boy had gone off with it.

But his body was sitting on the chair.

He heard a rustling sound. Bone Cracker was moving up and down the rafter perch. Its bald head was cocked on one side. It was staring down at Simlin and the seeing ball.

Simlin stuck out his tongue. Quickly he looked back into the ball. Swooping bird, swooping boy. Lucky boy, swooping out there in strange places, seeing new things, and not shut up with –

The spit arrived before she did, hissing in the flames with a small green explosion and making Simlin think he had jumped out of his skin with fright.

'Give that to me,' she shrieked. 'It's mine. You've no right to look in there.'

Simlin put his head down on his chest, to show her he was very sorry. If he did what she asked at once she might not punish him. He handed Mother the seeing ball and waited, hoping that he looked as meek as a little lamb.

'What did you see?' she snapped. 'Tell me, droolgob!' She hit him hard on the side of his head.

It hurt. His ear stung where she'd swiped it. If he told her, she'd know that he could see what was happening to the blind boy, and she'd never stop asking. So he kept quiet.

'I'll tell *you* what's happening, nincompoop,' she shrieked. 'The big brother has gone to the city to find his mother. So the little one will be without his protection.'

All Simlin could do was shrug, and think, *She's got the wrong brother.*

'That big boy likes his little brother so he protects him. Just like I protect you.'

Simlin frowned. That did not sound right to him. Simlin used to think that one day his mother would like him. She might even love him.

It just never happened.

Out of the corner of his eye, he saw a building loom in the seeing ball. It was dark red as a scab of blood, a scab that you pick when there's nothing to eat. The swooping bird was flying near it, holding the invisible blind boy inside.

And Mother can't see them.

Simlin decided that he was just as good as any blind idiot. There was something special he could do. He could see the boy in the ball. He made a *yip-yip-yipp*ing noise like a pig snorting. He had never made the noise before and he liked it.

'How dare you laugh at me!' yelled Vaskalia, twisting his ear. It hurt so much that he whimpered,

'Bird. Little bird. Bird with blue back and fork for tail.'

Vaskalia stopped twisting and began to gnaw at the copper bangles round her wrist. Her eyes swivelled as she plotted away to herself. She spat into the fire and stared at the lime-green flames. Then she looked up at the huddle on the rafter and whispered, 'Bone Cracker? Wake up, my dear. Off you go, into the night. There is something you must do.'

Bone Cracker dropped down and lumbered to the door. Before it went it glowered at Simlin over its shoulder.

Simlin thought, *She likes Bone Cracker best. Fed up. Fed up.*

Vaskalia busied herself around her pot on the fire. She ladled brown liquid into a bowl.

'Have some good hot broth, my sweet idiot,' she said. 'You *are* a clever droolgob, to see the little bird.'

Clever droolgob? Sweet idiot?

The words tumbled about in Simlin's head. He tipped up the bowl and drank the hot broth. He wondered if she was only feeding him because she wanted to know everything he saw in the seeing ball. But so what?

11

BLOOD-RED CASTLE

The air was cloudy with dust.

It took Luka a moment to decide that it was the city spread out below them, because it looked upside down. How alien it looked to him. There were broken buildings the colour of wet flour, with roofs open to the sky, crumbled staircases and sagging floors. Balconies clutched at the walls. In the middle of one wasteland was a vast crater as if a meteorite had crashed into the earth at lightning speed.

'That must have been a very big bomb,' Luka told the swallow.

I saw her in the city. Vaskalia's voice cut into Luka's memory. This grey desert was where his mother might be, in this unknown place, among strangers.

The city changed as they flew nearer to the centre. The houses that still stood were old, with timbers crossing their gables and roofs.

At the top of a tall timbered house . . . Was she there?

A tank with big caterpillar tracks came bucking down an alley. The houses trembled. Luka saw people hurrying with their heads down. A lorry packed with soldiers ground along a potholed road. The soldiers held up rifles as if they were spears.

Through the middle of the city flowed the wide river. It split to flow round an island and join up again. On this island sat a castle built of stone, the colour of old blood.

The swallow dived down and flew above the river.

'We haven't time,' cried Luka, but the swallow ignored him and swooped shockingly low, with its bill open, skimming the water, scooping it up and sipping so that Luka realised how desperately thirsty the bird had become. It turned and swooped back along the river, catching insects in its bill, from just above the water as if it had a little fishing net. Luka was dimly aware of scratchy wings and jointed, stringy legs.

With its stomach full, the swallow flew straight along the river towards the blood-red castle.

'She won't be in there,' said Luka, but the bird ignored him and coasted along a drawbridge lined with soldiers. They wore battledress, shadowed with brown and grey. The swallow flew up and circled the castle just under the battlements. From them hung little bundles, like rolled umbrellas with old faces, wizened as gnomes. *Bats.*

The swallow swooped under the drawbridge and through an archway into a tunnel full of sluggish brown water. It stank. Luka saw green slime on the walls where dank water had slopped for hundreds of years. He heard the splash of a fat rat. Worse, he heard people crying.

'I don't like it here,' he insisted, but the swallow ignored him, turned and flew back again.

Barely above the water were small windows. They were grilled with rusty bars. A hand reached out as the swallow flew past and snatched at its forked tail. Fast as an arrow, the bird flew under and out of the other side, into the light. It circled the turrets and flew close to the wall. Luka did not like this wall. The thick, blood-red stone sucked everything into itself. He could hear nothing from the other side.

They flew down into a courtyard in the centre of the castle, to a window, recessed deep into the stone. The window had wide sills and the thick glass was yellow with age and tobacco smoke, and netted with spiders' webs.

The swallow began to feed on the tiny prisoners in the webs, aphids and hoverflies.

Behind the yellowed glass, men sat awkwardly around a long polished table, which reflected the faint daylight as if it was water. Above it hung blue smoke from their cigars, cigarettes and pipes. They were dressed differently in robes, suits, and battledress. *The warlords.*

On the far wall Luka saw the glint of metal, from bunches of keys.

At the top of the table sat a man in a pale uniform. On his chest gleamed buttons of gold. Epaulettes shone on his shoulders. His head was abnormally big. It was shaven and bumpy. He swung up his legs and put his boots on the table, boots as brown and glossy as the conkers on Jez's chestnut tree. Luka thought, *He's not from our land.*

The shaven-headed leader glanced quick as a fox towards the window, then back again. The warlords shuffled in their seats. Now the leader was sneaking glances all around him. Luka knew that he was trying to guess what the others were thinking.

The swallow picked one last insect from the sticky webbing, then flew away from the castle and over a market place. Two women stood behind a stall. Their faces were taut, as if the skin was stretched tight over wood, like the skin on his drum. Their stall had a few potatoes and some cabbages, sliced open so that their middles gaped from pale yellow to dark green, like the contours on a map. All of a sudden, three boys about Jez's age ran forward and snatched up the food, stuffing it under their coats. The women cried out to some soldiers lounging against a jeep. The soldiers shrugged. One of them laughed and spread his arms wide as if to say, *So what?*

Luka and the swallow whizzed away from the market and along a small street, flying close to the high windows. *Down a little winding way, at the top of a tall timbered house.*

Luka thought, *She will be here.*

THE FACE IN THE MIRROR

The damaged street was uneven, as if it had been picked up and shaken. One front door stood ajar. The next door was gone altogether. The windows were tiny and the rooms beyond them low and shadowed.

Through the first window, Luka saw a room full of long boxes made of wood. One was broken open and Luka saw that it was packed with guns.

In the top room of the next house were two small beds with bright knitted covers. On each bed lay a teddy bear, but somehow Luka knew that children did not sleep in this neat room any more.

The third attic was full of rubbish. There was a battered suitcase and a broken cane chair. Not the kind of room his mother might live in.

But the next window was open. A net curtain billowed softly over the sill.

Luka could smell perfume.

At the back of the room was the reflective pool

of an oval mirror. A woman stood before it, lifting her long hair over her arm and moving the brush gently through it. The brush flowed over the hair, as if the woman was casting a spell. *Her face must be in the mirror*, but it was too far away for Luka to see her reflection.

'My mother had long hair,' Luka told the swallow. 'She had such a soft curve to her cheek. Her skin was brown like Jez's, and she had lips that turned up in a smile, and silver eyes, and a scar on her hand.'

The woman became aware she was being watched. She stared into her mirror. She set down the hairbrush, turned, and walked towards the window.

'*Mum?*' whispered Luka.

The woman moved into the light. Her eyes were deep with sadness. Under them were crescents of smoky tiredness, and lines ran down from her mouth as if her face had never smiled to smooth those lines away.

She opened the window further and reached out to touch the swallow's shining blue back with a fingertip.

There was no scar on her hand. Disappointment flooded through Luka. It felt so heavy that he feared they would drop out of the air. The woman sighed.

She withdrew and closed the window.

There was one more house in the street. It was completely empty. Everything must have been burned on the fire during the winter. The floorboards had been pulled up. There were no doors left in the frames.

'Oh . . . can we fly once more round the castle? We didn't go to the top. There may be a clue . . . *please*,' begged Luka.

So the swallow flew to the very top of the castle, and there on a turret stood Death, clutching his scythe. Around him crouched ghastly figures: a man pointing a rifle, a weeping woman clutching a skinny baby, a skeleton, and children cowering from a figure wielding a stick. Behind them was a big clock.

'They're not real people,' Luka said. 'They are made of wood blackened by fire, but where are the *other* figures? The happy ones?'

The hands of the clock were stuck at midnight and the awful figures were left outside to haunt the city. Time was halted in the middle of war, pain, hunger, and rage. Luka was sure there must be other figures from peacetime stuck inside, unable to be seen by the people of the city.

'Let's go home,' said Luka. The swallow looped

the castle and set off straight along the river. At once they were engulfed in a screaming black cloud.

'Oh Jez, if only I was at home with you,' wished Luka as they were buffeted by a swarm of devils with needle tails, turning and tilting on sickle-shaped wings. Yet the swallow was not frightened, just vexed at having to negotiate his way through this crowd of swifts, dashing home to their nests. They were gone as quickly as they had arrived.

Another agitation was catching them up fast. Over the river swarmed a cloud made of dark points. The cloud vibrated as it raced towards them. The points had wings. They made a sound almost too soft to hear.

'Here come the bats, setting out for the night,' cried Luka. 'It must be later than I thought, swallow. We shouldn't be out after dark.'

13

TORTOISE FROM HEAVEN

Big Katrin was still at the bakery. She wanted to stay and watch over Luka this evening. Jez sat by Luka's bedside too, fretting, imagining that heavy belt of metal effigies.

Dimitri tried to hide his worry from them. He was sure he would find the old doctor in the inn down the road towards the sea. He could ask him about Luka.

'I'm going to the inn for a drink,' he called up the stairs, 'I won't be long.' But Big Katrin had other ideas. Dimitri found it hard to have just *one* drink, so she steered Jez downstairs to go with him.

Dimitri strode down the road towards the sea, singing in the evening sunshine, with Jez slouching at his side. In the lush grass at the roadside bobbed wild roses pink as shells and creamy-white elder flowers, intricate as a lace collar on a woman's dress. Big Katrin should have a collar made of such lace, thought Dimitri, next to her rosy throat.

He smelled smoke. They had almost reached the five-sided house with the stove-pipe chimney. His singing died away.

'I'm not frightened of you, Vaskalia,' he said, not very loudly. The curtains twitched and Dimitri grabbed Jez's elbow to make him hurry past.

A shadow passed overhead. It blotted out the golden light, and something whizzed past Dimitri's face and crashed on to the road.

'Who's throwing boulders?' he roared, putting his fists up in front of his chest. He couldn't see anyone and whatever made the shadow was gone. Dimitri bent down and peered at the boulder. It had four waving legs and a face like a tiny dinosaur. He turned the boulder over and stood it up.

'Well, hello there, tortoise,' he chuckled.

'Did you see that big vulture?' cried Jez, gazing up. 'Poor tortoise. That vulture dropped you to crack you open so it could eat you, didn't it?'

The tortoise blinked tiny eyes at them. Dimitri sighed. He picked it up and said, 'You look like an Alfonso to me,' and slipped it into the pocket of his greatcoat. He wondered if tortoises got on well with kittens.

Tonight the inn was full and noisy. Jez felt shy

because he knew hardly anyone. Dimitri had not seen so many people in one place for months, and he knew most of them. There was the miller, the cobbler, the man who kept apple and cherry orchards, the donkey driver, Peter the bus driver, a herdsman and a carpenter from the next village.

'It's wonderful to see you all,' he cried. 'Ah! Here's the man I want to see most of all.'

'Why do you want to see me?' said the doctor. He stared pointedly at Dimitri's stomach and said, 'Hmm . . . a weight problem? If you take my advice, you'll lay off the cakes and buns for a while. Is Katrin still looking after you?'

'Yes she is, I'm happy to say,' said Dimitri, 'and she cooks me lots of cakes. Now, let me get you a drink.'

When the innkeeper had set their drinks down, Dimitri said, 'I want to ask your advice about Luka. You know, the boy who is almost blind? He's Gabriel and Evangelina's son. He ran away. This is Jez, his brother, who found him and brought him home.'

'Brave boy,' said the doctor, taking Jez's hand and shaking it. 'So what's the matter?'

Jez said, 'Luka has gone very strange.'

'What do you mean? Has he a fever? Does he shake and have fits?'

'No.'

'Then I don't know what you're worrying about,' said the doctor.

'This past day . . . he has . . . sort of disappeared from us. He is in a very deep sleep.'

'Perhaps he's tired?' said the doctor. 'There has been a lot to sap his strength: hunger, fighting and a long, cruel winter.' He swigged down his drink and immediately ordered more. Jez shook his head – one had been quite enough for him. Whatever they drank was too sweet and burning. He wanted to go home. The room grew hotter, the voices grew louder and Dimitri's voice was loudest of all.

'We live up here, minding our own business and making bread, for years and years, and look what happened,' he cried.

'What happened?'

'You know as well as I do, you stupid miller,' shouted Dimitri. 'People from one side of the mountain quarrelled with people from the other side. They argued about who owned the rock their goats stood on. They started to fight and get into gangs with warlords. One of them made himself the boss. He put himself in the castle and got a big shiny car. He locked up anyone he didn't like.'

'Then another tyrant took over,' sighed the doctor. 'More fighting. More cars. There was a bad harvest. Everybody started blaming each other and fighting.'

'The warlords stirred up the villages. They began to fight against each other,' cried Dimitri. 'All those old feuds and resentments and suspicions came back and everyone fought one another. Nobody really knows why.'

Jez listened to them. It sounded crazy.

Old feuds and resentments and suspicions . . . Jez remembered Vaskalia with dread.

14

GIANT CLAW

Simlin sat in a corner in the dark, sipping his broth. Bat wing struts caught in his throat and he had to stick in his finger and drag them out, but the soup was warm and it filled up a bit of him. He thought longingly of the orphans with their biscuits, apple crescents and their giggles. Would they give him a bite of biscuit?

Simlin waited. The fire died. Bone Cracker did not come back. Mother had gone out. She would screech at him if the fire had died out altogether, because then enemies and bad spirits could come down through the chimney and not get burned to death. So he built up the fire just a little.

You never knew with Mother. You never knew what she would do.

Simlin knew now she would not love him.

He crawled on all fours to her elephant bed. It smelled of her. Her smell was salty, like that wind that blew all the way up here from the sea, and it was like rotten cabbage. Tonight there was another smell, too. Old flowers. He saw the box of powdery white, the stick of greasy red and yellow glucky in a bottle.

He sneaked his arm up the side of the bed and felt under the rocky pillow. *There* . . .

He drew his hand back and looked at the tussock of dark hair. Curls. Clean, soft, dark hair. *Must be the blind boy's hair. Mother will make special boy doll with real hair locks, and stick in pins into painful bits.*

As Simlin pulled his arm back, he felt a sharp pain on his own skin, *ouch!* He stared down at a tear in his sleeve and watched as scarlet blood welled up and seeped through as if it was a weave in a pattern. He put his arm up to his mouth and sucked the bleeding place. Had Mother made a Simlin doll? *Please, no.*

He peered at the bed and blinked.

A claw was sticking out from under the mattress.

Simlin had never seen such a big claw. Whose was it? What was mother going to do with it? The claw had not always been there.

With his mouth still fixed on to his bleeding arm, Simlin backed away on bent knees until his back touched the wall and he could go no further. He stared at the claw. It twitched.

Simlin stayed close to the wall all evening. He dare not doze off. Whatever was under the mattress might come out after him.

15

TALKING MAN

Jez was bored. The men were still rambling on and on about what started the war. It was all such a muddle.

'I never knew what they were fighting about,' grumbled a farmer, 'but somebody blew up the bridge so I couldn't take my beasts to market.'

'Everyone was an enemy,' said Dimitri, 'one minute it was the way they prayed. Next minute it was if they ate chickens or pigs, or if they washed their hair on Fridays or Sundays, or their eyes were a different shape from the families in the next valley.'

'Then all the strangers came in planes,' growled the orchard owner, 'scaring the old folk and making a wind that swept all the fruit off the trees. Damn the Occupation. There is *still* fighting and shooting.'

'And looting –'

'And bombs –'

'And no electricity, no post, no schools or enough food or medicine for the hospitals.'

'One day there wasn't even any bread.'

There was a second's silence.

'That was not the war,' admitted Dimitri. 'I had a problem with my yeast, and I apologise with all my heart. But even that was because of quarrels from way, way back. Old feuds, jealousies and spells. The earth doesn't care about us. There was that terrible winter.'

'We brought it on ourselves,' moaned the miller. 'The earth was punishing us.'

'Listen to me,' roared Dimitri, leaping up on to the table. 'Here we are, stuck in this ruined village that used to be so prosperous and friendly. The village children are orphans in an old school that's falling down round their ears, and the Occupation have repaired *nothing*. They even bombed the ancient walnut tree.'

'No. That was the frost,' explained the orchard owner.

The landlord weaved his way through the tables with trays of drinks balanced along each arm. Dimitri took a drink in each hand, and Jez thought, *Oh, please, don't have any more drink, Dimitri. Katrin will be cross with you* . . .

He wished Dimitri would come on home, but the

baker swigged the liquid from both glasses and hurled them into the fireplace *smash* and stamped his boot so that the table rocked.

'We will re-build our lives,' roared Dimitri.

'Yes. Yes,' came the cry, making the old inn shake to the last of its rafters.

'We will demand the three M's.'

'What's them three ems, Baker?' shouted Peter the bus driver, burping like a giant frog.

'Money, men and materials,' roared Dimitri.

'Money, men and materials,' shouted everyone. They swigged their glasses empty and hurled them into the fireplace.

'Please don't do that. I can't afford it,' begged the innkeeper.

'So it's *to the city*, boys,' bellowed the baker, red-faced, fists up in front of him, weaving and bobbing like a prizefighter.

There was a long pause. The old doctor spoke.

'I am not shure that they will lishen to us. They will think we are a pheasant scrabble – peasant rabble – from the mountains.'

Everything fell quiet. There was only the fire crackling and Peter the bus driver burping.

'We should have a spokesh – shpokeman – a

leader to shpeak for ush,' said the doctor. He drank deeply, smacking his lips while everyone waited and swayed, respectfully.

At last he said, 'It ish time for a new Talking Man. Every village used to have one.'

'We've got the right man already,' burped Peter.

'No we haven't,' shouted Dimitri, teetering on the tabletop.

'Oh yes we have,' said Peter. 'We've got you. *You're* our Talking Man. All those in favour of Dimitri?'

'Aye!' they shouted, waving their hands in the air. 'Dimitri for Talking Man.' They rushed at Dimitri, grabbed his legs and carried him off the table and round the inn.

Jez was getting so hot, he thought he might explode. He wished they'd all stop shouting and smashing glasses.

'Dimitri, let's go back now,' he pleaded. 'Katrin will want to get home. I must take over from her and watch Luka.'

'Leave him be, boy,' shouted someone. 'Katrin will understand. She should know her place by now.'

But Jez could not bear the hot, smoky inn a moment longer.

He cried, 'See you later, Talking Man,' and

hurried out.

Dimitri was borne around the inn in wobbly triumph. He began to wonder if he was in someone else's dream.

'What have I let myself in for? I'm a baker, not a blinking politician. Put me down, boysh. I have to get up early.'

He fell to the floor and began to fumble his way into his greatcoat, frowning as he felt a weight in his pocket. He lifted it out and squinted close.

A strange little face peered up at him.

'Time to go home, Alfonso,' mumbled Dimitri to the tortoise and he lurched off into the night.

But what was that? A voice was softly calling his name.

'Dimitri? Dimitri . . . Come over here. I have something for you. Something you want.'

16

GHOST HEAD

Dusk began to fall as they flew away from the city.

'It looks different from the land we flew over this morning,' said Luka. The darkness of the night made him feel sad. He knew that when the swallow brought him back to his body, he would lose sight of the world again. And he had not found his mother.

'I wanted to find her for Jez's sake, swallow. And for my own sake, most of all.'

The swallow was longing to get back to his mate. The bird's whole body strained towards home. He was tired, and anxious. There was something not quite right about the air. The darkness felt as if it was holding its breath, waiting for something.

'Are you sure we are on the right course?' said Luka, thinking again how different the world below looked. There was no visible moon. The land had disappeared. Luka could not see any outlines, or contours. They might be anywhere. The swallow dived lower and the ground loomed up. Luka glimpsed small, luminous clouds in the darkness and realised that it was white blossom in the hedgerows.

The swallow rose again to miss the trees.

Luka heard them. *Wingbeats.* Loud and deliberate, beating through the sluggish air, coming steadily nearer.

'Don't worry, little bird,' Luka reassured the swallow. 'It's probably a night owl and anyway it couldn't catch you all the way up here.'

The sky was full of dense cloud. Part of it glimmered with a yellow green light. More and more of this eerie light crept around the edge of the grey cloud, like a halo. It defined itself into the crescent moon. Luka saw it gleam on the feathers on the swallow's head, and light up something coming through the air towards them.

He cried, 'It's a ghost's head. A head without a body.'

The moonlight fled away but the pale head flew steadily towards them. Luka saw that it was joined on to a body with narrow pointed wings. The creature turned up towards them. Luka saw that it had white-ringed eyes with blank, fierce middles. He saw a hooked beak, and felt the hot air moved by the relentless beating of its wings. *A vulture.*

Luka felt terror flood the swallow's body, but he knew he had a reserve of great strength to send coursing into the little bird. He had willpower without fear, and he urged on the swallow, putting his whole mind into its little body. *Fly, fly, home. Fly for your life.*

But the swallow was so tired.

The ghost-headed bird opened its beak and let out an eerie scream.

Luka recognised that sound. With awful clarity, he remembered what had attacked him at the top of that gorge, just before he had fallen down into the Depths of Lumb.

'Fly faster. Fly higher. We can do it, we can!' insisted Luka, but his hope was flagging. He feared the exhausted swallow might die with the effort. Only a few days ago, it had arrived from its flight over thousands of miles across the sea.

Below them flapped that ghost-headed bird. It would never give up until it had torn them to pieces.

Luka put his mind on escape, but there was searing pain, and desperate gasping. They were failing. They were losing height, losing speed, losing strength.

The swallow flipped and flew straight upwards. Luka felt fear set like ice around its heart. All it could do was climb and hope to lose the vulture that was waiting for them to fall to their deaths.

Far below them Luka glimpsed lights, as small and soft as fireflies. They disappeared almost at once. 'They're the lamps and candles from my village. The orphanage and the bakery. But if we fly down to it, the village, that vulture will get us. Keep high, swallow. Head for the mountains!'

Ahead, Luka saw a dark angel soaring in the sky. It was majestic. It flew towards them, haloed in gold all round its body. It was bearing down on them, nearer and nearer.

Luka and the swallow were caught in the dark centre of its eye.

'It's a golden eagle. We don't stand a chance! Between the eagle and the vulture we'll be pulled apart,' he cried.

The eagle beat steadily towards them and the fragile swallow rocked on the air wash of its flight. Luka saw the eagle's clear golden eye.

The dark centre was not fixed on them at all. It was hunting the ghost-headed bird below.

The eagle dropped from the sky, straight as a

machete, on to the vulture. The two creatures knotted together, tumbling and twisting as if beaks and wings and claws belonged to one turning bird.

The bewildered swallow darted to and fro through clouds of feathers, as if a giant had slashed his pillows with a knife, smothering them in a storm of down and feathers. Beads of bright blood fell to the earth. Wings thumped, beaks ripped flesh, and Luka heard the eagle's yelp, and the thin scream of the ghost-headed bird.

In between them was the helpless swallow.

17

HOW DOES YOUR GARDEN GLOW?

Dimitri could not see who was calling him.

'Dimitri? I have a proposition to put to you. It is a matter of life and death . . . Come into my garden.'

Dimitri realised he was at the five-sided house. He saw that dumpy outline and heard rustling and snapping as Vaskalia disappeared into the tangle of tall plants. Before he could stop himself, he lurched after her. A nodding lily tapped him on the shoulder. A jagged leaf scratched his hand. His knees were being nibbled and a fat soft moth bumped against his face.

Dimitri blinked at a flower leering at him. It had a luminous orange stamen that curled like a chameleon's tongue. He felt faint. If he keeled over in this garden, no one would ever know where he was. The plants would eat him.

What? The stars had fallen down on to Vaskalia's garden. The grasses and long hairy leaves were spotted with tiny beacons that glowed and winked at him. Some of the little lights sat on top of some slimy black mushrooms.

Vaskalia scuttled back to where Dimitri swayed, queasily. Her face was lit green. She picked up one of the little stars, grabbed his hand and placed it on his palm.

'Why has it gone out?' he asked.

'Put it down and watch,' cackled Vaskalia.

Dimitri flicked it on to a leaf. The green glow reappeared.

'Madame Glow-worm is shining to summon her true love!' cried Vaskalia.

She simpered up at him, fluttering her eyelashes. Dimitri saw that they were coated with black, and that she had plastered powder on her greenish cheeks. In his unsteady mind he pictured Big Katrin's outdoor skin, rosy with sun and wind. He wished with everything he had that Katrin would come and save him.

'But why are they all in *your* garden?'

'Magical creatures are drawn to me,' she crowed. 'I have a way with plants too. I could bring my glow-worms to light a summer festival. Not the ones on the inkcaps, of course,' she confided, flicking a dimming speck off a mushroom, 'because they have already been poisoned.'

Vaskalia sidled up close. Even the night-scented flowers could not muffle her cloggy unwashed smell.

'Summer is a time to pick our sweethearts, Dimitri.'

'Well please don't pick me.'

'I chose my sweetheart long ago. I chose Luka's father, Gabriel. But he refused me. Then *she* stole him. That Evangelina, that foreigner, that harlot!'

'She was from the other side of the mountain, that's all,' groaned Dimitri, 'and he married *her*, Vaskalia, and not you. It was years and years ago, so stop it, will you?'

Dimitri felt as if he could scoop her rage up in big slimy lumps and hurl it far away. Something was stinging his leg. He tried to move away, but she grabbed his elbow and hissed, '*I* could provide the perfect home for Luka.'

'He's happily settled with me.'

'But I understand his gift. From his dark past, there comes a terrible power. I know things about his family that no one else does. He is in danger living with you.'

'You're lying,' shouted Dimitri, so that the flowers backed away.

'*I* would be the perfect mother for Luka,' she wheedled. 'His short life will be full of danger. Only *I* know what to do. *And* I would make it worth your while.'

She whispered into Dimitri's ear. The garden began to spin, taking Dimitri with it. He was whirling round and round, helplessly, with dreamlike flowers and lights and sickly scents, and wondering why there weren't any *birds* in this garden.

He heard Vaskalia's words as if they were far away from him. She spoke of promise and delight. Green light illuminated her face, making her eyes multi-coloured as opals, shining on her dark lips. '*Go on*, Dimitri. I can make Big Katrin fall in love with you madly, passionately, so that she won't know what's hit her. With just one spell I can make her forget all about Big Wassisname who went off to fight. Think about it. I'll do my love potion number twenty-three, some pills in her tea, an incantation or two, fifty pins stuck in a doll of her man, and she's yours, Dimitri, she's yours! And I get the blind boy.'

Dimitri felt queasy. He batted moths away from his mouth, and scratched a rash on his arm. For a moment his head cleared and the nightmare lurched to a stop.

He yelled, 'Listen to me, you! I won't betray Luka. He has Big Katrin, and Jez and me to care for him. Why don't you look after your own boy instead?'

Ow! He gasped and doubled up, clutching his belly as if he had been stabbed. *Ow!* Another pain jabbed his left temple.

He saw five of Vaskalia's faces, each one twisted with malice.

'You'll be sorry you ever turned me down, Dimitri Founari,' she screamed.

SQUEAKING MICE, GROANING BEAR

Dimitri stamped in through the bakery door.

'Get me some coffee, fast,' he snapped at Jez. He pulled off his coat, was about to aim it at the hook high on the wall, when he stopped. He thought for a second and took Alfonso the tortoise out from his pocket and set him down on the floor. He glanced around and scowled.

'You haven't got everything out ready for me to bake,' he ranted. 'You know I like it all waiting the second I come downstairs.'

Jez did not risk saying that it was nowhere near the time yet. Instead he said, 'Luka still has not woken up.'

Dimitri was silent. He had his back turned to Jez. He rubbed his stomach round and round, as if he was trying to get a note from the rim of a glass. He started to pace up and down, hands rammed into his pockets.

Jez poured water on to the coffee. He waited for

the coffee grounds to settle and brew. He said, 'I'm glad you rescued the tortoise. Look, the kittens are pawing its shell. They want it to come out and play. Now . . . here's your coffee.'

Dimitri yawned and stretched his arms above his head.

'How did you get your muscles?' said Jez, trying to coax him out of his bad mood. 'Your arms look so strong. Mine just look puny.'

Dimitri turned and looked at Jez as if he did not know who he was. Then something cleared on his face and he said, 'Sorry, I was miles away. And I'm sorry I've been bad-tempered. I met Vaskalia on the way back from the inn. Or rather, she met *me*.'

'Is that how you got that orange blotch on your cheek?'

'Er . . . maybe.' Dimitri's hand went up to the pollen smudge. 'But Luka is safe with me.'

'What do you mean?'

'Oh, I'll tell you sometime.' Dimitri walked around Jez as if he was thinking of buying him. 'Why are you worried about your appearance all of a sudden? It couldn't have anything to do with that pretty young woman at the orphanage, now could it?'

Jez sunk his chin down towards his chest to hide his blushes.

'I just wish I had a stronger body.'

'There's nothing wrong with your body. We'd all like to be something else. Don't you think I would like to be as tall as you, Jez? Don't you think I'd like to look *down* at Katrin instead of up? The only way I can be taller is to stand on a chair with my baker's hat on.'

'That's another thing; my hair's *useless*,' moped Jez, trying to smooth it down. 'I look like a hedgehog.'

'At least you've *got* some hair!'

'At least you've got good muscles!'

'Ah,' said Dimitri, sipping the coffee. 'I have a secret, Jez.'

'Please tell me!'

'All right. As you have made me such good coffee, I will.' Dimitri set down his cup and wandered into the larder, muttering, 'Now, where did I put them?'

He staggered out again, carrying his weights and set them down on the floor by Jez.

'There,' he said. 'Now pick one up.'

Jez stared at the lumps of dark metal. He reached down. Dimitri shouted, 'No! Bend your knees or you'll hurt your back. Watch me.'

Dimitri's knees squeaked like mice as his legs bent. He reached down, shuddering, to pick up a weight in each hand.

'Wow, that's good,' exclaimed Jez. 'How far up can you go?'

Dimitri's teeth were clamped together in effort so that he could not answer. Sweat broke out on his nose and veins bulged blue on his forehead. He held the weights close to his chest for a few seconds, shaking and grizzling with the strain. Groaning like a bear, he raised them above his shoulders for a split second.

'Stop, Dimitri. Your eyes will pop out.'

Dimitri sat down on the floor, gasping for breath.

'Haven't done that for a while. Phew. But that's what made these muscles, Jez.'

'Lifting those lumps?'

'They're called weights, not lumps.'

Jez knelt by him, examining the weights.

'Where did you get them?'

'From the miller. He's got lots of them. For weighing out his flour. The blacksmith welded two together with this strip of metal in the middle, so that I could grip them. He made them to my specification, of course.'

'Of course.'

'You'll need to use them every day. Morning and night.'

'I will, I will,' cried Jez. 'They've certainly made you into a fit man. Dimitri . . . this might sound nosy . . . but why don't you and Katrin . . . I mean, you make such a happy couple.'

Dimitri got up and busied himself with things for the morning, his yeast and flour. Jez fetched the jar of blue poppy seeds, set out the jug of oil, wondering if he had said something wrong.

At last Dimitri said, 'Because Big Katrin is not free.'

'What do you mean, not free?'

'Katrin was married. At the beginning of the fighting, her husband – his name was Karl – saddled up his horse, loaded it with food, blankets, his rifle and some ammunition and kissed Katrin goodbye. Then he rode off to join the freedom fighters in the forest.'

'And?'

'A few weeks later, the horse came back. Alone. Katrin has not seen her husband again. She keeps the horse in the field by her house.' Dimitri sighed and his eyes filled with tears. 'She has not spoken one single word since.'

Jez had not known about Big Katrin's past before. It had not occurred to him that she *had* a past. Katrin just turned up at the bakery, smiled, made cakes and spoiled children. How little he knew about people's lives.

19

DIVE-BOMBING THE BAKER

Early next morning, the swallows whirled above Dimitri's yard as if he had thrown a handful of steely-blue anchors up into the sky. Every so often, they swooped down, dive-bombing the baker so that he had to wear his hat, which was a shame because he liked to feel the sunshine on his bald patch.

He stacked the wood into the wheelbarrow and took it inside. He piled the logs in the basket and turned to Jez.

'Has Luka woken up yet?'

'No. He hasn't stirred at all. That makes it a long time. Let me lift the trays, Dimitri.'

'I'm sure young Imogen likes you, with or without big muscles.'

'It's nothing to do with Imogen,' insisted Jez, blushing. 'I just – well, I like to be fit and ready for anything.'

Into Dimitri's unwilling mind came that

cunning, green face. He said, 'You'll *need* to be ready for anything.'

'What do you mean?'

'I mean that there is a burden your family must carry. You may well have to shoulder some of it.' Dimitri busied himself putting cinnamon bark into a pestle, muttering, 'It's time I made some cinnamon buns . . .'

'Stop changing the subject, Dimitri. *Please* tell me what Vaskalia was up to last night.'

'All right. Vaskalia wants Luka to live with her.'

'Over my dead body,' shouted Jez. He stormed across the bakery and kicked the oven hard. He spun round and glared at Dimitri as if *he* were the enemy.

'Vaskalia claims she knows all about your family. Things that the rest of us don't know . . . And she promised me things.' Dimitri caught his breath as he recalled Vaskalia whispering secrets in his ear. He realised that someone else was watching him, and spun round with a guilty look on his face.

'Katrin – you gave me a fright!'

She crossed to the table, picked up a mug, tapped it and glared at Dimitri as if asking him a question. He knew she had heard everything.

'No, Katrin, I didn't let Vaskalia make me a drink. Not this time,' he said.

Katrin placed the mug back on the table. She looked into Dimitri's eyes for a long moment and Dimitri's face slowly blushed dark as a plum. Katrin went upstairs to make some tea and Jez whispered, 'Dimitri, what's going on? What did Vaskalia promise you?'

'She said she could make Katrin fall passionately in love with me – if I gave her Luka.'

'Please tell me you didn't agree.'

Dimitri flung himself down at the table. Jez saw tears in his eyes, and felt a stab of hurt. Dimitri was so strong and good-humoured – what could make him weep?

'I'm ashamed to say I was tempted. *I still am* . . . I love Katrin. I want her to share my life. But –'

'But?'

'I love you two boys. And do you think Katrin would ever love me if she thought I had betrayed you? You're like my sons. Vaskalia knows she's getting no help from me.'

Jez put his arms around the little baker and gave him a big hug. 'Katrin cares about you *anyway*. You're such a great guy. Maybe she'll love you without Vaskalia's meddling?'

He thought, *And please never change your mind. Please never let Vaskalia get Luka in her clutches.*

20

BOWL OF SNOW

After the terrible screaming and ripping from the fighting birds, the silence of the mountains was profound.

Luka woke to silver light streaming in between the rocks. Outside, the sky was azure blue behind the clear peaks. Below him was a hollow like a bowl, filled to the brim with snow.

Some of the snow began to move. White creatures with long ears chased in a circle. At some unseen signal they turned, and chased in the other direction. Mountain hares, hundreds of them, bounding in the sun, tearing through the snow.

But up in the crevice, Luka's swallow did not move. Luka could not feel it breathing.

'You have pushed the bird too far.'

The voice was carried everywhere in the wind that blew around the mountaintops. The words echoed each other as if they were notes of music. Luka smelled the scent of burning juniper and birch wood, and knew it was the man with the hair of frost, the man from his dream.

'You chose well, Luka. Yet you drove him too hard. Reckless boy. You risked his life.'

'I didn't mean to.'

'You did not think with *his* mind. That is what a shaman must do. You exhausted his small body and drained his energy. Now he may never fly home again.'

'But the eagle came to save us,' cried Luka.

'The eagle did *not* come to save *you*. The eagle came to protect his nest and his larder from a bird that flew near his territory. Why should the eagle care about people?'

Luka sobbed, 'I did not find my mother.'

'No. Yet you may have found other things.'

'What good is this gift if I can't even get my mother back?'

There was no answer. Luka stared out down at the mountain bowl. The hares played as if nothing was different. For a brief moment he heard the howl and sob of the wolf choir. Why could he not see this man with the hair of frost? It must be him. Luka felt as if the voice had reduced him to nothing. He was worthless.

The voice spoke again. It was softer, and came

from a different part of the mountain.

'Luka, you know that I am watching over you but I can only offer my advice. I am a shaman from the past. You are becoming a shaman boy. The shamanic gift is for everyone but it speaks through you. Use it, or it will leave you. Learn from it, and bring life back to your village. Some you know may share a little of its power. Others want your gift for a bad purpose, and you are always in danger from them.'

The words echoed against each other, tumbling like dominoes.

'See the Cloud Cat? Take your strength from her.'

On the mountain opposite, the Cloud Cat stood in a crevice lined with fur. Two small cubs rolled on their backs in their warm home, batting her face with large furry paws. The Cloud Cat stretched her mouth open in a yawn. She padded out along the ledge. Luka watched her shoulder blades slide under her luxuriant dappled fur. She stopped. She turned her small, round head and stared across the chasm with her gold nugget eyes with their round pupils. She knew he was there. Luka felt himself pulled into those eyes.

He begged, 'Please don't let the swallow die.'

As he gazed into the Cloud Cat's eyes, strength eased into him, warming his body.

The frail swallow began to breathe light and fast. He was panting, his tiny chest rising and falling, his beak open. The bird was so *thin*. He shuffled to his awkward little feet, stretched out his wing and began to preen his cobalt blue feathers ready for the flight home.

'But first, little bird,' Luka said, 'you must eat and drink and get strong.'

21

CLOUDS OF MERINGUE

This morning, Big Katrin strode to work without her scarf. A gentle wind lifted her oak-brown hair. The clouds in the sky were puffy as egg whites whipped for meringue, and Katrin felt a spring in her step and a desire to smile. Everything was going to be better.

She wondered if she had been too hard on Dimitri the day before.

She opened the bakery door. The loaves were lined up on the trays ready to be baked. Dimitri and Jez hovered by them, fidgeting.

Katrin hid her smile as she marched past them and on up the stairs to make tea.

Jez and Dimitri relaxed, listening to the water filling the kettle, the cups and pot put down on the tray.

Then they heard Big Katrin cry out. No words, just an exclamation of joy.

Luka was awake.

At once, he wanted to go to the orphanage to tell his story to the children.

'Of course you can,' said Jez, grinning with relief.

Jez looked at the children, sitting all around Luka. Their eyes were smudged and dark. Those eyes had seen so much to make them mistrustful, but this morning they shone as they waited for Luka's story.

They deserve to listen to Luka and be happy for a while, thought Jez. *What a shame it's only a story.*

'And about time too,' cried Aidan, shuffling his bottom around on his cushions. 'I have had to wait ages and *ages* for the next instalment. Where did you go *this* time?'

'I went high into the sky, with a swallow. And it was like dancing,' cried Luka, spreading his arms wide, lifting his face up to the orphanage ceiling. 'I was the Sky Shifter. The swallow and I danced through the clouds. Over them, under them, round them and through the blue, blue sky. I saw the earth far below, like a big patchwork blanket, with woods and fields and a horse and shining water. I saw the village, and the bakery *and* the orphanage. They are so small.'

'Did you see me, Luka?' cried Lisa, jumping up and down.

'No, I didn't, I'm afraid. Maybe you were still in bed, Lisa.'

'What did you see up there?' asked Ellie.

Luka put his head on one side. 'A skylark. She shot straight up, *vooom*. She was so small, but she sang such a big song like when Eva used to sing to us. A rippling song, spinning up in the sky.'

He paused and Aidan began to drum his fingers impatiently on the arm of his chair. Luka heard it but he could hear something else too. That whispering again. *Milksop, idiot, saphead* . . .

'The swallow was kind to take you, wasn't he?' asked Ellie.

'Yes he was,' said Luka quietly. 'And he was the very best bird of all.'

'*Bam Bam Bam! Boom Boom!*' shouted Florin, cheek flat to the piece of wood he was aiming at Luka so that Luka jerked his head away, startled.

'Did you see any penguins up there?' asked Daniela.

'No. No penguins. But I saw swifts. And bats.'

'Were there any big birds?' asked Ellie.

'Yes. There was an eagle. Soaring and gliding, like a dark sail with gold all around it. Its wings beat like slow drums and it was as big as a sailing boat. It followed us.' Luka shivered. He did not say more. It would frighten the children. He did not want to remember that horrible fight.

Imogen said, 'Don't worry about the eagle, children, it's only a story,' but her voice faltered. She glanced at Jez but he would not meet her eyes.

Upside down in the rafters, Simlin hissed, *Idiot. Why wasn't Bone Cracker in your story? Mother sent him out hunting. Bet you saw him.*

'Luka,' nagged Aidan. '*Why* did you go flying off up in the sky with a swallow?'

Luka hung his head. Aidan always asked the questions he did not want to answer.

'Come *on*,' persisted Aidan.

'I was looking for someone.'

'Who? Did you find them? Maybe it was your father but –'

'Stop it, Aidan,' scolded Eva. 'You're as bad as a terrier.'

Luka could not answer. He wanted to cry again. That spiteful whispering had not gone away, and if his mother really was in the city, he had failed to find her. *Failed.* He did not want Jez to know who he had been looking for, or he would be so disappointed Luka had not brought her home.

So he just shook his head.

Why did that woman tell Jez she had seen our mother in the city? Again he heard the shaman's voice saying, *Others want your gifts . . .*

Luka slept late the next morning. He went to sit in the sunshine, listening to the swallows, and wondered why he had not dreamed of his mother. Usually he looked up into her silver eyes when he woke, but not today. Did that mean something bad? He tightened up his face against that other pain which Aidan had stirred. *Father.*

Luka would not think about his father. He did not want to remember *having* a father.

The door from the bakery was flung open.

'Yeah! Here I go,' shouted Jez springing into the yard. Luka heard him ripping off his shirt, followed by the grunts, footfalls, bounces and curses of Jez's exercise routine which now happened in any spare moment. Luka heard the clanging of the weights on the ground, and groaning and cursing as Jez lifted them.

Luka giggled at Jez's grunts and then heard excited voices out in the street, the click of the latch of the yard gate and the hubbub of children on the other side. Eva's voice protested, 'Wait, all of you. Stop pushing.'

Jez mumbled, 'Uh – hullo Imo –' and fumbled to pull his shirt back on.

'Don't scare the swallows, you lot,' said Luka, 'cos one of them is very tired.'

'Bossy Luka,' squealed Aidan. 'Put me down on that sack, Eva.'

'We were out for a walk. So we thought we'd call in,' said Imogen. Then she whispered to Jez, 'Some people came to the orphanage. I don't want the children to hear.'

Luka had already heard her.

'What people?' Jez steered her into the bakery, where Katrin and Dimitri were sitting at the table with the coffee pot.

'Two men and a woman. They tried to push their way inside but Eva fastened the chain across the door.'

'I had to. They were quite determined to get in,' said Eva. 'They said they wanted to take some children to new homes and families –'

'And I did not trust them one little bit,' cried Imogen. 'Jez, they said they would be back.'

'I'll build you all a safe home,' vowed Jez. 'For now I'll fix more locks and –'

'And you had better mend the hole in the roof too,' said Luka.

Jez stared down at him. 'You shouldn't be eavesdropping, Luka. And how could *you* see a hole in a roof, unless you were above the orphanage.'

Jez bit his lip. Luka's stories were wavering on the edge of their lives. Then Jez said decisively, 'If there *is* a hole, I'll mend it.'

'I have to go to the city, so I'll buy tools for you there,' announced Dimitri.

'Why are you going?' asked Jez.

Dimitri fiddled with his coffee cup, swirling the grounds round and round.

'I'm going to buy a van. I need a van to make deliveries. Katrin has started baking cheese pies again. Business is booming. People are returning to the village. And there is something you all should know.'

He pushed his cup away and stood up to face them.

'I have been chosen as Talking Man.'

Luka felt his way over to Dimitri and took his hand. He said, 'Then you must go to the dark red castle and demand help. And fix the Midnight Clock.'

'How come you know about this castle, Luka?' asked Dimitri but Luka ignored his question and said, 'When you're Talking Man, will you still play music? I want to dance. And I want you to sing again, Eva, with your beautiful voice.'

'Maybe I will . . .' said Eva doubtfully.

Jez's stomach was beginning to feel bad. He felt as if he was wearing his heavy belt of lead charms again. How could Dimitri afford to buy a van? Had Vaskalia been giving him money? And Luka was talking oddly again, believing his own stories, as if they were true. Jez felt his face grow cold and blanch with fear, like an almond slipping its brown skin in hot water.

Luka's lips turned up in that secret little smile that drove Jez mad, as if he was going somewhere without him, somewhere dangerous.

GANG OF GHOSTS

Simlin ran fast as a hare back from the orphanage. The five-sided house was heaving with a rich, meaty smell that made him want to eat and eat and eat. It certainly wasn't bat soup this time.

'Ah, there you are, my child!' Vaskalia said, in a pleasant voice he did not recognise. 'Guess what's in my stew?'

Simlin smelled and blinked.

'Guess orange carrots . . . tatties . . . matoes and onions, green bits and –'

Mother took over. 'It is brimful of good herbs and spices. Green peppercorns and salt from the sea.' She ladled brown stew into a spare tortoiseshell bowl.

Simlin sniffed hard. The scorpion on his forehead itched *oo-scrat-scrat*, but the smell from the pot was so tempting and the rumbling in his tummy so shuddering that he did not heed his scorpion. He held his hands out for the bowlful.

In the middle of the gloopy stew was a huge

wedge of meat. Was it a chicken? Simlin had seen chickens strutting around the village this springtime. He did not remember ever eating one. But chickens were not giants like this. Could it be Bone Cracker?

Simlin snatched the meat from his bowl and sank in his teeth. *Mmmm!* Never had he tasted anything so delicious. His fingers slid around the greasy hunk, fingers to lick later.

Mother watched with her head on one side as Simlin tore bits of bird off the bone and drank from the bowl.

'More?' said Mother.

Yes. Two more bowlsful. But when she asked the next time, Simlin shook his head. Suddenly he felt very sick.

She grabbed his wrist. 'But we need to fatten you up. Make you strong.'

She threw back her head and laughed so that her wattles wobbled. Simlin heard that high note in her cackling that meant *hurt*. He saw the cold flints glint in her eyes. His scorpion mark began to itch again, terribly. Mother stopped laughing and looked at him. Simlin liked it better when she ignored him. But he had to ask her, 'What for? Why make me strong?'

'You've got some secrets from me, haven't you,

Simlin? Well, I've been keeping something secret from you too.'

She stomped over to the bed. *Oh no. The claw.*

Vaskalia braced herself, grunting, and with her porky little arms she heaved her mattress over on to its side. There was jangling, cracking and a rotten fishy smell.

'Look, Simlin,' she crowed. 'Look what's underneath.'

Simlin thought at first the mattress had been lying on an enormous ghost.

He saw a vast pale skin, hung all over with dead things. A curling snakeskin, crazed like cobblestones. Two long wings. A beak. Yellow tombstone teeth. A pair of empty shells. Something he had never seen before – a speckled bag with dangling tentacles. A flat fish with empty eye sockets. A herringbone fringed with spikes. There were teasel combs, bits of rusty chain and a curved knife, and the mangy tail of some kind of cat.

At the top of the ghost skin were the antlers of a stag, still with tatters of velvet.

And there was that giant claw . . .

'Behold the shaman's cloak,' hissed Mother. 'This is the cloak of the spirit-changer, who dances in and out of creatures, and in and out of people too. Whoever wears this will be the Powerful One.'

She stroked the cloak lovingly and whispered, 'It has its own gang of ghosts, its own following. All those who have ever worn it will walk behind the new shaman.'

'Dead ones?' faltered Simlin.

'Dead *and* alive will follow the new shaman,' she crowed. 'And whoever wears this cloak will be strongest of all.'

Simlin wanted the ground to open so that he could slide down into it and disappear. He shook his head so fast he thought his teeth would fall out, *Not me. Don't want to wear big stinking cloak, never ever.* He scuttled away and crouched in a corner, plotting what to do, making his face blank so that Mother would not know what he was thinking of, *that little blind boy with power to be big cat and bird . . . how does do it?*

23

WHEN BIG KATRIN WAS
A LITTLE GIRL

Big Katrin put her tray of butterfly cakes in the oven to turn golden brown. Earlier this morning she had beaten eggs and lemon juice for the lemon curd. Now she began to mix pastry for her cheese pies. Her hands with their fine tapered fingers flew lightly through the butter and flour.

She heard birds and paused to look through the little window. The swallows were twittering as they whizzed in and out of the wood store. Syrup the cat rolled on her back and dreamed of catching one. The pupils in her green eyes narrowed to arrow-slits in the sunshine. Her kittens hid, pouncing on shadows. The orphans were playing in the yard. Katrin herself had put a bolt high on the inside of the gate out on to the street because she had never forgotten those three strangers. The children were clambering in and out of an old romany wagon, a vardo, that Dimitri had found abandoned on the road to the sea and told her: *I'm going to paint it and decorate it with gold stars and flowers and scrolls.*

Out in the yard, Katrin watched Lisa trying to persuade the reluctant dog to fetch sticks. Aidan sat in Dimitri's wheelbarrow. From there he directed everyone in his imperious voice and occasionally squealed, 'Wheel me, Eva.' Maria sat with the tortoise on her lap, stroking its shell while Erin tried to feed it tomato. Florin crept around the yard, going 'Neowm *bang* aaagh!' and falling over with his hand clutching his throat.

Big Katrin saw Luka standing by the wall. He was listening to the other children but he stayed apart from them. She decided that his mind was elsewhere.

When she was a little girl, Katrin's mother told her a story about someone called a shaman. Katrin loved this story. She had never seen a shaman. Until now.

Katrin's mother told her, *A shaman can make his spirit jump into another body, into a bear or a wild boar, or a hawk.*

Into an ant?

Yes, even into an ant. He can share the creature's power.

When can I see the shaman? Soon? What creature will be the power one? pestered little Katrin – because in those days she never stopped talking.

One day, perhaps, my darling, said her mother. *Sometimes a family has a shaman for a son or daughter. That brings trouble for them. The shaman moves among us in times of trouble. He journeys with his power creature and brings back life for everyone. When he dies, he leaves his voice in the mountains to guide the next shaman.*

Her mother told her that a shaman was a born storyteller, who was full of the gift, and loved the earth and its energy. Sometimes people were jealous of his power. But Katrin's mother warned that it was never certain that the shaman would use the gift for good. There were stories of extreme wickedness from the other side of the mountain.

So a shaman was a dangerous being, especially if he was a motherless child.

Like Luka. A reckless boy.

Big Katrin frowned down into her mixing bowl, because her mother had never mentioned a shaman being born into Gabriel's family. Yet Katrin knew now that Luka was the shaman. The gift drifted through these mountains like a thin mist. Katrin had a little of it, enough to see Luka in the glass ball, with that snow leopard waiting for him nearby. So, disastrously, so did Vaskalia and her skinny son. But Luka was full of it. Because he was blind he would look inwards, and watch his spiritual life. He would not be distracted by the everyday world his eyes would see if he was sighted.

Big Katrin felt close to Luka. She would always watch over him and make sure Dimitri protected him like a father. Katrin smiled as she thought of Dimitri. *He* certainly had no spirit gift. Katrin did not see it in Jez, either, but they were all there to love and support Luka.

PART THREE: SUMMER

The man with the hair of frost walks by the river.
Salmon leap above the rock and a pike waits in the
shadows. Bears sway at the top of the waterfall and an
otter slips down the bank.
The man with the hair of frost says: 'Luka, you are a
shaman now. You are full of the gift. But others will
want it for themselves. And beware – there is more
than one shaman's cloak.'

1

BAD MAGIC

Luka ran out into the summer heat, straight towards the runaway horse that came clattering down the street. It reared up around Luka, striking sparks that smelled like gunpowder from the cobblestones. He wrapped his arms over his head, crying 'Whoa, Beechnut, whoa.'

Jez strode out of the bakery, shouting, 'You could have been killed, Mr Reckless.'

'Rubbish,' said Luka. He stood on tiptoe and talked to the horse until it stopped trembling. 'You bolted from Katrin, didn't you? Bad horse.'

Then he began to dance. He clicked his fingers and sang, 'I'm going to the *Big Red Castle*. I'm going to the *Big Bad City*.'

'I'm not sure I should let you go,' grumbled Jez.

'You must, Jez. Dimitri needs my help to ask the general and the warlords for aid.'

'Dimitri looks like a gangster in his old striped suit,' sniggered Jez, but then he grew serious and said, 'Luka, stay by his side every single second. There will be bandits, and soldiers and . . .'

Jez stopped. He had remembered Vaskalia.

The Red Castle will be dangerous for Luka, but not as dangerous as it is for him here.

Jez and Dimitri struggled to put the prancing mountain horse between the shafts of the vardo and Dimitri yelled, 'Hurry up, Peter.'

'Why are we going in that rickety cart?' grumbled Peter.

'Because you overturned your bus to miss a goat and now it won't go,' snapped Dimitri.

'Stop arguing, you two,' said Luka. Jez helped him climb on to the seat, just as Big Katrin puffed up chasing after her runaway horse. She held out her arms for goodbye hugs.

Luka sat squashed between Dimitri and Peter as the vardo bowled away out of the village. He raised his face to the sun and heard ripe seedpods snap in the heat. The dry ground cracked beneath the big wheels. They bounced over a pothole and Luka shot up into the air, giggling.

'Ow,' grumbled Peter. 'You should let me drive, baker. I know this road like the back of me thumbs.'

'Katrin has lent this horse to *me*,' said Dimitri. 'It's my responsibility.'

'Where did she get the horse?' asked Luka. 'And it is a *he*, not an *it*.'

'Don't get cheeky, Luka,' said Peter. 'Everyone knows you're strange. You're an odd'un, like out of them old stories.'

Luka fell silent. Yes, he *was* different, and it made him feel very alone.

Next thing Luka knew, he was pushed down on the seat, with Dimitri hissing, 'We're passing Vaskalia's house. Get down out of sight.'

Luka felt something thrown over him. Judging by the stale cigarette smell, it was Peter's jacket. Luka stayed as still as he could. He listened to the hammering hooves and felt the tension from the men on either side of him, until Dimitri pulled the scratchy jacket away and said, 'You can sit up again. She can't see you now.'

Luka reached his hands up to Dimitri's face. He touched his forehead and hairy caterpillar eyebrows, and felt Dimitri's face crease with a smile.

'Jez says Big Katrin could sort Vaskalia out *any* day,' said Luka.

Dimitri was not so sure about that. Big Katrin was

strong and her strength came from kindness. Dimitri did not believe it could compete with the spells and incantations from Vaskalia's old magic. *Her* strength came from malice. So he said, 'Stay with those who love you, Luka. You're safe with me for the next couple of days, *and* you can help me find the right words at the Red Castle.'

'Is there anything we need to buy for the summer festival?'

'I don't think so,' said Dimitri. 'All we need is music, food and *us*. Now, when we're at the Red Castle, please don't go off into one of your trances.'

Luka turned his face away and smiled. *Trances* . . . That was how others saw his spirit journeys. How could he explain his gift?

This morning, he was just himself, travelling with Dimitri and Peter, through countryside sweet with the scent of hay and clover drying in the sun. He thought with sadness of the little animals killed by the hay-cutting, the lapwings and the hares that nested on the ground.

When they returned from the city he would shift his spirit again. This time he would think carefully, and try not to put the power creature in danger. He was going to make Jez happy by finding the perfect thing for him to carve.

Peter began to roll a cigarette. His sharp elbow kept digging into Luka's side. He said, 'Who lived in this vardo claptrap before you got it, baker?'

'How should I know? It was abandoned. I mended the wheels and painted it up. I've even nailed a horseshoe over the door and hung a bulb of garlic to keep out bad spirits.'

'Whoever lived in it buried their shadows underneath,' wailed Peter. 'That's what *they* do. At night, them shadows will come out and get us.'

'I can smell salt, Dimitri,' said Luka.

'That's the sea. The road divides soon. Left to the city, right to the sea . . . there's a tractor on the road, piled high with people.'

'They're very quiet,' said Luka.

'They're refugees. I can tell by their eyes'. He reined in the horse. 'Good wishes to you all. Where are you heading?'

The man with his arms resting on the wheel shrugged and said, 'We want to go home to our village, but there's nothing left to go back to.'

Luka heard despair in his voice and called out, 'Why don't you go to our village up the road? There's a good bakery.'

'Thank you. Perhaps we will,' said the man.

'Don't go inviting everyone to our village, odd'un,' hissed Peter.

'Why shouldn't I?' said Luka.

'Because you don't know 'oo they are or what bad magic they'll bring.' Peter grabbed the reins from Dimitri and shouted, '*Geddonwivyer.*'

The startled horse kicked up his heels and whinnied. He cantered down the road to the city, pulling the vardo with its bright paint and its three nervous passengers.

SOMEONE AT THE WINDOW,
SOMETHING AT THE DOOR

Simlin watched through the window until the horse and vardo had trundled out of sight. Vaskalia snored on her fat mattress. The wood fire crackled in the middle of the floor, wriggling away in a worm of smoke up the tin pipe chimney and out into the air.

Simlin tried to let go of the curtain but it stuck to his hand like a cobweb so that he had to wipe it away on the wooden wall.

Gold stars and flowers painted on a shiny barrel on wheels. You could sleep inside that barrel. Baker man sitting up with Peter Bus . . . so where is blind boy?

Simlin scurried to the shelf, reached up and groped among the pin-sticking dolls for the seeing ball. He put his face up close. Whenever he had seen blind boy inside, there had been another creature with him. One had shoulder bones as big as axe blades. Another swooped like a crescent of dark blue moon. Today there was nothing.

Blind boy must be at home with the bully brother, or at the orphanage with the pretty women and *biscuits* . . . Simlin licked his lips with a pointed tongue. He rubbed his stomach. It was getting fat, like a round bowl stuck on to his front, because Mother kept feeding him. She kept forcing back his top jaw and pouring a sticky river of stew right down his throat.

'I'm fattening you up all ready for the midsummer festival, Simlin, so that you're all ready to wear the shaman's cloak,' she gloated.

There was a tapping on the door.

Who could it be? Was it someone from the shiny barrel on wheels?

Pause. *Tap-tap-tap-tap*. Louder.

Simlin slid the seeing ball into Mother's crumpled shoe. He stared at the door. Something was seeping underneath it on to the earthen floor. It swelled into a little pool.

Simlin sniffed. *Blood*.

LUKA TELLS HIS SECRET

The mountain horse hammered along the road. Dimitri sang at the top of his voice and Luka felt proud to be with the brave Talking Man. He had hope in his heart, like the gleam of light on the curve of a glass.

Maybe his mother *was* in the city. Dimitri might see her hurrying down a street.

But as the hours crept on and the wagon wheels churned, Luka's spirits slid back down. Dimitri's singing died away. Peter snored, clicking his teeth with his tongue.

Luka remembered what he had seen through the swallow's eyes: the blood-red castle and the shaven-headed leader. The Midnight Clock where time was stopped, haunted forever by the weeping woman, the man pointing a gun, the frightened, starving children and hooded Death with his scythe.

Luka sighed. He smelled leaves and fresh sap from cut branches, and heard the wind moaning high in the trees. They were hurrying along the forest road now and the shadows were cold and full of resentment. Luka listened hard. Was that the beating of wings? Was it the vulture thing that had attacked him in the Depths of Lumb, and pursued him when he was in his swallow shape?

Peter woke up and farted. 'There'll be bandits behind them trees,' he muttered.

'Stop groaning and moaning, man,' snapped Dimitri.

'Suit yerself, baker. I'm off.' Peter crawled inside the vardo.

Dimitri said, 'Don't worry. This horse will move like greased lightning if we want him to.' He patted something on his right-hand side. 'And I've brought my gun.' Luka heard a wobble in his voice.

The horse stopped and snickered with fear. Peter crawled out of the wagon again, bawling, '*Geddon-wivyer*. Where's a stick?'

'Don't hit him,' cried Luka, tumbling down on to the road. He felt his way along the sweating horse to its taut neck, and ran his hand down the coarse cut mane.

'You are safe with us, Beechnut,' he whispered. Taking the soft nose between his hands he blew up into the horse's nostrils. The horse calmed. Luka took hold of the bridle strap and they moved forwards again.

'*That's* the way to talk to a horse,' said Dimitri. He grabbed Luka's hands and swung him back up on to the seat. Luka listened to the brisk thud of the hooves and wondered what it was like to be the horse. He daydreamed of running, hooves hammering, mane and tail streaming on the wind. He felt a rhythm of energy running though him. They were going to the city to put things right for everyone. He thought of Imo, Eva and the orphans and little Stefan in his cot, but most of all he thought of caustic Aidan. Aidan loved Luka's stories because they made him forget his own pain for a while.

He thought of his home at the bakery and grinned. 'Dimitri, we will be fine in the castle,' he cried. 'You're not just our baker and our Talking Man. You're our hero, too!'

When Luka began to taste dust on his tongue, he knew they were near the city.

'It's a desert of bomb craters and rubble,' said Dimitri. 'There's the frame of a block of flats still standing, like an empty egg box. There's nobody around.'

'That's because they're all dead,' wailed Peter.

'No, they're not,' said Luka. 'They are indoors. In the evening, soldiers fire their guns on the castle battlements, and everyone goes in their house.'

''Ow do you know, Odd'un?' asked Peter suspiciously. Luka did not answer.

'I'm off inside *my* 'ouse,' said Peter and Luka heard him crawling back inside the vardo.

Dimitri said, 'He's right, Luka. How *do* you know? You haven't been to the city. When you go into those deep sleeps, what *really* happens?'

'I shift my mind into other creatures,' said Luka. 'The more I practise, the better I get. I'm powerful and I can see. I ran across the foothills with the Cloud Cat. I flew to the city in my swallow shape. I saw the blood-red castle.'

Luka waited for Dimitri to laugh in disbelief. Instead, he said, 'I've heard old stories of spirit-shifters. I never thought I would meet one. Do you really believe you are a shaman?'

'I *know* I am. I can't tell Jez, because he wouldn't understand and he would be afraid for me. Please keep my secret, Dimitri.'

'I won't tell, Luka. Thank you for telling me.'

Dimitri squeezed Luka's hand, but he felt fear

settle in his mind. Now he understood why Vaskalia wanted Luka.

'We'd better camp out here for the night,' he said, reining in the horse. Luka heard again that wobble of fear in his voice.

'What will happen to the horse while we are asleep?' he asked.

'We'll tether him so he can reach his hay and water.'

''Orse won't be there in the morning,' warned Peter, trying to push his way back on to the seat. ''Orse'll be in someone's stew pot with is 'air stuffed inside a sofa.'

'Oh shut up, Mister Doom-and-Gloom,' shouted Dimitri.

Nobody slept soundly that night.

4

THE MIDNIGHT CLOCK

The next morning they reached the city. Luka felt it was closing in around them. He realised that now there was no birdsong, and a burst of gunfire made him jump.

'*Oi.* Peasants in your gypsy cart,' jeered a voice. 'Where do you think *you're* going, fat man?' Luka felt Dimitri taut as wire next to him, and Peter on his other side, quaking like a jelly. He thought he heard that word *Idiot*. Had the Whisperer followed him here?

The voices stopped.

'Vagabonds,' said Dimitri. 'They're gone now,' but Luka still felt someone was watching them. Jez was right. The city *was* dangerous.

'Look at that castle,' shouted Peter. 'It really is as red as blood.'

'That's where they keep the prisoners,' said Luka.

'What prisoners? I dinna want lockin' up.'

'Oh, shut up, Peter!' said Dimitri. 'Now, we need to get the feel of the place.'

'We've already *got* the feel of the place, baker, and I dinna like it,' grunted Peter. 'I'm getting me spare bus parts and I'm off back 'ome, fast.'

'Aren't you coming with us to the castle?' asked Luka.

'I am *not*. See all them figures stuck up by that Midnight Clock? That's no party. That's Mr Death with 'is big sharp scythe, and Mrs Hunger, and Mr Madness beating them children. They say every midnight those statues slide down the tower, and run all around the city, grabbin' folk to tek back up with 'em. *I* dinna want to be around when they do.'

'If they took you, we wouldn't have to listen to your moaning,' snapped Dimitri. 'Now, there's the garage.'

As they got closer, Luka smelled petrol. He heard cautious steps approaching their vardo.

'Good morning to you,' called Dimitri. 'I want to buy a van.'

Luka heard the garage man's gruff reply. 'There it is.'

'Oh. Have you only the one?'

'There's been a war on, country man, or hadn't you noticed?'

'Try it out, Dimitri,' whispered Luka, grabbing

Dimitri's arm as they stepped down from the vardo.

'I want a test drive, please,' said Dimitri. Luka heard keys jingle and the man said, 'It's not been driven for months. It won't want to start.'

Luka heard them trying to fit a key in the ignition and curse when it would not fit. The man tried a whole bunch. At last he heard a key turn and a door open. In they climbed, and after three false starts the engine spluttered into life. They chugged and bounced around the waste ground. Luka squirmed at the springs sticking into his bottom.

'This is perfect,' cried Dimitri. 'There's room for bread trays in the back, and I can put cushions on these old bucket seats.'

'But will Katrin like the colour?' asked Luka as they climbed out of the van.

'Yes. It's white,' said Dimitri. 'White and orange.'

'The orange bits are rust,' sneered Peter. 'Wait while I get the parts for me bus,' and Luka heard him rummaging around. At last he found what he needed and grunted, 'There! Bus will be good as new. I'm off out of 'ere and back to the village.'

'Mind you take good care of that horse and vardo,' warned Dimitri.

Luka listened to the horse's hoof beats clop away

out of the city. He pictured the vardo arriving in his village, and felt homesick.

When he could no longer hear the hoof beats, he linked his arm through Dimitri's, took a deep breath and said, 'Let's go and buy tools for Jez.'

They set off, leaving the van to collect later.

'These old streets are like rat runs,' said Dimitri. 'There are people begging on every corner and the drains stink.'

Luka jumped as a hand clawed at his leg and a voice whined, 'What have you got for me, little boy?'

'Here we are, mate,' answered Dimitri. 'Have a piece of bread. Hey, there's no need to pull my hand off.'

Luka heard the beggar smacking his lips over the bread. Dimitri said briskly, 'Come on, Luka,' and a few minutes later he said, 'this is the place for us.'

He opened a door and a bell tinkled. Luka smelled fresh wood, oil and varnish. He sensed people. A voice said, 'What do you want?'

'Good morning. What a splendid shop,' said Dimitri. 'I want to buy some tools, please.'

'What kind of tools?'

'For carving wood and stone,' piped up Luka.

'You're in luck. We have a small stock of tools

that's survived the war,' said the shopkeeper, searching at the back of a shelf.

Luka felt his way around the shop, touching brushes and paints, pencils and knives, chisels, files and hammers.

'And what are these, please?' he asked. 'They feel soft and a bit oily.'

'They're pastel crayons. Different colours, very subtle, delicate shades,' said the shopkeeper.

'Can we get some for Imogen, Dimitri? And some inks for her drawings?'

'They're on my list,' said Dimitri, and Luka heard the smile in his voice.

As the shopkeeper wrapped the tools, crayons and paints in brown paper, tying the parcels with string, Luka became aware that he was being watched. He touched Dimitri's hand. Dimitri turned. At the back of the shop, behind the counter, shone two faces. Dimitri saw a man and a woman. They had wind-burned skin, cheekbones flat as plateaux of rock, and dark oval eyes shaped like plum stones, staring at Luka.

The man spoke quietly to the shopkeeper who said to Dimitri, 'I've taken these two refugees in for a few nights. They want to know who the boy is and where he comes from. They say, does he play a drum? Seems a strange question.'

Luka smiled and held out his hand. The man stepped forward and reached over the counter to take it, and the woman followed. She was pregnant. Her man took Luka's hand and touched it to her belly.

'She's lovely,' said Luka, knowing there was a baby curled tight as an ammonite inside. 'She'll have a mother and father, just like I did. My name is Luka, and I am from a village in the north, near the mountains.'

The man's voice was light, but his accent was marked so that Luka had to listen hard. 'I'm Sith and this is Ribi, my wife. We *know* you. But listen to us, Luka. You must tread carefully wherever you go.'

'How do you know Luka?' asked Dimitri. 'He's never been away from home before.'

'We recognise him,' said Sith. 'We know what kind of being he is.'

Luka glowed at their words.

Dimitri frowned. How could these strangers know what he was, when his friends and family did not? Dimitri did not want Luka to be set apart from everyone. Nevertheless, he felt he could trust this man because Luka obviously did.

He asked, 'Where are you from, Sith?'

'The other side of the mountains. We had to leave. The shaman's cloak threw too dark a shadow over our village. It is a cloak for those who seek out bad sprits. I am a musician, but now I am not allowed to play in my own village.'

'A shaman should not cast a shadow like that,' mused Luka.

Luka's stories may be true after all, thought Dimitri. *I must protect him.*

Out loud he said, 'I'm a musician too. Come and play in our village, Sith. You'd be welcome there.'

'We rode through your village in the middle of winter,' said Sith.

'Then please ride through our village again.'

'There,' said the shopkeeper as he piled the paper parcels before Dimitri. 'Now for the part you won't like.' His tongue poked out in concentration as he wrote the prices on the paper and added them up.

Dimitri fumbled in his pocket for his spectacles and perched them on his nose. He peered at the shopkeeper's sums. 'Blimey. I had forgotten how expensive shopping can be.' He took his moneybag from inside his shirt and counted out the coins into shiny piles. He thanked the shopkeeper.

'Goodbye for now, Luka and Dimitri,' said Sith.

'Goodbye Sith . . . Ribi,' said Luka. 'Come and see us in our village.'

'And bring your instruments,' said Dimitri. 'We'll make some fine music. Luka, hold on to my jacket. I haven't got a spare hand with all these parcels.'

Luka grabbed the corner of the jacket and skipped alongside Dimitri, thinking how happy Imogen and Jez would be with their presents.

His daydreams were spoiled by the harsh, deliberate rhythm of marching boots, heading straight for them. A voice snapped out a command. The boots stopped dead, *crunch*. Luka heard the breathing of men on guard, and smelled nervous sweat and gunpowder. They were near him . . . now they were either side.

'Dimitri? DIMITRI,' he cried as fingers dug hard into his arms.

'Get your hands off us!' shouted Dimitri.

Luka was rushed along to the rhythm of boots. Behind him he heard kicks and punching and Dimitri cry out in pain. Luka struggled like a fish on a hook. He felt hysterical, and he tried to shout out. Instead his face streamed with tears.

There was no point struggling. Luka let himself go limp. He knew where they would be taken, but he did not know why.

5

GARLANDS OF BULLETS

Luka heard the boots stamping across the drawbridge. He heard again those insistent cries from the dungeons below. The boots stopped. Luka's feet touched ground. With a clanking of chains and a rush of air, the drawbridge was pulled up behind them. A door shuddered open. Luka was lifted and carried with his feet dangling, and his arm hurting. The boots marched on, this time on cold stone, up a staircase, through another door, into a room that echoed, across floorboards that dipped. They stopped again.

The room was hot. Luka sniffed. He could smell tobacco and garlic, horses, gunpowder, goatskin and sweat. He heard men shifting from one foot to another, heard the clatter of a gun thrown on to the table, the pull of a long knife from its sheaf. These must be the warlords, who had fought over his land for years. Now they were in an uneasy truce, under the Occupation from across the seas.

'D-Dimitri?' stuttered Luka.

'I'm here, Luka,' whispered Dimitri. The parcels still hung from his fingers by the knot of string made by the shopkeeper, but someone wrenched them off. It hurt. Dimitri raised his head and glanced fearfully around. He saw fierce, watchful faces and garlands of bullets worn as if they were flowers.

A tall man strode into the room. The soldiers clicked heels together in deference. The warlords stirred and murmured like wasps. The newcomer wore a forest-shadowed uniform with gold epaulettes on his wide shoulders. He strode to the chair at the head of the table, lowered himself into it and swung his feet up on to the table. The soles of his conker-brown boots were so clean that Dimitri thought he could knead bread on them.

At his shoulder hovered a pink-faced man in a black peaked hat. The pink-faced man turned to Dimitri and said, 'The general wants to know who you are.'

Dimitri took a deep breath and tried to control his shaking. 'D-Dimitri Founari. Baker. I am the Talking Man for my village.'

The man interpreted for the general who threw back his head and guffawed, showing shiny-white teeth. He took off his cap with its gold badge and placed it on the table. His shaven head gleamed and Dimitri thought of cuttlefish bones washed up on a beach.

'The general says, he is a Talking Man too. We all are Talking Men. Or are we Talking Women? All women talk a lot, don't they?'

'No. Big Katrin does not talk at all,' whispered Luka. 'Who's that speaking?'

'A pink lollipop in a cap,' said Dimitri, but not quietly enough, because the lollipop announced, 'I am Captain Lazslo. The interpreter. I also work in Intelligence. What are you doing with that boy, fat baker? He can't be your son, because he doesn't look like you. Are you a child trafficker? Have you kidnapped the boy to sell on the black market?'

'No,' cried Dimitri. 'He has come with me to ask for your help. Our village is in ruins after all this fighting. So many times we've had *no* clean water, *no* electricity, *no* medical supplies at all. Everything was broken down by war. Everything needs fixing. There are orphaned children from miles around.'

'One of them has no legs, another is deaf and some can't speak or play,' cried Luka.

'The general wants to know why you brought

a blind boy to the city, Talking Baker.'

'And I want to know why you keep people locked up in your dungeons,' retorted Luka.

'Do you, indeed.'

This was the general. His voice was deep, like an engine turning over, and Dimitri realised that he did not need an interpreter at all.

The general's face was white with rage. 'Be careful, boy,' he growled. 'That is seditious talk. This land is like a barrel of gunpowder waiting for a match.'

'I *know* there are prisoners,' cried Luka. 'I've heard them weeping. And I know that everyone is terrified by the figures stuck up there on the Midnight Clock. Why don't you mend it? My brother could mend it. Everyone would feel better.'

'The boy is young,' begged Dimitri. 'He has suffered in this war. We *all* have.'

'Go on, Talking Man in your Al Capone suit, tell us all about it,' sneered Captain Lazslo.

Luka dipped his head at the cruel laughter. *Bullies.* Dimitri put his hands behind his back and tried to stand up tall and proud, as Big Katrin had shown him, moving his shoulder blades back and down and sticking out his chest. He opened his mouth, but fear stopped his voice from coming out.

So Luka said, 'The orphanage is a wreck. It will fall down on us. We must build a new one. We need toys. And a dress for Ellie, a wheelchair for Aidan-who-has-to-be-carried-everywhere, and lots of books because he is so bored he gets spiteful. Maria needs a thing to help her hear, everyone except Aidan needs shoes. And we need a *real* bed for Eva so she doesn't have to sleep on the floor.'

When he heard Luka's courage and remembered just why he was there, Dimitri forgot his humiliation. He demanded, 'Give us the bricks we need to rebuild our lives. Give us cement mixers, and men who can work hard. Give the children proper food, blankets, beds and clothes they're not ashamed to put on in the morning.'

Luka said, 'My brother is going to carve things and sell them for money. And just look at this.' He reached inside his shirt. He laid a piece of paper on the table and smoothed out the crinkles, lovingly. 'Why don't you buy this painting? It is by Imogen who looks after us. She says it's the mountains. She will sell it. I bet it's good.'

The general said, 'Mmmm . . . it is good. In fact it is excellent. I can arrange for more of these watercolours to be collected and sold. Does this Imogen paint birds and flowers?'

'I'm sure she could.'

'Does she paint animals?' This was the smarmy voice of Captain Lazslo. It made Luka think of thick sugar icing. 'I have heard rumours of white leopards hiding up in the mountains.'

'Oh no,' said Dimitri quickly. 'They were all hunted and killed long ago by fur traders.' He looked away, so that they might not see the lie in his eyes. The Cloud Cat must stay a secret, or be killed for her fur.

The general said, 'Hmmm . . . a boy and a baker . . . you behave like conspirators. Tell me, boy, if you are blind, how do you know about the figures on the Midnight Clock?'

Luka shrugged. 'Everyone's heard about them. But *you* haven't heard about our village. Why don't you come and see what it's like? Come to our summer festival! You know nothing, stuck here in this castle.'

'Be careful,' hissed Dimitri, but Luka ignored him and shouted, '*I* can't see you, general, but everybody else can. Do you want them to think you have no heart?'

In the cold silence that followed, Dimitri shut his eyes and waited to be marched away and locked in a dank dungeon full of rats.

The general said, 'I *do* try to be fair, Luka. You are cheeky and outspoken, but I admire your courage. I shall take up your offer and send men to help your village. Find yourselves some land and build a new children's home. Baker, you shall have your bricks and cement mixers. Who knows . . . perhaps I shall come to your festival after all. Here,' the general wrapped Luka's fingers around some notes of money, 'take that to pay for this watercolour. But be careful, baker and blind boy. We shall be watching you.'

Dimitri and Luka were escorted back across the drawbridge to the city. Dimitri was sure they were being followed, but now that the meeting with the general was over, all Luka could think about was his next change. It must happen very soon.

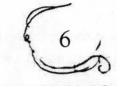

6

IN THE SEEING BALL

Simlin crouched in the corner of the five-sided house, watching blood seep under the door and spread across the earthen floor

Mother shuddered with a warthog snore. She sat up.

'My darling bird,' she wailed. 'What hurt *you* like that?'

Bone Cracker's bony bald head glimmered white, but its beard feathers were stuck together with blood. One eye was closed with a powdery eyelid. It tried to stretch out a wing. Simlin saw that its flight feathers were snapped off at the shafts.

Bone Cracker dragged itself towards the fire, *shuffly-hop*. It flopped to the floor and turned its head. Its one eye stared at Simlin.

'You must have found the wrong bird to fight. You're starving, aren't you? What shall we give you?' Mother gnawed at her copper bangles, and spat into the fire so that it flared up lime-green.

'Give it my stew,' said Simlin.

And she did. *Good.*

Simlin sat in his corner with his long arms wrapped round his knees and pondered while Vaskalia made medicine for the Bone Cracker. 'White bellflower . . . fennel . . . yarrow and dark dock. And very special juice.' Her tongue poked out as she concentrated on her grinding bowl and stick, pounding away at a stinky mess. 'Did you kill that nasty little boybird, my darling?' she whispered.

Simlin wanted to look in the seeing ball to see what was going on. He sneaked it from Vaskalia's shoe where he had hidden it. The seeing ball responded to him quickly now. It was his secret friend. He put his face right close. The ball stank of Vaskalia's shoes, rather like a mouse's old nest.

And there was something in there. The creature was patchy beechnut brown and white. It made big noises. Simlin shook the ball gently and put it close to his ear. He heard a snicker from high to low, like someone plucking strings on an instrument. It was the mountain horse that he had seen pulling the shiny barrel on wheels.

'Where are you, idiot boy?' he whispered.

'The idiot boy is right here, in front of *me!*'

screeched Vaskalia, snatching the seeing ball right out of his hand. '*Eeooyaa*. It's always empty when *I* look.'

Simlin shouted, 'Gone! You frightened horse away, spoil witch.'

Thud on the side of his head, *smack, thwack*, with a pain like sheet lightning so that Simlin feared she had cracked the seeing ball. He sat rocking on the floor with a shooting pain in his head, but gloating that Mother could not see the boy in the ball like he could.

He had made that power his very own.

7

THE DARK BETWEEN THE TREES

The engine spluttered. The van leaped forward and stopped dead.

'Like a frog with a cough,' said Luka. 'The horse and vardo were better, Dimitri.'

'The van and I are both out of practise,' said Dimitri, in a hurt voice. 'Oh, how I want to get out of this city. There's no life here.'

Luka kept quiet. He knew they were being watched, all the time. The van shuddered and jumped, and Luka thought his head would come off. After a few miles, the van ran smoothly again, but Luka could tell something was wrong when they turned on to the road to the north by the way they bounced over the potholes.

'There's someone sitting by the edge of the road,' said Dimitri. 'It's Peter.'

'What's he done with Beechnut and the vardo?' asked Luka.

'I don't know. I can't see them anywhere,' said

Dimitri angrily, slamming out of the van. Luka fumbled with the door handle and climbed out after him. Dimitri bellowed, 'What have you done with them, Peter?'

'That 'orse, baker, put is 'ed down and set off into the forest,' said Peter. 'I think them shadows crawled out from underneath and frit it. I 'ad to jump down quick and 'urt me bum. What are you goin' to do about that, baker?'

'Never mind your bum. What are *you* going to do about my beautiful vardo, and Katrin's horse? It belonged to her husband, Karl. How will she ever forgive me?'

Luka did not know Big Katrin *had* a husband. He always thought of Katrin and Dimitri together.

'Stay here and don't move, Peter!' ordered Dimitri. 'Watch the van while we find that poor horse.'

'What about the lad? Let 'im stay wi' me.'

'Leave Luka with you, when you've lost a horse? You must be joking.' Dimitri grabbed Luka's hand so hard it hurt. 'Come on! We'll follow the wheel ruts and hoof prints.'

They plunged out of the heat and into the shade of the forest as if they had dived into a cold pool. Luka's feet sank into a crunchy mat of pine needles.

The air was sweet with resin. It made him dreamy and light-headed. He heard squeaks and trills and the soft thump of feet, and something big blundering through the trees ahead.

'Are there still bears in this forest, Dimitri?'

'Yes. And deer. And wild boar and wolves.'

Luka was aware of the trees arching all around, as if the forest wanted to close over them, and hide them away inside itself. Dimitri said, 'The war lingers here, as if it is caught in the dark between the trees. But I can't see any tracks now. I'm afraid we may be lost . . .'

'Let's call him,' said Luka. 'Beechnut. *Beeeechnut.*'

'*Horse Horse Horse,*' bellowed Dimitri.

But he did not come. Luka's feet felt heavy, as if his spirits had sunk down into them. He said, 'I can't go any further, Dimitri.'

'The path is blocked with boulders. The earth has thrown them up. There are crannies between them. Hiding places. It is like a secret fortress.'

Luka shivered. 'I think something horrible has happened here.'

A little way beyond the rock fortress Dimitri could see mounds in the earth. Graves. Grass was beginning to grow on them.

'Luka . . . listen to me . . .'

Luka whispered, 'You don't have to say anything.' In his mind, he heard gunshots and cries of pain. He hung his head in that sad place.

An extraordinary noise shattered the quiet, as if a demon was hollering and dragging something gigantic behind it and breaking branches.

'What is it?' gasped Luka.

'I don't know . . .' said Dimitri.

Beechnut came charging through the trees towards them, dragging the vardo, and snorting his pleasure at not being alone in this place after all.

'Where have you *been?*' shouted Dimitri, angry and delighted at the same time. 'I'm telling Katrin what a bad horse you are.'

Luka ran forward, breathing in the horse's warm smell and flung his arms round his hot neck. The horse turned and walked away, with the vardo trundling after him.

Dimitri could hardly bring himself to look at the mounds of dug earth. Some of them were marked with crosses of wood.

'What do you see?' said Luka.

'There are names. Now I know why the horse ran back here. He was looking for his master.'

'Katrin's husband?' whispered Luka.

'Yes. Karl. This is his grave.' Dimitri turned cold thinking of Katrin's grief.

'You will have to tell her,' said Luka.

'I suppose I must.'

'Do you recognise any of the other names, Dimitri?'

Luka dare not speak the real question in his mind: *Is my father here? Is Gabriel one of the names scratched on the wood?*

'No. It's such a waste of life,' said Dimitri. Tears flowed down his face. He struggled to cry noiselessly, not to sob or whimper, but Luka knew.

The horse pawed the ground and whinnied, anxious to be away.

'Can we go now, please?' said Luka.

'Yes,' said Dimitri. 'Let's go home.'

They stumbled back through the forest. The horse put his head down and plunged after them, pulling the vardo.

The van was where they had left it. Peter Bus snored behind the wheel, a damp cigarette hanging from his lip.

'Wake up,' cried Dimitri. 'You're supposed to be keeping watch, not snoring. Open the windows to let the smoke out and get up on that vardo. Let me pick a few roses for Katrin and then we'll go.'

The summer night was still. The land stretched far away out of Luka's reach, vast and desolate. After the graves, and the warlords and the general, he wanted to call the Cloud Cat to him and run away from the awfulness in his land.

He thought, *My mother's gone. My father is gone too.* He sighed sadly. *But . . . the general is going to help us after all.*

After a long silence he asked, 'What's that scent, Dimitri?'

'Honeysuckle. It's sweeter at night. There's a fine crescent moon, Luka. It's like a silver earring. I wish you could see it.'

Through the grimy window of the five-sided house, Simlin peered up at the moon. It reminded him of Mother's yellow toenails. Did anyone live up there? No, they couldn't live on the moon, because when it went thin, they would fall off and hurt themselves. When the moon went round again, it looked like a big seeing ball.

A white van went past, with the baker inside, and after it came the horse that had been in the seeing ball, pulling the barrel with the gold scrolls. Only it was all scratched and dusty now and there was someone slumped on the seat . . . Peter Bus.

Where was the blind boy? Mother had put the seeing ball back up on the shelf, surrounded by her pin-sticking dolls, so that Simlin could not look into it without her knowing.

All of a sudden, Simlin knew the boy's where-abouts *without* the seeing ball.

Yipyip snort. Boy is returning to the village.

8

PARCEL OF DELIGHTS

'Get back, Katrin,' shouted Jez, pulling her away from the bakery door. 'That's gunfire.'

His heart thumped. Could he get to Imogen at the orphanage in time? But he should stay here to protect Big Katrin. If the war was back, where was Luka? How many men were outside?

Someone chuckled out in the street.

Jez flung open the door and there was Dimitri, peering at the back of a rusty van. 'That van sounded just like a gun battle,' cried Jez. 'It's a great little van. I want to learn to drive it.'

'Hmmm . . . I don't know about that. It is a good little van but the exhaust backfires,' said Dimitri. 'Take these parcels, Luka.'

Dimitri strutted inside, tripping over the tortoise propping open the door, and stooping down to put it the right way up again. He presented the wild roses to Katrin and turned to survey his little empire. Everything was laid out ready for an early start next day. There was the yeast, the weighed-out flour and clean baking trays, dishes of poppy seeds, cinnamon and brown sugar.

Luka grabbed Katrin's hand and said, 'It's all right, Katrin. The horse is coming soon. Peter's driving the vardo.'

Dimitri looked longingly at his chair by the fire, piled high with cats. He nodded as Big Katrin spooned coffee into the jug and said, 'It's good to be home.'

'So how did it go, Talking Man?' said Jez, 'and are any of those parcels for me?'

'Give Jez his presents,' said Dimitri. Luka held out the parcels and squealed as Jez ripped them open. He jumped up and down waiting for Jez's reaction.

'Fantastic,' shouted Jez. 'Now all I need is something to carve.'

Luka grinned to himself. He knew what that something would be: blue sparkling rock from that cave he had been to with the Cloud Cat. If *only* he could find the way back there. He felt for a chair and flopped down on to it. The dog laid her head on his knee, digging in her chin so that he knew she was there. Luka stroked her head, and said, '*I'll* tell you how it went, Jez. Dimitri was an amazing Talking Man. There was a jumpy general, but he will help us build a new home, and sell Imo's pictures for us. I bet he'll sell your carvings too. *And* we met some mountain people having a baby and invited them to play some music, didn't we, Dimitri?'

'Yes,' said Dimitri. He made himself look up to meet Big Katrin's eyes. He dreaded telling her about Karl's grave. Perhaps she already knew. He said quietly, 'Katrin, when the vardo is back, I'll unshackle the horse and walk you both home.'

Luka was wavering on the edge of sleep, but his mind went on making plans. *I'll find the way back to the Cloud Cat's cave and get a piece of sparkling blue rock. Jez can carve it. With the money we make, we can change the orphans' lives.*

After baking was done the next morning, Jez took Luka to the orphanage.

'Will you look who's here,' Aidan squealed. Luka heard the children rush towards him. He stopped and began to ease the lid off the tin he carried.

'Hey, everyone,' he said. 'Big Katrin has sent you crumbly apple slices.'

'Where have you been *this* time? What did you see?' Luka heard that edge of envy in Aidan's voice.

'I went to the city with Dimitri, and you know perfectly well that I didn't *see* anything at all, Aidan.'

'At least you can walk. Tell us the story. What was it like in the city?'

'Very dusty and smelly with beggars everywhere.'

The children shuffled around on the old carpet, munching their apple slices, and Maria trotted across the room to feed some to Stefan through the bars of his cot.

Luka began, 'We went in the vardo that Dimitri painted for you lot.' He told them about the horse and the mountain people in the shop. 'And Imo, look what I chose for you!'

They all held their breath while she untied the string from the parcel and cried with delight, showing the inks and pastels and paints one by one to the children. Jez wished *he* had chosen them. He vowed that one day he would buy her even *better* colours.

Luka said, 'A man in the castle bought your picture, Imo.' He dug in his pocket for the money and handed it to her saying, '*And* he will buy more.'

'That's wonderful,' said Imogen. 'But do you know what I shall paint first? Your portraits. Every single one of you.'

'Don't you dare paint my picture, Imogen,' said Aidan, reaching for another apple slice. 'And Luka won't be able to see his anyway. *Yum.* Katrin has stuck this crumble together with honey . . . Food is nice, isn't it.'

'Yes, and I'm going to bring some salmon for you all later,' said Jez, 'because Luka and I are going to the river this afternoon.' He leaned close to Imogen and whispered, 'Paint a portrait of Luka for me, wild hair, white face and all.'

'Of course I will,' she said. 'Now, Luka, tell us about Dimitri the Talking Man.'

'That was scary at first,' said Luka. 'The soldiers marched us off to the Red Castle because they thought Dimitri was a child trafficker. That general is suspicious of everyone, but Dimitri won him round.'

'Dimitri told me it was *you* who persuaded him,' said Jez.

'I want to hear about Mr Baker in the castle, Luka,' ordered Aidan.

'Mr Baker was a hero. He said they must mend what they had spoiled and the general said, "As you are such cheeky little people, maybe we will".'

'Do you *really* think they will help us?' said Aidan.

'Yes,' said Luka. 'The general even said he might come to the festival. He said, "Find land to build new homes".'

Imo clapped her hands. 'That would be so much better than patching up the old orphanage. Jez spent all yesterday mending the hole in the roof, Luka.'

'I still need to fix more locks to keep you all safe,' said Jez.

'A new home would be fantastic,' cried Imogen. 'There's some empty land north of the village. It's common land, but I'll ask everyone about it. Oh Jez, this is wonderful. Will you help me draw a plan for the home?'

Imo's voice was so full of emotion that Luka thought she might burst into tears.

He did not tell the children about the Midnight Clock, or how Peter said the figures ran about the streets at night. He did not tell them about the graves deep in the forest. Why should their minds have to look at any more horrible pictures?

He still felt despondent. He wanted to make his next change, for everyone's sake, especially for Jez. He must find his way back to that cave.

Simlin's shadow stretched across the flagstone floor of the orphanage porch. His head was on one side, straining to hear what they said. Their mouths were stuffed so full. He dare not move forwards. They might catch sight of his nose, or his toes.

He could smell sweet apple. It made his mouth sprinkle. He wanted his own crumbly apple slice.

The blind boy was talking about a festival. That was when Mother said he would have to wear that cloak. The boy did not know about that, did he?

9

UP IN THE ALDER TREE

That afternoon, the brothers headed up the riverbank. The dog lumbered after them, her tongue lolling in the heat.

Luka was preoccupied. He was planning his next change. The river would be the start of his journey because he remembered that it was below the Cloud Cat's cave.

'We'll go to the waterfall,' said Jez. 'I'll have more chance of catching fish there. *Wow*. A kingfisher just flew past. Blink and you'd miss it.'

'I'd miss it anyway.'

'It was emerald and turquoise and brown as cinnamon . . . like a stained-glass arrow. And there's a heron, standing on one leg, glaring down into the water.'

Luka heard a rasping call, *Kra-ack* and the *whup-whup* of the heron's wings as it flapped ponderously over them. He imagined that they were on hinges.

He heard another sound, too . . .

'There's the waterfall, Jez.'

'Good. Give me your hand,' said Jez. He guided Luka around an alder tree, along the bank and around the river bend. Then the noise was deafening. The waterfall plunged out far above, from a darkness crested by rowan trees flamed with berries. It was a water avalanche, pouring into a cauldron of black rock and seething there, so that Jez caught Luka's arm and pulled him back.

'But I like the drops on my hot skin,' yelled Luka.

'Hold on to me tight, stupid,' shouted Jez. 'It's dangerous. We're going underneath the waterfall to the bank on the other side.'

Luka felt the shape of each rock with his free hand, trying to remember it, because the next time he came here he would be alone. He taught himself to recognise the sound of the water which changed note wherever it fell. Holding on to each other, the brothers clambered across the wet rocks. The world behind the waterfall sounded close and secret, and then Jez cried, 'We're out the other side.'

The roar cleared from Luka's head as they moved into sunlight. The worst was over. Away from the plunge and froth of the waterfall, the pool was calm. The water slowed and almost stopped, before trickling and bubbling down tiny falls into the river. Luka felt the wet stones, and stuck his fingers deep into a pillow of moss lodged in a cranny.

Jez steered him toward a large, smooth rock. Luka's fingertips traced indentations, shells and fronds and curves, the fossils of tiny creatures that lived millions of years ago.

'Why do the fish come here, Jez?'

'They leap back up the waterfall to the place where they were born. It's their instinct. They swim back up from the sea and they'll spawn. You know what happens then. I watch, grab them out of the pool and put them in my bucket. They'll die soon, anyway.'

'I see. Jez . . . What's making that chittering noise?'

'Dunno . . . it sounds like a lapwing when it's courting over the fields, but it wouldn't be a lapwing on the river. Lapwing, flapwing. There *is* something down there. It looks like a cat.'

'A cat *swimming*?'

'Be quiet, Luka, or you'll frighten the fish.'

'I *am* quiet,' retorted Luka. 'You're the noisy one. Something is on my face.'

'It's just a butterfly,' grinned Jez. 'It's got long blue feelers and they're tickling you.' Jez blew softly so that the apricot-coloured creature fluttered from Luka's white skin.

Luka wished he had his drum. Next time he would bring it and drum softly to draw the creature to him. He still did not know which creature that would be.

Simlin sat at the top of an alder tree, with his legs wrapped tight around the trunk. His knees jutted out at either side like the corners of a set square. The sun was on his back and sweat trickled down between his shoulder blades. He could see a long way. If he looked down he saw lots of little poached egg flowers floating on the water. If he looked ahead there were mountains. If he looked the other way he saw that iron-grey thing they called The Sea.

Best of all, Simlin could watch the brothers. The bully brother was looking into the water for fishes. He kept dabbing in his hand to grab one. The blind boy was sitting on the rock.

Simlin wanted to see Luka perform one of his tricks.

The top of the tree swayed gently. Simlin swayed with it. He liked being on the treetop. He could hide up here forever. He gripped his knees tight to the tree, as if he was riding a wild horse. Leaning backwards, he rolled an alder cone between his palms and hurled it down at the blind boy. It landed in the pool near him and bobbed on the water like a tiny turd. The boy glanced towards the splashy landing noise, but that was all.

Bully brother yelled that he had caught lots of fish and they should go. Simlin shimmied a little down the tree trunk so as to hear them better.

'I don't want to go,' the little one whinged. 'Can't we stay here longer?'

'No,' bawled bully brother. 'I'm taking this fish to the orphanage so Eva and Imo can cook it. After that I want to go for a spin in Dimitri's van. Now *come on*!'

The blind boy turned and cupped his hand to his mouth, talking to something down in the water. Simlin leaned far from the tree trunk, listening hard.

The blind boy whispered, 'I'll be back tomorrow. Early.'

'So will I,' sniggered Simlin up in his tree.

10

BOYFISH

Simlin woke, soaking with sweat. There was no breeze. Heat had draped itself over the land all the short night long. He went to peek out of the window. He blinked. The sun was already up there in the startling blue sky. He was late. Even Mother was up. He caught her salty smell as she stroked poorly Bone Cracker.

Simlin spied on her, slathering grease on her mouth with a fat stick that turned her lips as dark as elderberries. She squirted perfume, *pfff! pfff!* making Simlin sneeze and his eyes water. Pulling a face at his sneeze, she turned away and counted out some money. She stuffed it down between her breasts and left the five-sided house at last.

Simlin waited a while. Peeped out. Mother was nowhere in sight. *Good.* He had an important job to do.

In a corner of the five-sided house there was a silver bucket. The winter snow had melted through the holes in the roof and filled it. Flies floated on the scummy top. Simlin grabbed it and tipped brown water over Bone Cracker's head. The bird woke up and glared at him with its one good eye. It struggled and flapped heavily up to the rafters.

Simlin stuck out his tongue and skedaddled along the road, up around the village to the gurgling river. He bounded like a hare on his long white feet, scrambled up the rocks, careful not to bang the bucket, under the waterfall and out the other side.

There was the clear pool. Above it sparkled spray from the waterfall, a mist of small rainbows in the sunlight.

Simlin heard a soft thudding sound. He hung the bucket on a branch, reached up his long arms and pulled himself into his alder tree. He stared down and saw the blind boy perched on that rock again, legs crossed. He was tapping a drum. The pool was a tumult of turning silver sides as fish flipped and leaped, drawn towards the beat of the drum.

The boy stopped drumming. He placed his drum on the rock next to him.

The fish frenzy increased. Then it stopped.

Simlin blinked and stared hard. Butter-coloured marigolds and emerald weed long as girls' hair streamed across the pool, but now he could not see the fish.

Simlin waited. The boy sitting on the rock did not move. He was pale as Mother's mushrooms. His eyes were white and motionless.

The boy must have slipped out of his body. Like changing clothes.

But where had he gone?

There was a fish mouthing near the surface just below the rock.

The boy must be in the fish.

Simlin slithered down the alder tree and unhooked his bucket. Light as a long-legged crane fly, he stepped on to the rock and waited.

The fish was opening and closing the flap things on the side of its head. Its tail swished. Simlin must not let his shadow on the fish, or it would dart away.

NOW. Simlin swung down his silver bucket and scooped.

GOT YOU.

Simlin scampered to the bank and set down the bucket. Hands on hips, he watched the fish panic and thrash. It twisted tight in the bucket, flipped over to ripple on its side. Look at its gills, gaping, silver flaps opening and closing fast, as if they would tear right off its head.

Yee hee, yipyipsnort! You don't like being in there do you, boyfish?

Simlin capered around the bucket in a wild, celebratory dance. He picked it up by the handle and set off home as fast as he could go, with the water slurping and slopping and triumph roaring in his ears.

COOKING LESSON

Simlin stood the bucket on the table. He peered in. The fish was gasping. It was on its side with its silver flap open and its eye stretched. Simlin jumped up and down. If he watched this fish, he would find out how the blind boy could change out of his body into other creatures. Simlin could find out how to do it.

Whatever he did, Mother would not love him. So he could keep the secret for himself. He could take the boyfish and run away to a fair. Make the fish change back to the boy and the boy change back again to the fish. People would pay lots of money to see it. Simlin would be so rich. He could have his own cook in a hat like the baker man.

Up on the rafters, Bone Cracker stirred. Simlin saw its good eye fixed on the bucket. It opened its beak and stuck out its hard tongue and hissed.

'No, leave fish, featherbrain, or I tie you up with ivy ropes.'

'*What* fish?' The flames slanted in the draught as Vaskalia threw open the door. A new smell came in with her, a furry-hairy-slurry smell. Still shielding his bucket, Simlin glanced over his shoulder.

'Why got a mule?' he asked.

'No, Simlin, it is a donkey, a *strong* donkey. He has to carry something *special*.'

'But where will it live?'

'Here, of course.'

Bone Cracker gave an eerie scream, *ee-ark*. Its one good eye was lit on the donkey. Plops dropped down on to the dark cross on the donkey's back. The donkey's ears went back. Its top lip wrinkled over its slab teeth and it brayed deep, chest-heaving sobs.

'What are you doing with my very best bucket? If I had known you were going to the river I'd have told you to get more leeches. I'm right out of them.'

Mother looked down and saw the boyfish twisting in the shallow water.

'Ooooh! What a lovely salmon! I didn't know you were a fisherman, droolgob.'

She spat into the fire. Flames sprang into an emerald crown and Mother began to build up the fire, saying, 'I fancy chargrilled fish with herbs for flavour. Five parsley leaves and tatties on the side. No dill. Dill harms the constitution of ladies such as myself. So does garlic. I tell you what, slubber-degullion: *you* cook the fish.'

'But –'

'It's time you learnt. After all, I won't always be here.'

No, you won't. Simlin tried to straighten out his face and hide the beginning of some *yipyipsnorts*. He tried to look a bit sorry and sad, but did not manage it.

Vaskalia's eyes went into spins of many colours and ended up dark violet. She plunged her hand into the bucket, grabbed the fish and held it close to her face, so that its mouth opened and closed as if it was kissing her.

'Put it back,' cried Simlin. 'Fish will flap and die up in the air.'

Mother plopped the boyfish back in the bucket. She said, 'First cooking tip: make your fire big and *very* hot!'

'We should keep fish for one week. Get it ripe,' he said.

'Apples and hares and pheasants get ripe. Fish don't. They just go off and stink.'

'Leave it to get bigger?' he tried.

'Get bigger in a bucket? If you want the fish to grow, you must put it back in the river.'

'*NO NO NO.*'

'Then shut up. *OW.*' The donkey had nudged her in the back. There was a splattering noise and a hot, grassy smell.

'Outside with you, dungbum,' she screeched and chased the donkey into the garden.

Simlin peeped into the bucket. He must fool her. He would pretend to cook the fish until the very last moment. Lifting the trivet with his toes, he dropped it square over the flames. She wanted herbs for flavour. Quick as an adder, Simlin sneaked outside. Mother was at the end of the garden talking to the donkey, wagging her finger at its long face. Simlin snatched parsley, chervil *and* some sprigs of dill and scooted back inside. Stopped. Thought. Scooted back out. Dug with his fingers in the earth for a plump little bulb of garlic.

Simlin knelt by the fire and ripped the herbs into tiny pieces. He peeled the papery case off the garlic bulb. Inside were juicy pink cloves. He popped a clove under the rim at the base of the bucket and pressed hard until it was flattened. Then he put the bits of parsley and garlic on the trivet so that anything Mother cooked would taste of them.

Simlin jumped up and down. He hid the rest of the garlic cloves up among the pin-sticking dolls, which recoiled from it, wrinkling their noses. They did not like garlic any more than Mother did.

Vaskalia stomped back in. Shoving Simlin out of the way, she pulled the fish from the bucket and whacked its head on the tabletop.

Simlin almost fell backwards in shock.

So much for his pretending to cook the boyfish.

Now he would never find out how Luka did his tricks.

12

GOODBYE, BOYFISH

The wood squeaked as it burned. The shredded parsley and garlic curled and blackened on the trivet and the fish scales charred and crackled and began to smell strong. Simlin's mouth dropped open. Would the blind boy swirl out, like a genie? Would he be crying?

Simlin poked the crispy skin and leaped back, appalled.

The boyfish was cooked right through.

Vaskalia pushed him out of the way, snatched up the fish and juggled its hot body between her palms. With a low growl, she bit off its head and dropped the body back on to the trivet. She winked at Simlin, took the head from her teeth and scrabbled out an eyeball. She held it up to the dust-filled slant of light from the window and cooed, 'Farewell, dear fishy-wishy,' then popped the eyeball back into her mouth and swallowed it.

'Delicious. River fish will make you strong,

Simlin. Here . . .'

She tore a morsel from the fish's cheek and pressed it to Simlin's lips. He forced himself to swallow, although his gorge threatened to bring everything up out of his stomach and throw it on the earthen floor.

What had he done? Now he could not run away from Mother with the boyfish in a bucket. Now he would not be rich. Nothing would change. Life would always be the same here, here with Mother, *always*.

Vaskalia lip-smacked her way along the fish's body. She picked out the bones and arranged them in a little pyre on the table. She flossed her furry teeth with a piece of root, and collapsed on her elephant bed. Her bottom roared, sending out hot smells that made Simlin's eyes water.

He edged across the room and reached up for the seeing ball among the pin-sticking dolls. He peered in. *No boyfish in ball. Because boyfish is cooked and eaten.*

The blind boy was dead. Simlin felt warm and wet down his trousers.

Something moved in the seeing ball. It was brown as a nutmeg and covered in fur, wet fur, stuck up in points. Small, bright eyes. Tiny ears and big curly whiskers.

Oh! There you are again, blind boy.

He wasn't a fish after all.

13

RUBBLE GARDENS

'I'll go and wake Luka,' said Jez. 'Imogen wants to paint his portrait today.'

Big Katrin turned to him and shook her head. Her brown eyes darkened.

'Has he gone off on his own again?' groaned Jez. 'I bet I know where. He didn't want to come back from the river yesterday. It's dangerous there. Little pest.'

Off he went with the dog at his heels.

Dimitri said, 'I'll explain to Imogen. Are you coming, Katrin?'

Katrin nodded, head lowered. Dimitri had told her that he had seen Karl's grave. It seemed to him that she already knew her husband was dead. Now she covered her bowl of butter and sugar with muslin, and untied her apron. Together they walked through the village. They saw a woman collecting her hens' eggs, and Dimitri chatted to an old man who wanted Katrin to bake him egg custards sprinkled with nutmeg. Sunlight mellowed the ruins.

All around the orphanage had been cleared and swept.

'What's going on here?' called Dimitri to the children outside.

'Rubble gardens,' cried Lisa, sloshing water from a jug into a low circle built from a jumble of stones. Pools of water and earth dribbled down the sides.

The rubble gardens were already planted with big daisies, rosemary bushes and purple cranesbill. Big Katrin tapped Dimitri's arm. She pointed at orange and red nasturtiums helter-skeltering down the sides of an old olive oil can.

'Still more to do,' said Ellie. She pointed to a heap of plants, foxgloves and speedwells, rosebay willow herb, blackberry and elderflower roots and granny's bonnets of pink and amethyst. Poppy pods lay drying in the sun ready to burst with seed. Dimitri could smell a warm coco-nutty-almond scent and saw a gorse bush planted in an old paint tin. It was covered in yellow blossom, shaped like little kidneys.

'We got the flowers from the bomb gardens,' said Lisa.

'That's dangerous,' warned Dimitri. 'There might be landmines and unexploded bombs.'

'But there weren't.'

'Good. Well, I'm glad you're gardening. I'm gardening too. I've planted a greengage tree near the wall in my yard.' Dimitri ignored the pitying look Katrin gave him. All right, there wasn't much soil there and he wasn't much of a gardener, but he would guard that little greengage tree with his life.

There was a surprise in the porch.

'I see the village geese have moved in,' said Dimitri.

'They like the cool shade,' said Lisa, opening the door straight into a game of football. *Bang bang aagh!* Florin fired his block of wood at them. 'Stop it, Florin,' said Dimitri.

Big Katrin strode to the cot where Stefan lay, turning his head from side to side. A thin teddy bear was threaded through the bars. Its head was jammed. Big Katrin rescued the teddy and picked up Stefan. He gazed up with his round hare eyes and reached towards her face. Katrin carried him to a table set out with thick paper and beans and jars and sat him on her knee to watch. The little girls scooted after her. They set to work, winding paper round inside the jars. They put in beans and watered them.

'We're going to making a wigwam of beanstalks,'

Ellie said. 'We can eat green beans. But don't worry, Stefan. There won't be a giant.'

'Hey, is that you up there, Aidan?' called Dimitri, to the small figure with sun-bleached hair, perched at the top of a stepladder. 'Have you put your hands in any wet paint lately?'

Aidan did not answer. His fierce blue eyes were glaring at something by the wall.

Dimitri followed his stare, and at once felt sick with foreboding.

Vaskalia.

Imogen hurried over.

'Dimitri. It's good to see you,' she said. 'This lady has offered to make a scented garden for children who can't see well.'

Dimitri heard Imogen's soft, cello voice and thought, *How pretty she is. No wonder Jez is in love with her. But she's shaking. Even she is frightened of Vaskalia.*

He took her to one side and said, 'Imogen, Luka won't be coming today. Jez thinks he may have gone back to the river.'

'Open the door, Mr Baker. I am so hot I cannot breathe,' commanded Aidan from his stepladder perch. Dimitri wiped the sweat from his face and tramped back to open it. In rushed a flurry of white feathers. A gander. Its serpentine neck was stretched right out, as it fast-waddled across the room, hissing, aiming straight for Vaskalia. At once Vaskalia snatched little Maria in front of her as a shield.

'You should have kept the door shut, you cripple,' she shrieked at Aidan.

'Don't shout at him like that,' cried Dimitri. 'It was me. *I* opened the door.'

Big Katrin sighed. She looked at Dimitri and she looked at Aidan. She stood up and strode across to the gander where it had trapped Vaskalia and her little hostage in the corner, orange beak wide around its spike of a tongue. Katrin scooped it up and clamped her arm across it, holding its neck in her other hand so that it was quite helpless.

'You look like you're playing the bagpipes, Big Katrin,' yelled Aidan.

'That gander thinks I cooked its mate in my stew pot,' sneered Vaskalia.

'And did you?' asked Dimitri.

'Perhaps I did . . . perhaps I didn't,' she smirked. 'Goose necks are so tough.'

She let Maria go, and the little girl fled across the room into Imogen's open arms.

Dimitri feared the way Vaskalia was behaving. It was as if she knew something they did not. But at least if she was here with them, she could not be harming Luka.

The children fidgeted and whinged and squabbled. They stayed out of Vaskalia's sight as much as they could. Every now and then they glanced secretly at her, wanting her to *go*. So did Imogen, still cuddling the sobbing Maria.

At last Vaskalia arranged the dead foxes around her neck and simpered, 'Farewell, my dears . . . It has been *delightful* to meet you all.' She set off at full stomp towards the door.

'It has been *disgusting* to meet you,' spat Aidan from the top of his stepladder.

Vaskalia stopped. She turned towards Aidan. Her face glinted with malice. Aidan's stomach was sick with fear, but he wasn't going to let *her* see. He stuck out his tongue, crossed his eyes and put his thumbs in his ears, waggling his fingers around his head like the feathers on a crested grebe paddling on the river.

Dimitri tried not to laugh. 'Be careful, Aidan. Remember *you* can't run away from her.'

Big Katrin returned without the gander. Lisa and

Ellie ran to drape daisy chains around her neck, and Dimitri's too.

'I hope Luka comes back soon,' said Lisa. 'Please bring him here to tell us his story.'

Big Katrin smiled down at them, but her smile faded fast. Vaskalia carried harm wherever she went. It might be poisoned cherries in a basket, a bad wish posy for the door, a spell of hatred, or a curse. What was it today? There must be something.

Katrin strode out to search by the rubble gardens, and there she found today's bad magic: monkshood, crimson torn heart, burning nettle and devil's tongue fern, with its knife-shaped leaves. There was a shell-pink mantrap orchid, and three big bulbs. From them would sprout cannibal eclipse lilies, orange and black, strong enough to gobble up a goldfinch or bite off a child's ear.

Dimitri and Big Katrin carried the armfuls of plants back to Dimitri's yard. They threw everything over the wall and left them to shrivel in the sun, ready for a bonfire.

Katrin made Dimitri wash his hands and arms meticulously under the outside tap, and then she washed her own.

As she turned her hands over and over in the cold

water, her mind went from the dangerous plants left by the orphanage to plants in the market. She remembered Vaskalia by her stall years ago. Vaskalia was showing off with a wand carved from blackthorn wood. She was mimicking a song and dance act. She stopped and pointed the blackthorn wand at Evangelina's belly, which was full of baby Luka.

Blackthorn could cause miscarriage. That time it did not, but Katrin wondered if the blackthorn wand had harmed Luka's sight.

14

LUKA LEAPWATER

The otter slept on the riverbank. In his dreams, he was munching fish.

His eyes snapped open.

There lay his white pebble, close by his paw. He had been juggling it on the riverbank before he fell asleep after last night's fish. He rolled on to his back, threw the pebble up and caught it, juggling it between his forepaws, then dropped it and watched as it rolled away. He yawned, and sat up, forepaws held high in answer to the summons of the drumbeat. Twitching his whiskers, he called a shrill answer and slipped from the tangle of grasses down his toboggan slope into the river.

Once in the water he became a sleek, dark shape. His webbed feet were powerful paddles, driving him low across the pool. He pulled himself up on to the rock, shuffling into the sunlight and shaking himself from head to tail. Water droplets flew away from him like a shower of diamonds.

The otter rolled on to his back. He preened his coat and smoothed the wet spikes ready for his journey. It shone, reflecting green and gold from the trees and water all around him. When he had finished grooming, he sat up, and chattered to Luka, eager for this new game.

Luka let the otter fill his mind. In this otter shape, Luka wanted to travel along the river, surging through the water and snaking across the land to find that cave again. No fish could do that. Water voles and frogs were small, and they had too many enemies. The otter seemed the perfect choice.

'Leave now,' pleaded Luka and the gleeful otter slid into the water. He paddled along the surface like a dog, before diving down into the deeper water where he swum fast and supple as a dancer. Luka felt quick, shallow breathing and watched the water world of the pool through low-set eyes. The otter circled, powered by his big fan feet, showing Luka what he could do.

They were twisting through an underwater garden, filled with fronded weeds. Beetles dived and rose again, scrabbling up the water. Fish fry whizzed in shoals, and Luka saw tadpoles with back legs twice as long as themselves. Above them steamed the bulky shadows of ducks and coots, driven like paddle steamers by the tumult of their feet.

The underwater world flowed past. It was as unpredictable as a dream. All around rushed currents of water, each one playing its own note. Colours shifted and merged, from turquoise, quartz and fern-green to white, rock-dove grey and caramel.

On swam the sinuous otter, through shadows that were never still.

One long shadow lurked among the weed, pointed as a torpedo. *A pike.* It hovered in the water, opening and closing its mouth. Luka saw a portcullis of fangs and small sharp teeth but the otter swum boldly past.

A black chick with orange tufts around its neck circled above them. The otter paused. He surfaced, scooped up the chick and popped it into his armpit as a toy to play with later.

'Don't, or it will drown,' cried Luka. The otter let it go. The chick shot back up to the surface and dashed away to find its parent.

The otter changed tack and swum across the pool. The water began to rock. Wind furrowed the surface as if it was a transparent ploughed field. Light sparkled on the points of the ripples and bubbles rose as big as cherries.

They were approaching the waterfall. Luka was fearful and exhilarated at the same time. The otter squeaked with glee in the foam that seethed at the bottom of the waterfall. He scrabbled on to a rock to shake himself dry.

The leaves on the trees stirred and threw down shadows on to the water. Luka saw wild roses of intense pink on the bank, and shimmering in the water too. Dragonflies glittered emerald green and blue damsels whizzed on wings as transparent as the veined skeletons of leaves.

The otter scooped a golden iris flower with his forepaw. He sniffed it. *Sneezed*. Gave a low whistle and a chirrup that sounded like the squeaky oven door at the bakery. Luka giggled. He stopped as he saw the salmon. They were waiting to gather energy before hurling themselves into the sky like silver sabres. He remembered Jez telling him, *They leap back up the waterfall to the place where they were born.*

The otter climbed up the rocks to the very top of the waterfall and turned to look back. The avalanche of water surged over the edge behind. Ahead, boulders blocked the river and on the boulders waited three brown bears, swaying heavily on short hind legs. They swiped at the salmon that came flying over the top of the waterfall.

'Will they eat us too?' The otter wound swiftly along the bank to a bend, and slipped back into the water. The bears were so engrossed with their fish game that they did not even notice him.

A golden eagle sat on a swell of air, stern eye fixed on the river. Luka saw its golden halo, like the sun behind a dark cloud. The eagle hovered and dived, and rose with a fish in its talons.

Luka thought that their last moment had come, but the otter wasn't anxious at all. He spun in the water like a top, round a fir cone that bobbed on the water. He pushed it with his nose, and dribbled and chased it as if it was a ball.

'You're such a clown,' giggled Luka and the otter chirruped in response and swam on up the narrowing river, swift and supple as an eel. Once he paused to play with an emerald feather from a mallard duck. Another time he chased a willow leaf across the surface and leaped out of the water, turning somersaults until they were dizzy. Luka laughed as he had not laughed for a long time. It was a joy to *see* at all, and it felt as if years had passed since he had played, really played.

On they swum, up the river until the way ahead was blocked by stones, strung from one bank to the other like a necklace of huge pearls, buffed by water over thousands of years until they gleamed silver-blue.

'These are Jez's stepping-stones, so the cave where I sheltered with the Cloud Cat must be nearby.'

The otter clambered up and lolloped from one stone to the next, like a tubby, whiskered clown on short legs. Up the bank they went, along the ledge to the cave which vaulted overhead like a blue night sky, sprinkled with stars. Small galleries honeycombed away from the large cave. They were full of midnight darkness. If you looked for long enough, the roof of the cave sparkled as if stars a million miles away were signalling to the earth.

The otter had no such feelings of awe. He began to bat a small piece of sparkling blue rock around with his paw as if he was playing football. Then he raced across the cave, turned, and pushed something towards Luka with his nose.

'So *that's* where I left it.' It was the little wooden drum he'd taken from the orphanage when he'd run away to follow the Cloud Cat. 'I'll ask Jez to bring it back.'

Now his Cloud Cat was up in the mountains with her cubs, living her secret life. Luka remembered the strength she had given him. Much as he loved the little swallow, and the otter too, it was in the Cloud Cat's spirit he had lost himself. She was an outsider, like him.

Luka willed the otter to tuck the small, sparkling rock in his armpit to take back for Jez.

'He'll be happy when he can carve all day, like our great-grandfather,' Luka told the otter.

On their way back, the otter turned over a stone in the river. Out dashed a small eel, wriggling straight into the scooping paw and up into the munching mouth, quickly followed by a fresh-water crab. The otter clamped his jaws shut and crunched open the shell as if it were a walnut.

'You're *so* greedy,' squealed Luka.

The mellifluous river flowed towards the sea. It was growing dark. Shadows by the riverbank shimmered with unknown presences. *Pike again*. It shot away and the water held only its disappearance, a puff of disturbance where it had been.

The white moon rode high in the sky, and down in the water too. The otter chased the moon that wavered on the river surface. He kept trying to touch it, trying to catch the cold white disk that split into many and wriggled on the water, but roll as he might he could never catch it in his paw. The water shook the moonlight into a hundred pieces.

Twice the blue stone fell from the otter's armpit. Twice he went back to fetch it.

Night time arched over the earth. Luka looked up at the crackling stars and wondered how many night-creatures were flying across those vast spaces.

The river began to flood faster and faster. The stars rushed through the sky. All they heard was water, torrents of it, tumbling and crashing, far ahead, then far too near, rushing them down into a maelstrom, over and over, screaming with the thrill and the terror of being swept over the edge of the rocks. Down, down the waterfall, *Luka Leapwater*.

A face flashed past, a face with a flaming creature on its forehead . . . *Gone*.

The last thing Luka saw, before they were dashed into chaos again, was the body of a small boy sitting on a rock, waiting for his spirit to return. The last thing he heard was a voice that echoed among the rocks like music: 'Welcome back, Shaman Boy. Your change this time was perfect.'

15

BIG BROTHER WAS CRYING

The white gander glimmered on Vaskalia's garden path. Big Katrin had carried it from the orphanage to share the field with Beechnut. Immediately it dashed back to the five-sided house in case its mate returned.

Inside the little house, Vaskalia put more wood on the fire. She would never let that fire go out, even on such a hot summer day. It discouraged unwelcome spirits from abseiling down her chimney.

Picking up a mottled mirror, she puckered her lips at her reflection and told herself, 'When he sees me at the festival in my scarlet dress, Dimitri will realise *I* am the woman of his dreams. *Eee!* what's this?'

There was a scrap of paper on the windowsill. Vaskalia put her hand through the missing pane and grabbed it, waving it under Simlin's nose.

'Read it to me, slubberdegullion.'

'Says . . . *build new children's home on land north of the village . . . want to be sure that land belongs to everyone . . .'* Simlin lowered the paper. He knew what was coming. Mother's eyes levelled and looked straight at him. So she was going to tell him a lie.

'That land belongs to *my* family,' she said. 'They can't have it.'

'Doesn't belong,' said Simlin, 'and Mother never goes north of village.'

She spat in his face three times, once on each cheek, once on to his scorpion birthmark, and then said, 'Beauty sleep for a gorgeous girl,' and launched herself up on to the twanging bed. Soon it bounced her off to sleep.

Simlin wiped the orange spit off his cheeks and his scorpion. He let himself quietly out of the door and scarpered past the haunting gander on long and soundless feet. He ran all the way back to the river and shimmied up his alder tree.

There was the boy's body sitting on the rock, still empty.

Simlin heard twigs snap and alder cones crunch.

Someone else has come to spy . . . it's bully brother with yellow dog.

The brother went up on to the rock. He prodded the boy. Peered into his face. Looked worried. Said,

'Luka?' close to blind boy's ear. Louder. '*Luka!*'

The dog sniffed at the empty boy body and wagged its tail. Big brother picked up that drum and stared at it. Tapped it. Went to sit on the rock. Rolled up his sleeves to show his bulgy muscles and Simlin thought nervously, *Brother could thump me one.*

There was a gleam on the big brother's cheek. Simlin blinked and stared again. The gleam caught the sunlight. *Bully brother was crying . . .*

Simlin felt a little catch in his chest. He wanted to climb down and say something to the brother. But what could he say? So he stayed silently up in his tree. Big brother stayed down on the rock.

Twilight. Bird song shimmered in the air, shivery-tuney, not like Bone Cracker's *eee-ark!* screams. Darkness followed. Simlin could not sleep. He shimmied down the tree trunk and crept on all fours up the waterfall rocks. He waited. He nodded off, sat up fast, because something had hurtled down the river, with a cry. Quick! Was that the gleam of an eye? It sank below the surface again. Simlin capered back to his tree, scrambled up and waited.

At last he heard water splash, twig crack, grass rustle. Something was moving on the riverbank, among the tall pink balsam flowers, sending off the seed heads popping. It was lying on the bank now. It looked like a log of wood, shiny brown in the early light.

The log slid into the river, making a water-gurgle noise. Simlin saw a ream, a swirl on the water. A streak of nutmeg-brown streamed through the water, eeling in and out of the weed. The yellow dog got up and wagged its tail. The streak-creature hauled itself up on to that rock and turned its small head towards the big brother, who jumped up, wide-awake now.

The streak-creature twitched its whiskers. It dropped something from under its arm by the brother's brown foot. Simlin almost fell out of his tree trying to see what it was. Sparkling blue, shiny wet . . . The brother turned it over and over in his hand. The streak-creature shook itself from head to tail and Simlin saw that it was an otter.

The otter chirruped. It flipped around and slid back into the pool, and twisted away. Now that it was safe in its own watery element it looked like an alien. The blind boy's body stirred. He was back. He was in himself again. Big brother wanted to pick the little one up, but the little one wanted to walk, holding on to his brother with one hand, drum in the other.

When they were gone, Simlin shimmied down his tree and trotted all the way back home, chattering to himself. As he approached the five-sided house he saw Mother leaning against the wall, flumping her breasts and pouting at a man standing by an army truck. He had a bright pink face and a black hat with a peak.

Simlin spied. Simlin listened. The pink-faced man was wheedling, 'Come across the sea with me, you gorgeous woman. You could be a healer in a rich country. People would pay for your spells and potions and your advice. Love potions, hate potions, thin spells, hair spells . . . You would be a celebrity. You could get lots and lots of money.'

Simlin saw that Mother had made the pink-faced man her Special Drink in a little copper cup. The man glugged it down and smacked his red lips. He held up a piece of glass in the sunlight and shone it at the wall. It charred the wood and made a little curl of smoke. Vaskalia sucked on her copper bangles and spat at the wall. The charred wood glowed up green. The man spat too and the charred wood sputtered and went out and they both *yipyipsnorted* very much.

The man turned the glass towards the donkey

tethered in Mother's garden. Simlin clapped his hands over his ears to keep out the donkey's horrible noise and ran through the garden into the house. No one came to look for him.

16

TATTOOS AND TOADSTOOLS

Back from his river journey, Luka sat on the chair in the bakery yard, soaking up the sunshine, with the dog lying by his feet. He listened to the scissoring of swallows' wings as they swooped inside the woodshed. He had already tried to explain to Jez and Dimitri how to find the blue cave. Now he smiled as he imagined the otter basking in this sunlight, warming his wet pelt, and juggling a marsh marigold between his paws.

Luka dozed off. He was woken by barking, and the clatter of iron on the cobblestones. Jez and Dimitri were back! They led Katrin's horse into the yard, snorting and sweating, for he was laden down with panniers of rock from the cave.

'We followed your directions, Luka,' said Jez 'and I remembered the cave as soon as we got near. It's like the night sky. It's where I found you before. And all I had to do was swing the pick once and the rock fell in blue showers.' He knelt by the chair and

318

studied his brother closely. When he'd found Luka's body near the waterfall, his face was still and tight. Now it was softer. His eyes moved under the black chaos of his hair. His hands were relaxed, not clenched into fists and there was a little colour in his cheeks.

Jez said, 'You're in much better shape than the last time you went away.'

'Did you remember to bring my drum back?'

'Yes.' Jez took the drum from off a pannier and whizzed it like a frisbee, on to Luka's lap.

'Whey-hey!' cried Luka, running his hands round the honey-coloured wood feeling the figures carved on its side.

'I thought we'd never reach that flippin' cave,' sighed Dimitri.

'As soon as I saw the stepping-stones I remembered,' said Jez.

'I had an otter to help *me*,' boasted Luka.

'I only had a baker,' said Jez. 'Hey, feel this rock.'

'It's ice-cold,' cried Luka. 'Give me a file to smooth it. I could make a stone egg.'

'I'll carve little bowls, and decorate some tiles, a candlestick maybe,' mused Jez. 'I can't wait to get started. Oooh, here's food. Thanks, Katrin.'

'Everyone is so busy,' said Luka through a mouth full of cheese pie.

A voice complained, 'I'm not busy, Odd'un.'

'Peter . . . Have some pie,' said Dimitri. 'I'll find something to keep you busy. You can be a woodcutter. The trees round the square have grown thick as a forest. Cut them back for the festival and stack the logs for next winter. Then polish the furniture the carpenter has made from the walnut wood.'

Behind the wall of the bakery yard crouched Simlin. He stared at tiny emerald forests of moss glowing on the stones, and copses of golden lichen. Meticulously he picked them off, listening. The pretty woman arrived, and Eva with the sad face, carrying Lazy Boy No Legs. All those loud children came too. They scrambled inside the painted barrel and over the top. A little girl grabbed that tortoise and tried to teach it to jump over a stick.

Bully brother was hanging around the pretty woman, flexing his arms and showing off his bumpy muscles. She could not speak for smiles. She had white flowers woven into her plait. The brother blinked, dazzled by her smiling. A blush crept up his neck and over his face, right up to his scarecrow hair. He gave the pretty woman something.

'What a beautiful stone,' she exclaimed.

'I'll make you a decorated bowl, Imogen,' boasted the brother.

Lazy Boy squealed, 'So you've been on another journey, Luka? You look all ghostly and used up. Like you have no insides left. *We* are going to have a party. Dimitri says we shouldn't, because of that Vaskalia. He says she is a stump of ill-will.'

Mother?

'We must give her a second chance, Aidan,' said Pretty Woman. 'She wants to make us a scented garden . . .'

Head on one side, Similin listened to the pretty woman's calm, low voice.

Dimitri's voice was gruff with frowns. 'You say we should forgive and forget, Imogen, and I know you're right. So Vaskalia can come to the festival. But what will come *with* her?'

Scented garden? Mother says plants don't have eyes, but do have minds. Plants creep about and hide and disguise themselves. Stinging ones grow near safe ones and pretend to be nice. Mother can make plants do what she wants them to do. Want to go from her . . .

'Come on, Luka, I want to hear your story,' squealed Lazy Boy.

'I *will* tell you, Aidan, if you carry this drum back for me and get it put away in the cupboard with the other one. And –'

A shuddering out in the street shook the bakery walls.

Jez hissed, 'What the heck is that?' and from the roof of the vardo Florin yelled, 'Bang Bang! Soldiers, and a pink man!'

'Has anyone seen a blind boy and a Talking Fat Baker?' shouted someone.

'We're here in the yard,' answered Dimitri before he could stop himself. Luka heard the boots of the soldiers as they jumped down. The gate creaked open and the sugar-icing voice of Captain Lazslo said, 'Well, well. I did not know people still lived in places like this.'

'It was lovely before all the fighting,' said Luka.

'And the general has sent us to make it lovely again, because you are such a persuasive boy. But he is uneasy. He has heard stories of bad magic in this land.'

'Not here, he hasn't,' snapped Dimitri.

'Baker, you'd better understand that I am in

charge of all the soldiers detailed to build. So *you'll* be able to get back to your bread and fairy cakes.'

Dimitri's voice rang out like a trumpet: '*I* am Talking Man. *I* shall oversee what happens to *my* village and *my* people, and don't you forget it. And listen to me, city boy, we have found the ideal land to build a home.'

'The wise woman from the house with five sides says it's *her* family's land.'

'What wise woman? It's not hers! We are building the new homes there and there is nothing Vaskalia can do about it. Jez? Show us the plans.'

Imogen and Jez had covered sheets of paper with drawings of the new homes. Now they spread them on the bakery table. The children grew round-eyed as they saw the bedrooms with bunk beds, playrooms, the garden and playground full of swings and slides.

'Luka,' squealed Aidan. 'They've drawn a lift. I will go upstairs, I *will.*'

'And so, corporal, I hereby command you to begin building at once,' proclaimed Dimitri. 'Level the land and lay the foundations.'

'Address me by rank, Fat Baker, if you please,' snarled Lazslo. 'You know perfectly well I am a captain.'

So next day, the work began. The soldiers started early to avoid the heat. At night they stayed at the inn. When Dimitri asked how things were going, the soldiers groaned, 'That lazy Lazslo tells us what to do. Then he disappears off down the road out of the village. He never even picks up a brick.'

'I wonder where he goes . . .' mused Dimitri.

In the five-sided house, Vaskalia was tattooing herself with a pair of pike jaws. Droplets of blood fell to the floor as she stuck bones in all along her throat and chest.

Simlin squinted at spirals, stars, crosses and ancient-looking signs.

Vaskalia climbed up on to the table and pirouetted in her scarlet dress, so fast she almost fell off the table.

'Look at me, Simlin. I'm a gorgeous poppy in a field,' she cackled, turning fast to make the skirt swirl around her. 'I've dyed this dress with lords-and-ladies berries. And look. I've sewn these tiny pieces of white satin. Well?'

Mother is a spotty red toadstool.

The scorpion birthmark on his forehead was itching, as if the tail had curved over on the back, ready to sting.

'Have you nothing to say to your own mother, droolgob? The men of this village will be fighting over me. Dimitri and the captain will come to fisticuffs. Will anyone be fighting over you?' She pinched his arm. 'No muscle there, is there? I've fed you fat goose and hare hung until it is black and falls off the bone, but you are still soft as a maggot. Oh well, I suppose that the grease from that goose I cooked will keep us warm next winter.'

She gnawed at her copper bangles.

'But things may have changed by then,' she said.

Yes, Mother. Things will have changed by then.

17

FESTIVAL

The village square was set ready this light summer night, as if it was a stage waiting for a play to begin.

Peter had polished the tables carved from the old walnut tree until they shone like dark mirrors. He had cut the trees back just enough. The stones of the square were dappled gold as if fingertips touched and moved new coins. In the cool evening the fragrance from the lanterns of blossom on the lime and lilac trees was elusive, delicious. Everyone breathed deeply, hoping for more of the scent. Eva and the children filled china jugs with honeysuckle and roses, and set one on each table.

Big Katrin had made Dimitri mend an old trestle table. She scrubbed it three times, before setting out the feast.

Aidan squealed, 'Luka, you should see what we're having. Crusty rolls and golden pies, tomatoes, cheese *and* chicken, *and* red fruit, *and* gingerbread, *and* apple cakes as big as millwheels. But Katrin is covering it all up again.'

Big Katrin laughed as she shook out her white muslin. It floated and settled over the landscape of food like a mist.

'Summer certainly smells good,' said Luka.

'And everyone is all dressed up,' said Aidan. 'Look at my waistcoat. Sorry – I mean, feel the embroidery. Imogen has a blue dress and her hair all curled up with flowers.'

'Wish I could see her.'

'She thinks Jez looks handsome. She's never taken her eyes off him.'

'He spent ages getting ready.'

'And Big Katrin has left her apron at home, and her hair is all down round her shoulders. It's a pity Mr Baker looks so silly in his horrible striped suit.'

'It's his *only* suit,' giggled Luka. He reached out and stroked Aidan's face. Sometimes it was pinched and lined with pain. Aidan's hurt came out in his anger, but this evening his face felt soft and relaxed. He continued to give Luka a running commentary on the festival.

'There are loads of people. Everyone looks a bit shy.'

327

'Why are the children screaming?' Luka asked.

'They're pretending to see faces in the olive trees. And Stefan keeps scuttling around like a crab. He'll get stood on. Oh, and there are two brown-faced mountain people.'

A voice Luka recognised said, 'It's Luka, isn't it? We met in the city.'

'Sith and Ribi, hello. I'm glad you're here. You can stay in our old house if you like.'

'Thank you. Luka, you have certainly brought life to this village.'

'It's not just me,' said Luka. 'It's everybody. Meet my friend Aidan. This is Sith and Ribi. There's going to be a baby.'

'Hello, you three,' squealed Aidan.

Ribi touched Luka's face and said, 'We'll talk later on. We must say hello to Dimitri.'

Aidan continued his commentary: 'There's the pink lollipop captain, and the soldiers, and that family who arrived on a tractor. There are some I don't know. I can't see their faces because they're wearing sunglasses. *Everyone* is here. Except you-know-who.'

'Come on, you two rascals. Sit with us,' said Jez. He hoisted Aidan on to his shoulders, grabbed

328

Luka's arm and took them to a table where Eva was sitting with George the shoemaker. He was telling her that he had been poorly.

'Poor George. Are you feeling better now?'

'A bit better. I thought I'd have to miss the festival,' he moaned. 'That Vaskalia woman came in to my shop yesterday. Hadn't seen her out for years. She demanded red dancing shoes. *No*, I told her, *there's not enough time to make them*. At once my feet bent up with cramps. I couldn't walk. So I stayed up all night making her shoes, but I still feel sick . . .'

'The music's beginning, George,' said Eva. 'Listen and let it make you better. Look at dear Dimitri with his eyes closed for the music . . .'

Dimitri led with his fiddle. Sith played a three-stringed lyraki and Ribi's mandolin made notes that sounded like peals of bells. Peter's cousin came to play the pipes, and their sweet, wild call drifted across the square.

Luka stood up. He was the first to dance. Imogen took Jez by the hand and led him out. The children grabbed hands and danced in a circle while Aidan clapped and beat the table, shouting instructions from his chair: 'Round you go again. STOP! Change direction, and LOOK OUT everyone because Stefan's escaped.'

Peter drummed two stones against the inn-keeper's wooden barrels, as his father and grandfather had done at festivals years ago. Luka danced faster to Peter's rhythm. The music wound around the square and up into the sky and Luka thought, *I have Jez and Dimitri, Katrin, Imo and the orphans. I have a good family. I am happy, aren't I?*

Dimitri called out, 'Eva? Come here and sing. It's too long since we heard your angel's voice,' and Eva sang, so movingly that Luka heard Big Katrin having a little weep.

The evening air was warm and scented, full of insects drunk on nectar, staying up after their bedtime. The music spiralled into the night sky and away to the listening stars.

Yet Luka was nervous. He was waiting for something extraordinary to happen.

FLAME DANCER

Dimitri put down his fiddle and pulled on his white hat. A griddle had been set up over charcoal, sprinkled with fresh rosemary and thyme, and he began to cook. Soon, sausages and peppers sizzled.

Hungry people crowded around the barbecue. Luka was right at the front, his inside mouth sprinkling with hunger.

'This plate's for me and Aidan,' he said.

'Better keep room for the pastry wheels and cherry pie,' said Dimitri, piling Luka's plate high. 'Hey, Jez – can you run and get more bread?'

After they'd eaten as much as they could Aidan shouted, 'More music, Mr Baker, please,' and the band began to play again.

Dimitri was ecstatic, deep in his music dream. He played folk songs they all knew, and wove wild, fast tunes that made them want to dance and dance. Aidan turned to Luka and said, 'You're lucky. At least you have legs. Dance instead of me, will you?' but just as Luka stood up, he heard Aidan's sharp intake of breath.

Someone was already dancing in the middle of the square. Shoes tipped and heeled with metal hammered in a relentless rhythm.

'It's *her*,' hissed Aidan and Luka felt the happiness draining out of him.

The staccato dance steps rang like bullets. Dimitri forced himself to open his eyes and saw a blur of red whirling on high-heeled dancing shoes, snapping fingers as if they were castanets. On her head was a crest of scarlet, fixed with a pike-bone comb, holding a veil of black lace to hide her eyes. Down her back hung a snake of oiled hair.

Dimitri had to admit to himself that she was an accomplished dancer. He could not look away from her. *Vaskalia.* She was dancing a spell, a red flame in the twilight. He wanted to put down his bow but he *had* to keep on playing.

Someone else moved into Dimitri's sight. Someone tall. Big Katrin. Her eyes were dark as pools. Dimitri always wanted to topple into those pools and drown. This evening those eyes held his, and would not let them go until he had done what they wanted him to do. *Stop playing your fiddle. Now* . . .

With an effort that hurt his chest, Dimitri slid his bow away as if he was dragging a sword out of a wound, and dropped it to the ground.

Vaskalia stopped dancing. Luka shivered like a leaf in a hailstorm, waiting, until he heard those shoes hammer towards the bandstand, and Aidan squeal, 'Look out, Dimitri. She's coming to catch you.'

Dimitri ran across the square, wheezing and gasping, and the dancing shoes clacked hard after him. Aidan thumped the table, hollering, 'She's got him trapped round a tree – behind a chair – but oh no, he's out of puff.'

Thankfully, Luka heard Big Katrin's steps pacing, as calm as an empress, into the middle of the square, and Dimitri sigh as he fell into her arms.

Vaskalia's voice cut the air, as white cold as lightning.

'You'll be sorry you ever turned *me* down, Dimitri. Your friend Gabriel made that mistake and took that trollop Evangelina instead of me. And where are they both now, eh?'

Yes, where are they? echoed in Luka's mind, and tears trickled down his face.

'I shall settle a devil in your pantry and a fire

fiend in your ovens, baker. And *you*, dumb ogress, watch out for your head in every doorway, or you'll lose it.'

Vaskalia's curses writhed like malevolent wraiths among the villagers, even after she had pounded away across the square and into the trees.

The people were silent until the atmosphere cleared. It was as if a storm had passed. Olive leaves rustled like shavings of silver in the breeze. Aidan put a drink made from elderflower and peaches into Luka's hand. He said, 'She's gone, Luka. But you know, someone else was watching from behind the olive trees.'

'Did he have a scorpion on his forehead?' asked Luka, remembering the face he had glimpsed as he fell down the waterfall.

'Yes. Eva says that's Vaskalia's son. She thinks he climbed up in our roof.'

'The Whisperer,' said Luka sadly. 'All my life someone has whispered names at me. I hear him up there in the orphanage roof.'

'Jez has mended that hole now, so he can't hide up there any more. Here comes Jez now with more bread. Dimitri's going to play music again. Let's enjoy the festival now she's gone.'

The music wound on into the night again, but Luka did not want to dance.

He knew Vaskalia would be back.

19

THE GHOST IN THE OLIVE TREE

Owls called softly across the square. Mice scurried to the crumbs underneath the tables. Bats flickered, clever as tiny fighter planes, and vanished behind broken walls. Candles of citronella glowed orange-yellow with the scent of lemons.

Peter kept complaining, 'Ah'm *so* thirsty.' The band put down their instruments to get a drink. A nightingale began to sing, filling the space they had left her.

Dimitri lolled against a beer barrel. He saw Jez and Imogen with their heads close together. He was pleased by their happiness, but he hoped Luka would not feel too alone.

A soft arm encircled *his* shoulders.

'My dear Katrin,' murmured Dimitri, letting her lead him across the square. 'I know the war has been terrible for us all . . . and I know you must miss . . . but . . .'

He stopped. The square had fallen silent.

Dimitri turned.

Up on a tree flapped a white ghost, as if it hung on a cross.

The ghost was hung with trophies, yellow bones, animal skins, knives, gold and silver coins and a tiny skull. A snake wound around the neck. Jagged antlers reared up behind the shoulders. Scallop shells clapped together in the night breeze. A giant pair of harsh wings crossed on the breast.

Around the hem was a fringe of sharpened teeth. A claw hung on the front like a sickle.

The apparition was lit with wavering green lights.

Simlin shivered behind his tree. His teeth rattled like jacks. Mother had brought that thing, that cloak, from under her mattress, spread across the donkey's back. Who had put it up *there*? It was monstrous. Simlin knew that its folds hid sinister presences.

Aidan squealed, 'She's back, Luka. And her mouth is all slathery red. She's swaying and there's a big ghostly cloak with bones and skulls and skins and teeth all round the bottom. It's hanging on an olive tree.'

Luka could hear Vaskalia breathing. Quick, harsh, angry breaths, short with rage. He thought he had always heard it.

She howled, 'Let us meet our shaman boy and see who will wear the cloak tonight?'

That's me. I am the shaman boy. I am the shape-shifter. Luka's heart dived. He had not known there was a cloak like *this*. He sensed that held within it were the kind of powers he did not want: malevolence, old magic, superstition, ill-will, hurt and harm.

Vaskalia drained his energy as if she had stuck leeches all over his skin. But Aidan grabbed his hand and Luka knew that Aidan's strength of mind would help him. And they *all* came, clustering round him in a circle of safety.

The voice howled as if Vaskalia was possessed. 'Who will wear the shaman's cloak?' It was not the shaman's voice he had heard in the cave, or the echo from the mountains or the waterfall. This voice was steeped in hatred.

Luka concentrated his mind on the Cloud Cat, on her deliberate prowl, her axe shoulder blades sliding under her thick white fur and her gold-nugget eyes.

He opened his mouth wide and cried, '*I will not wear that cloak!*'

To Luka, his voice sounded frail as the twitter of the goldfinches that lived in the trees near their old house.

To everyone else, it was the yowl of a great leopard. Luka's eyes blazed cold gold, and sent Vaskalia flying across the square as if someone had punched her full-face.

She struggled up again, and the awful voice reverberated, cracking a jug of lemonade on a table.

'Whoever wears the cloak will shift his spirit, through the air, water and fire, over the earth and under it too. He will bring fear to his people. He will hold live coals in his hands, suck souls out of ears, spit plague, cough gold and banish those we do not want.'

Vaskalia raised her arm and stabbed her finger at something across the square. The faces in the square turned together, a field of pale sunflowers in the night, following the pointing finger to a thin figure disappearing under a table.

'And there he is. Come out, Simlin, and wear the shaman's cloak.'

20

GABRIEL'S SON

Luka heard whimpering and he knew it was the Whisperer.

Aidan said, 'It's her son. He's fallen to his hands and knees. He looks as if he's waiting to be executed.'

But Vaskalia's voice commanded, 'Stand up, Simlin. Soldiers, dress my son in the shaman's cloak.'

'That Captain Lazslo is getting the cloak down off the tree. He's telling the soldiers to drape it on Simlin. But he can hardly stand up in it,' said Aidan.

Luka heard the teeth around the hem of the cloak tapping, and the totems jangle against each other. A cold shiver of moonlight ran through his head and body, like an electric shock. This cloak had been worn for shifts into evil.

He heard Simlin's knees creak as he sank in a huddle, snuffling like a poor small animal, and he could not bear Simlin's misery. He forgot about the whispering and the name-calling. He did not want Simlin to suffer.

Luka stepped forward, pushing away the hands that tried to restrain him.

'Take the cloak off him, Vaskalia,' the Cloud Cat roared through him. 'He doesn't want to wear it.'

'So out *you* come, blind boy, and put it on instead.'

'Don't you dare harm my brother, scumbag sorceress,' shouted Jez.

'You keep out of it, scarecrow, or you will be sorry. Gabriel's family were lords of change. If Simlin won't wear it, then a son of Gabriel's must put it on instead.'

'And a son of Gabriel's *will* wear it. Here I am!' cried Jez. He strolled into the middle of the square. 'Put the cloak on *my* back,' he commanded the soldiers. 'I am strong enough to take it.'

'Jez, be careful,' cried Imogen, as the soldiers lifted the cloak off Simlin and placed it on Jez's shoulders. There he stood, wearing the shaman's cloak like a king. He held out his hand and called Luka to his side.

'You can't do that,' howled Vaskalia.

'I *can*,' said Jez. 'And I just have. I am Gabriel's son, too. I am very strong. Do you really think I am going to stand here and watch you hurt the only

341

member of my family I have left? Luka is my little brother. I love him.'

A babble of abuse and curses streamed from Vaskalia's mouth. Sith warned, 'Beware, Luka's brother. In the mountains we learned to dread the power of that cloak. The cloak will possess you. See how it possesses that woman. There is wickedness in every fold.'

Jez began to moan as if he was in pain. 'It's so heavy, it's bringing me down.'

Luka said, 'The cloak itself isn't wicked. It's just what people *believe* it can do. They make it like that and give it power. That's why Jez feels so bad.'

'You are a wise boy,' cried Ribi. 'That might have been your mother talking. That was her kind of wisdom. We knew her, Luka.'

Vaskalia howled, 'But *Luka* must wear the cloak. He has inherited his father's gift. Let me be Luka's mother. Let me look after the gift that Gabriel gave him.'

'No, Vaskalia. You are wrong. He has not inherited his father's gift.' This was said by a woman. The woman's voice was low and melodious, and it was one that Luka did not know. Dimitri thought the voice came from the woman standing next to him.

The woman next to him was Big Katrin.

Katrin smiled. She walked forward and stood looking down at Vaskalia.

'You are wrong,' she said. 'There was no such gift in Gabriel's family. No shaman, no spirit leapers. They were good people, builders and craftsmen, but that's all they were.'

'How dare you *speak*, ogress. Luka has the gift.'

'Yes he has. But it was his mother who passed it on to him, not Gabriel. It was Evangelina's family who had the gift.'

Vaskalia's gape of a mouth opened and closed, and opened and closed again. No words came out. She bunched up her skirts into a scarlet puffball and pounded across the square, her heels clacking. One of them broke off and the shoe lurched sideways. Vaskalia wrenched off both shoes, hurling them from her, and ran to vault on to the donkey, thrashing her heels into its ribs. The donkey stumbled away into darkness.

Dimitri kept saying, 'Katrin . . . Katrin?' in his bewilderment.

Aidan begged, 'Big Katrin . . . please say some more. Why did you speak?'

'Because something needed to be said.'

Sith went over to Luka and said, 'We knew your mother Evangelina. That is why we felt we knew *you* in the city. We saw her in your face. Katrin speaks the truth. Your mother comes from a family of gifted ones but they would not use the power in *that* cloak.'

'If only she were here,' said Luka forlornly.

'Well she isn't,' snapped Jez.

'Jez, take off the cloak,' begged Luka. 'It smells rank, and I can hear you shivering.'

Jez turned his face down towards Luka and sneered, 'You're not just blind, you're a little fool, aren't you!'

Luka shrugged. 'Aren't we all, sometimes?'

'Not as stupid as you. *I* should be the one to get the gift.' Jez snatched his hand from Luka's, and strode away. The cloak belled around him. The bones and chains rattled. A fox head hanging from his back opened its jaws and snarled at Imogen. The snake around the hem swung out its full length, as if it was made of steel, and hissed at Luka.

'Get it *off* him,' cried Sith, pulling at the cloak.

'No,' shouted Jez. 'It's *mine.*' His eyes were blood-shot and veins stood like ropes in his white face.

'Jez, please take it off,' pleaded Luka. 'Stay here with me!'

Jez's knees gave way. He sank to the ground and began to cry like a little boy. Dimitri and Sith ran to lift the cloak from his shoulders. As he did so, Dimitri saw a movement in the corner of his eye. It was Simlin slithering away. He turned just once to look back and the scorpion on his forehead glowed.

'Take that cloak far away into the woods and bury it,' ordered Dimitri.

Luka heard a voice wailing through the night and knew that they would not be rid of the cloak so easily.

Imogen dipped her sleeve in water and cooled Jez's face, murmuring, 'Hush now. It's gone, Jez, it's gone.'

'You'll be glad to know that her son Simlin has gone too, Luka.' Jez spoke tightly, his teeth clenched together. 'I should have given him a good kicking to help him on his way.'

'No.' said Luka. 'That might have been me.'

'What do you mean?' said Jez.

'I mean, if things had been different. If Vaskalia had married our – our Dad.'

'He means, Jez, we should show Simlin a little mercy,' murmured Imogen.

21

THE HONEY-COLOURED DRUM

The wolf choir sang through the night on the edge of the village. Luka sat with his back against a tree and counted seven different notes from the pack.

Eva and the children had gone back to the orphanage. Jez and Imo were sitting at a table nearby. Luka heard them murmuring and thought, *They are a couple now*, and missed his mother yet again.

Jez said, 'Come on, my little brother. Let's see Imo safely home.'

As they came near the orphanage, they breathed the perfume of the tiny night stock flowers the children had planted in the rubble gardens.

'Slip inside and whisper goodnight, Luka,' said Imogen. 'They'll all be fast asleep, but the wish will stay with them and keep them safe from bad dreams.'

Luka stepped into the porch, thinking, *Imo and Jez just want to kiss.*

The stone porch still hugged the warmth of the day. Luka reached out for the handle of the door but did not find it.

'Imo, did you leave the door open?' he asked.

'No,' she cried, pushing past him. 'Children? Come out.' Her voice echoed in each corner of the hall. The silence, the waiting, made Luka feel ill.

'Don't hide from me,' shouted Imogen. 'It's not funny. *Please*. Where are you?'

Only one voice answered. One unmistakable voice squealed from the far end of the room. *'I'm still here . . .'* It was Aidan.

'What's happened? Where are they all?'

'Gone. There's just me and Stefan left. The lady picked him up from his cot. She went *"Eugh*, he's wet,"* and put him back again.'

Then came Eva's voice, sobbing, 'I couldn't stop them. I just couldn't.'

'*What* woman?' cried Imogen.

'There were three of them,' said Aidan. 'Two men and a lady . . .' Aidan's breath caught in his throat and he began to cry.

Luka remembered the general's warning: *Child traffickers are here in the land. They steal children. They sell them for a good price.*

He bowed his head at the tears around him and said, 'Jez. Fetch me my drum.'

PART FOUR: AUTUMN

Seven wolves wait at a distance, hearing the soft drumbeat.
Their tongues loll and drip. They lower their heads to the
black-faced wolf with the silver eyes and their tails
thump in obedience, because he is their leader. When he
howls and runs, his pack will run with him.
The black-faced wolf is waiting for the shaman boy.
The man with the hair of frost walks by himself, as a
shaman always will. He says, 'A wolf choir does not
always sing of death, shaman boy. Take strength from
your Cloud Cat and from those who love you.
In the end, turn back to your life.'

1

SEVEN WOLVES RUNNING

The scent of the children was in everything Jez brought out for the wolves.

In the cool midnight their scent was sharper still. It was so strong that Luka in his wolf shape reeled from it.

He sniffed the wooden block that was Florin's gun. The smell was resinous wood and nervous boy. Maria's hairband had caught her faint, flowery scent. Luka knew it at once. A wisp of her curly black hair was still caught in the band. Maria would not have heard the child stealers creeping up on them until the very last moment. How frightened she must have been. Lisa's cardigan held her odd, toffee smell in the midst of the coarse wool.

The toys and clothes held the essence of the children and there was more, because Luka the black-faced wolf smelled an extra scent that both shocked and tempted him. It made his tongue curl around his muzzle. It was the smell of something alive. Something to be caught and eaten. *Flesh*.

His pack waited at a distance with their heads down in deference. Luka flung back his head, pointed his muzzle to the sky and howled. One by one the six wolves took up his howl. Each one sang a different but close note, their black lips drawn back over their teeth. Luka had always thought wolf howling a desolate, lonely sound. Now he learned that it was the sound of wolf souls longing to run together, trusting each other.

His friends had been stolen. How would they cope? The orphans had become their own family, living together with Imogen and Eva. Imo and Eva would be heartbroken and Luka knew he must bring his friends back to the village. He shuddered as he thought of what might happen. They might be separated, abused, sold into slavery or taken away to a foreign country, lonely and lost.

He remembered that shaman's cloak, steeped in wickedness, still in the forest, waiting for a wearer. Luka Wolf shook himself, put his nose down to find the scent on the ground, and loped away to find those who had left it. His pack was with him.

The wolves raced through the night village, past the square still littered with food and chairs and glasses from the festival, past a pair of red shoes lying abandoned in the middle, past the ruined church and houses and the open door of the bakery.

Behind them came a backfire, like a gun, from Dimitri's van.

Glancing back, Luka saw the pale shape of the dog leap at the van, but he did not falter in his stride as he loped on down the road out of the village.

He paused, one paw raised. There was a new scent on the ground. His pack waited, shivering with eagerness. There they were, his pack, tense and gaunt; two yearlings and his white female, two pup-wolves and the grizzled male.

Through the eyes of the black-faced wolf, Luka saw the tracks of big tyres in the dust. He smelled petrol and a hot engine as well as the children's strong human smell. The child-stealers must have put them in a lorry or a truck. Luka thought of them pushed inside into the dark, only half awake, terrified, travelling far away at speed.

The pack must travel fast. Luka Wolf pointed his muzzle to the black, star-shattered sky and howled and his pack howled too, their voices weaving together in mournful music. So intent was he on finding the children, he did not notice that the wolves had paused outside the little house with five sides.

2

SEVEN FLOWERS OF WOLFSBANE

Simlin crouched in the corner. He stayed as still as if he was made of wood. Behind his knees he had tucked the seeing ball to keep it safe.

He had crouched motionless ever since he had fled back from the festival and the terror of that shaman's cloak.

Mother snored on her elephant bed. Her skin was grey as a mushroom. Simlin saw her feet sticking out from her red dress. They were podgy and blunt and covered in filth. He had run home and found her sulking on her bed, swigging purple brew from the jar, whining to herself until she had fallen asleep.

Simlin heard running, something running. *Must be something coming after me.* He wrapped his arms over his head and squeezed his eyes tight shut. *Howling.* When the howling began it sounded like those bagpipes starting up at the festival, droning from another strange world.

These were wolves howling. *Right outside his door.*

Simlin wondered if the blind boy was with those wolves, inside a wolf's brainbox.

Mother shuddered and juddered awake. She slid off the bed fast, like a sack of flour down the chute at the mill. She stood up and cupped a hand behind her ear.

'Hear them out there, Simlin?' she said. 'Hear the wolf choir.'

He dare not reply. That bone-jangling cloak was still out there in the night, weighty with totems and wickedness.

His hand reached out for the seeing ball.

Sure enough, when the glass cleared, Simlin saw a wolf with a black face and long, bony legs. It ran on arched paws as if it was on tiptoe. Around its shoulders the wolf wore an extra mantle of thick silver-tipped fur, like a stole to keep it warm.

The wolf turned as if it could see him. Simlin gasped. Its eyes were pale silver, clear as river water in the sunlight. Behind the boy-wolf Simlin saw the six shadows of its pack. Simlin knew about wolves. Once they had you down, you were done for.

'Give it to me.'

Vaskalia pulled the ball from Simlin's hands.

'Is it him? Is he a wolf now?' she screeched with

her nose squashed up against the glass. 'Tell me.'

'You can't see in there, can you?' cried Simlin. All of a sudden he was helpless with *yipyipsnorts* and no time to dodge her smacking fist, but then he was angered and turned on her, yelling, 'Yes. Boy spirit is in black-faced wolf, leading his pack. For six wolves do follow him. Boy is cleverer than *you*, smelly old toadstool, mushroom Mother.'

He ducked but there were no more smacks. Her head was on one side as she listened to the wolves' wild, ever-changing howling.

'A wolf choir sings of death,' she crooned. 'But whose death will it be?'

She peered up at the rafters and called, 'Bone Cracker? Off you go and get me some meat. Quickly.'

She opened the door and clapped her hands up at Bone Cracker. The vulture flopped sleepily down from the perch and stretched its wings before waddling out.

Vaskalia peered out at the night and called, 'Hurry up with the day, you out there. I need to find the yellow flowers of wolfsbane. I will need *seven*.'

3

STILL, SILVER LAND

Luka led his pack swiftly along the road. A slight
wind blew up, gusting the scent at him, until he
paused, nose high. They were coming to the
crossroads where Dimitri had called out to that
family on the tractor. Now Luka saw the crossroads
through the lead wolf's eyes. The horse and vardo
had bowled along that rough road to the city. On the
right, to the east, he saw a rocky uneven track
leading into the dark. Luka sniffed the air and
shivered. He smelled a foreign, salty place and knew
that somewhere soon they had to come down to
the sea.

Luka sensed that the mood of his pack had
changed. They yipped and whined, ears back. They
could smell that water. They were nervous of the
unknown stretch of silver, but Luka in his wolf shape
was driven to follow that scent down to the sea and,
still running swiftly, he turned on a single paw to
follow it.

The pack loped on along the bumpy road marked by the tracks of that vehicle heavy with children, strong with scent. They ran easily on long legs, through grass and sedge and rock, until Luka Wolf felt light touch his eyes and he paused.

Ahead, a band of yellow on the horizon was spreading fast up into the sky and down into that shifting, pewter-grey spill in front of it. This was the first time in his life that Luka had seen the sea. It pretended to be a still, silver land, but Luka saw it swell and move and knew that it was dangerous. His wolf's ears pricked to its deep sound.

On they raced. His wolves trusted him but still Luka felt their reluctance as the sea wind began to gust. It parted their fur and lifted their earflaps.

They were running along a headland on and on to the edge where the track turned to sand. The top of the cliff was thick with pink thrift flowers.

The wolves glanced anxiously towards Luka. He was their leader, their measurer of threat. The scent of the children ran on ahead, tantalising him, but he slowed and waited at the edge of the cliff, because far below was a place where people might be. There were cottages with roofs made of red tiles that overlapped like a tortoise's back. There was a harbour and a jetty. Sitting on the water was a boat. Luka saw the truck they had followed all the way here from the village. No children.

The pack whined and touched noses as they waited for their leader to make a move. His wolf nature focused on finding the source of the scent immediately, but at the back of his boy mind hung that terrible cloak. It was still there, near his village, trickling malice.

Luka Wolf set the image of the shaman's cloak aside. First he must find his friends and save the heart of his village.

The track wound like a helter-skelter down the steep cliff, to the secret harbour and the wild sea. Down it raced the wolf pack, with Luka in the lead, scuffing up clouds of sand, twisting and turning until they skidded to a stop where the track widened out and ended on the jetty. There they shivered, edging together so that their breath met together in one phantom cloud. Big gulls waddling on the jetty took fright and battled up into the air and away out to sea, screaming.

Luka Wolf slunk forward, belly low to the ground, up to the back of the truck. He leaped over the tailgate.

The truck was empty. Yet the smell of the children was all around.

Luka Wolf leaped down and crept along the jetty. He sniffed at the boat's rope wound around the capstan. The boat rose and fell on the swell of the tide, a small chasm away. He dared to look down. A jumble of rocks showed as the grey tide shrank away from them, then covered them again. The scummy water slapped against the harbour wall, deep and dark, not dappled with sunlight like the shallows by the riverbank.

For a moment Luka heard whimpering, as if animals had been hurt.

The children were in that boat.

Water slapped at the harbour wall. Far out to sea the waves tumbled and rolled endlessly. The sand carried in the wind filled the wolves' nostrils and mouths. The scent of fish was strong and made them slaver, but the whimpering came again and the wolves flinched. Whimpering turned into weeping. The wolves trembled.

The grinding of an engine drowned out all sound.

It was above them. It was racing down the sandy track.

Out from the nearest cottage ran a man. He

uncoiled the rope from the capstan as fast as if he were spinning a top and jumped across the chasm of harbour water on to the deck of the boat. As he jumped he lost hold of the rope and it snaked down into the water, but he backed across the deck to the wheelhouse, shouting, 'Go, go now,' and a woman yelled, 'Get on the boat, Sergei.'

The wheelhouse door flew open and Luka Wolf sprang on to the deck of the boat and his wolves followed, and from a place far inside him rose up a summoning howl, a fanfare.

Luka Wolf faced the man backed against the boat's wheelhouse and snarled, keeping him there. His pack stood with him. The grinding engine stopped in a swirl of dust. Brakes screeched, tyres burned and something yellow hit the water with a splash. *The dog.* Summoned by Luka Wolf's howl, she padded desperately to keep her head above water. In her mouth was the rope from the boat.

'Give me the gun,' screamed the woman from the wheelhouse, and Luka feared for the lives of his pack.

The boat shuddered as its engine started and died, started again, full throttle, and stopped. Luka and the wolves leaned close together for reassurance, and Luka Wolf saw his brother running along the jetty.

Once again the engine spluttered into life. Once again it petered out. With a rush of air, Jez landed on the deck. The wolves snarled and glanced to their leader Luka. He yipped at them, *Stay there on guard, keep them there,* and ran to peer overboard at a second, louder splash.

Down in the murky harbour water bobbed a round shape. The short arms and legs worked furiously like a paddle steamer. *Dimitri.* His legs were too short to make the same successful leap as lanky Jez, but his arms were strong enough to grab hold of the rope from the deck and pull himself, hand over hand, up on to the deck.

There he stood, glowering, with his hands made into fists, dripping dirty water on to the deck.

'Where are the children?' he roared, and was answered with small cries from the hold below the deck.

'Dimitri. We're here and we're hungry. Help us,' cried voices Luka knew and loved, but the boat began to shake. The engine was in full throttle now. The dog gave up her futile struggle to hold on to the children and the wolf she dimly recognised as Luka.

Exhausted, she let go of the rope as the boat turned and headed out to sea, parting the water as easily as a blacksmith working molten iron in his forge.

The wolves whimpered in fear as the ground beneath their paws rose and fell and the smell of the land they knew was left behind them.

THE SLANT OF THE SUNLIGHT

Luka Wolf ran across to his pack, who were poised by the wheelhouse, their lips drawn back above their teeth. The faces of the three traffickers scowled through the window, contorted with anger that their plans had gone wrong. One of them bawled, 'We were just trying to make a living.' Dimitri remembered that voice. It sounded like the toe of a boot swirling gravel. He knew he had seen the three before, in the inn, last winter, sitting in the nook of the fireplace, wanting to hunt animals and take pelts to sell. The men wore hoods and the woman's face was framed in white ermine. Now her yellow hair was wet with spray and the men had hats pulled down above their set faces.

'There's always someone doing well out of a war when the rest are suffering,' growled Dimitri. 'Jez, we have to take them.'

'But what about the children?' said Jez. 'How long will they last down there?' Secretly he was thinking, *How long will I last up here without being sick? This boat going up and down, up and down on the waves.*

'If we can get into that wheelhouse, we can save them,' said Dimitri.

The wolves swayed on their thin legs as the boat rose and sank on the swell, and Luka knew that all the power was with that tight-mouthed woman steering the boat.

The door was flung open and out came the third man brandishing a gun. Dimitri and Jez hesitated. Luka Wolf did not. He leaped to grab the man's wrist in his jaws. The gun discharged its bullets on to the deck right by his paws, three times, exploding like the worst night of the war.

There was a pause.

Luka saw Dimitri stoop to snatch the revolver up from the deck and push the man inside the wheelhouse with the other two traffickers. He was right up close, shouting into the man's face.

The man stumbled backwards, crying, 'It was that woman who sells spells. That one in the little house . . . she wanted to buy a snow leopard pelt . . . She kept whining on about white fur . . . *She* told us there were children in the old school. She said,

"Take them away, they're nobody's children, nobody wants them."'

'You piece of dirt under life's floorboards!' snarled Dimitri. 'Last winter it was wild animals you were hunting, not children.'

'It's just a job,' wailed the man.

Dimitri pushed him back inside, slammed the door shut and leaned against it, with the revolver trained at the ready. As the wolves slunk up to stand guard, he stepped back, smirking in triumph.

Jez threw himself to his knees and wrenched open the trapdoor down into the hold. *Don't think about food . . . Don't think about food.*

Lisa climbed out first, waving. The other children followed, smiling with relief, all except Florin. He was terrified by the sounds of a gun and cowered down in the hold so that Jez had to climb down and carry him up.

'Wolves,' shrieked Maria, pointing at the pack, for she had not heard the nails of their paws click on the deck or their howls as the other children had. They were frightened and fascinated at the same time by the lean shapes with the crazy eyes.

'Yes, that's right,' said Dimitri, edging past them. 'Let's put those thieves in the hold.'

371

Down went the three at gunpoint, furious, swearing so foully that Dimitri told the children to cover their ears. He knelt on the deck, roaring, 'Don't mess with *our* children,' and slammed down the trapdoor. 'That's that,' declared the baker with smugness in his voice.

'No it's not,' said Jez. 'We're heading out to sea. I'm just a little nervous with all these wolves around.' He glanced at the pale silver eyes of the elegant lead wolf. He could not make himself look into them for long. Waves of panic washed around his stomach at the thought of his little brother's change. Eva had carried Luka's limp body back to Big Katrin at the bakery, but his spirit was right here, in that wolf, on this boat out in the sea.

'Please let him come safely back,' Jez prayed silently, to the wolves, the sea, the sky, anything that might hear him.

Luka Wolf gazed up at tall Jez. He admired the fearless way he had leaped on the boat and rescued the children from that dark hold. Dimitri was in the wheelhouse now. Somehow he turned the boat back towards land. A memory stirred in Luka's mind, something this man had once said to Aidan-who-had-to-be-carried-everywhere. Dimitri had worked as a seaman, many years ago, hadn't he?

But what was Jez doing now? He had staggered to the rail of the boat and was leaning over it. His face was the colour of the green weed on the rocks at the edge of the sea . . .

Dimitri was bringing the boat into the harbour and up to the jetty. Luka decided not to wait for Jez to moor the boat to the capstan. He leaped across on to the jetty and his pack followed. Luka ran down the stone steps on to the wet pebbles. The shivering dog was crouched on a rock, staring at them. Luka Wolf knew she wanted to run with them but he barked a command to her to stay.

He paused. The sea had such an overwhelming smell. He dipped his nose in the icy water and drank but at once spat it out. The water was far saltier than tears.

Up the sandy track ran the wolves with the sea wind snatching at them. They leaped to the grass at the side, flattening themselves as a jeep roared down to the harbour. The driver was an Occupation soldier. Next to him sat the general.

He must have arrived at the village too late for the festival, thought Luka, *but I'm glad he's here now.*

The wolves paused on the top of the headland,

tails waving, heads lowered politely to their leader. Luka raised his muzzle to the air and sniffed. Petrol. Another vehicle was coming. He smelled cigarette smoke drifting from the window. He took his pack away from the road as Peter's bus trundled past, following the general's jeep to bring the children home. The pack must hurry north.

Luka saw that the sky was wolf-grey. The sun slanted sharply under the clouds, streaming on to the edge of the sea so that the sky too looked as if it was underwater. Luka knew that they must all hunt and then rest. A little way up the road was a small wood, full of the smells of rabbit and deer. The hungry pack quickly killed and ate, finishing with berries, the occasional worm and some fat crickets still clinging to the grasses. The wolves licked themselves to clean away sand and the taste of salt. Then they leaped and twisted and rolled on their backs, displaying their fluffy tummies.

The pups had a play fight. When it grew aggressive, and more than play, Luka snapped at them to stop. The pups thumped their tails obediently and smiled with their whole bodies.

The last sunlight of the day fell at a slant that

told of autumn coming. In the far distance the mountaintops were as vague and lonely as breath blown on glass.

The pack rested. Owls gathered, calling to each other with their five hoot phrases. From out of the twilight drifted the soft call of deer. The wolves slept.

Luka Wolf woke when the night scents were sharp on the cooled air. He stood up and shook himself down to the tip of his tail, sensing that they were being followed.

The pack roused themselves and waited, shivering with eagerness, sometimes nipping each others' tails, always watching their leader.

The black sky was still encrusted with stars. Luka and his pack loped back up country, never having to think hard, for wolves have maps in their heads. The night smelled of autumn. They ran on steadily, sometimes snapping at a whooshing night bird, or starting at a pig-faced bat, but never faltering in their stride.

The sky lightened. Luka saw that white frost had painted an outline round the blades of grass and the leaves. The sun climbed the sky and dissolved the frost. The pack ran on, intent on its mission, over the crossroads and on up to the village. Luka found their presence comforting. It was as if seven creatures had just one mind.

And then Vaskalia changed everything.

Simlin knew it was the Bone Cracker's fault. One day, it would get its come-uppance. It had waddled in, dragging a brown animal with small soft hooves up to Vaskalia. The brown animal quivered. Its eyes flickered and then clouded.

Mother had taken up her cleaver and struck *woomph woomph woomph woomph woomph!* She counted six chunks of little brown deer. *Woomph!* Seven chunks now.

Mother had whipped off the skin with a sharp knife, fetched her pestle full of wolfsbane mix and began to smear yellow spell all over the meaty chunks. *Stank. Pooh.* She trotted outside, strewing the chunks around her on the road.

'That's the end of them,' she cackled. 'I hate that howling. Now for a good long sleep.' She packed moss inside her ears and launched herself on to her mattress.

When the wolves came, Simlin crept to watch round the door.

The smallest pup yipped. He was turning over

something on the road with his slender white muzzle. The second pup stopped too and sniffed at another find by the side. *Meat*. Lumps of it were strewn across the road. They glistened, red flesh marbled with white fat, all smeared over with a yellow film like a skin. Luka leaped at the pup, sending him spinning. His white female barged against the second cub, knocking her away from the lump of meat. The pack pushed the cubs on up the road, past the five-sided house, but the smallest pup still licked the stuff from his lips and then began to cry. His legs buckled. His frantic mother ran backwards and forwards, snapping, then picked up the smallest cub by the scruff of the neck and ran on a little way. The pup was too heavy for her to carry far and she soon set him down.

The pup's legs gave way. He curled up, legs squirming, writhing at the pain in his belly, while the other wolves waited, turning their heads and whining.

The smallest wolf staggered up on to his paws. He gulped. His tummy went in and out, in and out like a bellows and he threw up all that smelly poisoned meat in grey-pink lumps all over the road.

Simlin glanced at Mother on top of her mattress.

She was still fast asleep. He jumped up and down a few times in his excitement and set off to follow the wolf pack into the woods.

5

THE RICH EARTH

The wolves travelled at an easy slow lope, stopping to rest often, so that the youngest one could get back his strength. Outside the village the land began to slope towards the mountains. The going was slower as they ran among the trees, so close together. Luka Wolf could smell the change of season in the wind. It stirred the fallen leaves and blew their loamy scent through the woods. Autumn was here, suddenly, on this higher ground. Already leaves had turned red, acid yellow and bronze. The evergreens stood sombre as their new growth darkened.

As the wolves ran, squirrels scurried away up trunks to disappear in tops of the trees. Rabbits fled down their burrows and owls into their tree holes, but there was no need for them to fear danger because the pack was hunting something else.

The deeper into the forest they went, the more Luka Wolf became convinced that the shaman's cloak had travelled further among the trees *by itself.* Dimitri had called to the soldiers to bury it. *But where?*

As the land sloped up towards the mountains, it had a thin covering of copper leaves and beechnuts. The earth smelled damp and rich, peppery. Leaves scuttered and rustled in the breeze and the wolves' paws in them made a sound like the rushing of that sea they had so feared. Plump toadstools, soft as dormice, sat among the leaf mould. There were rings of huge scarlet mushrooms with white spots, like poisonous parasols, and ripe blackberries bobbled on scratchy tendrils among the bronze bracken.

It's here, I know it is.

Luka Wolf ran on, nose to the ground. His pack kept looking to him, wondering why he was leading them around these woods when there was so much food trying to hide from them. At last, behind a wide grey oak tree, Luka felt the ground beneath his pads change. It swelled. It was hot and growing hotter. A foul smell seeped out. There were drifts of acorns, plump and golden, still in their small cups. The squirrels had not wanted to venture over this swollen ground to take them.

The broad trunks of the oaks swarmed with ivy. Autumn had turned the trees into strange, two-coloured columns, the strong dark green of the ivy and the papery copper of the frilled oak leaves. The trees had already shed many of their leaves and now Luka Wolf scratched them back with his paw.

There it was.

Luka uncovered an edge of grinning teeth, a snakeskin, and a chime of jangling bones. The pack joined him, digging furiously until they had uncovered the whole cloak.

It lay stretched out on the ground, white and winged as a giant squid beached in the woods. From it seeped malice that stunk like a bursting of bad goose eggs and made the ruffs around the wolves' necks rise in dread.

Luka's sharp ears heard rustling, up in the oak tree, among the crisping leaves. He heard what sounded like a sneeze. How could it be? He glanced around the circle of his pack. Their large ears were pricked at the sound in the oak tree but they did not recognise it. A human sneeze was not in their wolf memory.

The pack was weary, but if he acted at once they would be with him. He was strong. They all were. The strength was the pack. Alone, the wolves could not survive.

So Luka made the move. He put his paw down firmly on the skin, seized the edge of the cloak in his mouth and began to tear with his searing teeth. The noise from the cloak was extraordinary. It shattered the woods as if the ground was cracking open. The wolf pack slathered and joined in with Luka, ripping this ghastly fabric apart, tearing and shredding, holding the cloak between them as if they meant to fold sheets after washing.

Then they went mad, shredding it to pieces, loudly and with satisfaction.

Luka stopped, sensing a new shape between the trees. A pale shape with a tongue lolling with exhaustion. It was the dog. She had followed them all this way. Her tail wagged hesitantly and Luka whimpered back a welcome. There was no threat to the pack from this newcomer and they did not chase her off, but accepted her to help, although she soon lay down to rest.

The ravening wolves worked through the dusk. They threw the debris of bones and snakeskin and teeth over their shoulders until the cloak lay around them in a thousand shreds. As the light fled back to the sun, the outlines of the trees softened so that they seemed huge crouched beasts. The grey tree stumps lurked in the shadows. Luka struggled to keep his wolf mind focused on what they must do: destroy this cloak so that it could not be worn again, ever.

The wolves rolled over and over in the torn mess, marking it with their scent of victory. Now that the cloak lay in a thousand pieces, the scavenging creatures, carrion crows and foxes, ants and beetles would carry it away and finish off the task.

It was done.

Luka threw back his head and howled in triumph and his wolves joined him, and the dog. The song of their choir wove in and out of the trees, out of the wood and down the slope to the village. They loped away again, the dog panting behind. Now at last the pack could hunt and eat and rest.

Luka thought, *I'll be parted from them soon. I'll be blind once more. So I'll fall asleep and hope that my mother's face will look down at me from my dreams.*

In her elephant bed, Vaskalia rolled over, twitched and turned at the wolf choir's song. She whimpered as if she was in pain. In her dreams the shaman's cloak billowed away from her. She chased after it with outstretched arms, but it sailed through the sky straight into the sun's inferno.

Back in the bakery, Jez turned to see a wolf through the little window. He hurried to the door. That big black-faced wolf was slinking away up the street, a shadow-double behind him.

'Dimitri,' he whispered. 'I think Luka's back.'

At the top of the oak tree, Simlin wanted to holler and shout, because the stinking clanking drag-me-down cloak was gone forever. It couldn't put itself back together again like the glass seeing ball, could it? *No*. It couldn't get him, couldn't swamp him now!

The blind boy and his wolves had beaten Mother. *Good*.

Simlin scratched at the birthmark on his forehead. It itched so much. *Ow!* He reached round to his back. There was an angry hurt at the very base of his backbone. He felt a knobbly bit, as if something was growing from the end of his spine, like the stinging tail of a scorpion.

6

AIDAN STOPS BEING BORED

'Where is everyone?' whispered Luka as they walked into the silent orphanage.

The shout of, 'Luka! Surprise!' almost knocked him off his feet. Children grabbed his hands, Lisa kissed him, he could hear Imo's gentle chuckle. Someone threw a bunch of strong-scented marigolds at him, and Maria shouted, 'Where's the wolf?'

Over it all rang Aidan's imperious squeal. 'Luka, how comes you are walking and talking this morning? When Imo took me to see you at the bakery, you were lying on your bed like a rag doll with your mouth hanging open.' The children giggled and Florin began a wolf howl.

'No, Florin, it's not funny,' Aidan insisted. 'Everyone else had been stolen. Luka was no-braining it at the bakery. I had a dreadful, boring time with no one to talk to, except Imo and Eva and they just cried all the time. Big Katrin called round with cakes that nobody felt like eating and *she* never says anything *anyway.*'

'You still had Stefan,' said Luka doubtfully.

'Stefan don't talk. He never even *cries,*' said Aidan. 'So it was very boring for me, Luka, stuck here while you were running with the wolves. That's what Jez told me, anyway.'

'Luka was a big wolf with a black face and silver eyes,' said Lisa. 'He rescued us. Now he's Luka again.' She clapped her hands and skipped around Luka.

'Aidan, I'm sorry you were lonely,' said Luka, 'but that's all over now.'

'So when do we get the story?'

'You'll have to wait until after the cakes, Aidan,' said Luka, hearing his tummy rumbling loud as a clockwork motor. 'Then I'll tell you all about wolves going to sea.'

An engine growled to a halt outside. Imogen said, 'I'm afraid you'll have to wait even longer than that, Aidan. We've got visitors.'

There was the hard sound of boots in the porch.

'*Oi,*' shouted Aidan. 'Who are you?'

'Quiet, boy. This is the General in Chief from the Red Castle,' announced the sugar-syrup voice of Captain Lazslo.

'So you're the general with the gold bits?'

'Yes, I am. And I think I know who you are.' In the high-roofed orphanage the general's voice boomed and echoed. 'Your name is Aidan.'

'But – how do *you* know that?' Luka had never heard Aidan sound bewildered.

'Luka told me. There!' A loud bang of something dropping on the table made Luka jump. 'That pile of books is for everyone, but especially for you, Aidan. Because you get bored and naughty.'

'Me? Naughty? Did Luka say that? But when?'

'When he came to the city with the Talking Man. He said you need a wheelchair too, and that Maria needs a hearing aid. He gave me a long list of things that *all* of you need. They will be with you as soon as I can get hold of them. I've just been to see how the new homes are coming on. They're looking very good. The soldiers have worked hard and fast all summer and you'll be in there soon.'

'General, thank you for following the wolves that night and rescuing our children,' said Imogen, and the children joined in, shouting, 'Thanks, general. Thank you.'

'It was a pleasure,' said the general and Luka heard a smile in his voice. 'The three traffickers are awaiting trial. There won't be so many broken hearts with them out of the way. Of course, the person you must really thank is this boy here.'

The general rested his hand on Luka's shoulder. 'Somehow he persuaded a pack of wolves to follow your tracks down to a secret harbour. The rest of us just followed.'

'No. Luka *was* a wolf,' announced Lisa.

'No. You're both wrong,' squealed Aidan. 'Luka was slumped at the bakery dozing away with his mouth open for hours and hours. He certainly wasn't running about on all fours howling.'

'Aidan, I don't understand it any more than you do,' said the general.

There was a silence. Aidan sighed, a deep long-suffering sigh. 'Luka's a bit of a shaman really, isn't he, general? Being a wolf? *And* I think he's been a bird.'

And a snow leopard, thought Jez.

'Yes, he is rather like an old shaman, Aidan,' said the general. He turned to Jez and said, 'I was impressed by your bravery on that boat, Luka's brother.'

'He's called Jez,' said Luka proudly.

'I am pleased to meet you, Jez. Now, when Luka came to see me, he said you might mend the city clock. It has stopped at midnight. Luka suggested that the suffering figures stuck outside make the people feel angry and restless. He might have a point. Could you make the clock work again so that the peaceful figures come round too?'

'*Wow!* I most certainly can,' said Jez. 'I'll bring Ivan the blacksmith with me to help.'

'It's quite a climb . . .' said the general but Jez said at once, 'I'm not scared of heights.'

I'm not scared of heights either. Simlin folded himself right into the corner of the porch. *I like climbing around roofs. Oh!* Fat Baker man was coming with the giant woman. She was carrying a tray covered with floaty muslin. Simlin licked his lips with his pointed tongue because he could smell cakes sitting underneath that muslin cloud. He could smell their sweet, buttery, new-baked-floury smell that made the inside of his mouth sprinkle. What cakes today? *No cakes for Simlin. Not fair, not fair . . .*

'Well, if it isn't Vaskalia's boy,' said Dimitri. 'Why don't you come inside with the others?' Simlin pressed himself even further back against the stone.

'Come on. After all, you're one of the village children too,' said Dimitri, hoping he sounded kinder than he felt. Simlin could not look up and meet the baker's eyes. He did not know what to say, so he mumbled some of Mother's nonsense spell words to himself and scratched his itching scorpion.

Big Katrin frowned. This skinny boy's forehead was becoming red raw with scratching.

Katrin disappeared inside. A few moments later, Eva came out. She was carrying her medicine tin. Cornering Simlin, she smoothed a piece of lint over his scorpion and stuck it down firmly with a plaster at each end.

'That'll stop you scratching, lovey,' said Eva.

Big Katrin reappeared and handed him a golden bun topped with raspberries. It was still warm. For a few moments, Simlin was in sweet, buttery heaven as he gobbled it up. He peeked around the door. '*Bang bang*', shouted someone, and Simlin fled away down the path.

7

INTO THE MIDNIGHT CLOCK

Dimitri scowled as his van roared up the narrow street without him. Dust flew. Rubber burned. Since Jez had been learning to drive, the tyres were becoming as bald as the baker's head. The van stopped dead, reversed, jumped forward, turned, reversed, turned and roared back down again, its wheels squealing on the cobblestones.

Dimitri's arms were folded. His worried forehead looked like a ploughed field. His swallows had flown south weeks ago, leaving him with the prospect of another harsh winter. Someone had already helped themselves to the stack of logs by the square, even though they were to be shared fairly among the villagers. Now young Jez was going to the city in his precious new van to repair the Midnight Clock.

'D' you think I'm a good driver?' cried Jez to his brother in the passenger seat.

'Yes. You're great,' screamed Luka, because he could not see the walls looming up fast in the windscreen and chickens dashing for safety as his big brother flung the wheel around. It was fast, noisy and exciting being driven by Jez. Luka loved it.

'Why are you pulling that face, Dimitri?' cried Jez. 'If we get stopped, I just tell them I'm working for the general.'

'You take care of my van, Jez,' said Dimitri darkly, 'and take care of Luka too. I've had a word with Ivan. He'll look after you both.'

'I'm seventeen,' sighed Jez. 'I don't need looking after. Are you sure you've got everything, Luka?'

'Yes,' said Luka, patting his chest. Inside his jacket was a drum. He never went out without a drum now, and in his pocket was a bag of cherries to eat on the way.

'Bye, Dimitri,' yelled Jez. 'Be careful Alfonso doesn't snaffle your greengage.'

And away they roared, to collect Ivan the blacksmith. The van bumped down the potholed track to the forge, Luka squealing and bouncing in his seat.

Luka smelled the molten iron before he heard the hiss and sputter of the fire and the ring of Ivan's hammer.

'Give me a few moments, Jez,' said Ivan. 'These

are the gates for the new orphanage, but I'm just at a tricky bit.'

Ivan's few moments lasted for ages. Luka got out of the van and wandered around the yard. It smelled of horse.

When Ivan was finally ready, Luka had to travel in the back of the van with the bags of tools. Dimitri had removed his trays, but the van still smelled tantalisingly of fresh bread. Jez swerved to miss a goat and Luka was flung across the van, so he lay down on the floor as the van lurched and roared its way south, shuddering over the potholes in the road. He wanted to sleep, but there was no chance of that with Jez at the wheel.

At long last the air changed and he knew they were in the city.

'There are the soldiers waiting for us at the door to the tower,' cried Jez. 'Do you want to stay down here in the van, Luka?'

'No, I do not,' retorted Luka. 'I'm coming up there with you.'

'You take care, little boy,' said the soldier gruffly. 'The general didn't say there was a blind boy coming too. So how are you getting up and down a spiral staircase?'

'On my feet, of course,' said Luka.

Luka felt his way up the staircase behind Jez. It was like climbing round and round enclosed inside a snail shell. Up and up they crept, round the dank, mouldy-smelling steps. Behind him, Ivan stopped to wheeze every few steps and complain about his lumbago.

Luka began to feel sick and wished he had eaten before they started climbing. He thought of tombs and graves, as if the walls would move and close in on them, but Jez grabbed his hand and said, 'Hold on tight,' as they stepped up and up.

At last the air opened out around him. He could stand up straight. He felt the cold wind across his face and spread his arms like wings, laughing. Reaching out for Jez's hand again he grasped another instead, made of rough wood.

'You don't want that one, lad,' said Ivan. 'That's Mister Death. You'd be better holding hands with the hungry children.'

'I don't want to hold any of them, thank you, Ivan,' said Luka.

'Yeah, well we need to get on, or it'll be dark before we've finished,' fussed Jez. 'Luka, I think you'd be safer sitting inside the clock tower with us.'

'No, I like it out here,' said Luka. He was remembering his fantastic flight with the swallow, thinking of all those creatures of the air, the birds and the bats.

'That's tough,' snapped Jez. 'Go into this corner and stay there.' Jez steered him by the shoulders through a little door, into a space that felt cramped and smelled of wet metal.

'So that's where they are!' cried Ivan. 'All the other statues. I can remember people looking like this.'

'How do they look?' asked Luka.

'They look content. Peaceful and busy. Not soured and angry like the statues out in front.'

Luka listened to his brother and Ivan delve around inside the clock. They unscrewed the mechanisms that controlled the figures. Both were damaged. He heard them mutter and curse, shout, 'Yes' followed by 'Um . . . no.'

Jez said, 'The clock is stuck at a minute before midnight.'

'I don't think it'll ever work again,' muttered Ivan.

Luka sniffed. There was a smell of burning as Ivan tinkered and soldered metal. Luka dreaded him setting the wooden figures alight.

Far below them, the city lay silent. Luka was

beginning to feel hungry and he thought it was getting late. Certainly it must be time for the curfew. He wondered if there was anyone out there, gazing up at the clock tower, wondering what was going on. Perhaps by now people had stopped looking up at those horrible figures which only reminded them what life had become.

He must have fallen asleep.

He woke up shaking. The whole tower was moving.

8

IN THE BAT OF AN EYELID

L uka clapped his hands over his ears. He felt as
if he was inside a machine like the one Dimitri
used to grind up his coffee beans. There was a deep,
bass *Thrum Thrum* and whirring as if an enormous
bumble-bee was trapped inside a honey jar.

The *Thrum*-ming separated. It made sense now.
It was the deafening ticking of the clock. *Tick-Tock-
Tick-Tock.*

Luka backed against the wall as the whirring
increased and huge shapes shuddered past him, and
stopped. For a moment, the clock took a deep
breath from its insides.

And then it chimed. The chime was joyous, a
deafening clangour that happened twelve times.
Luka giggled helplessly and clasped his head, in case
it came off his shoulders and rolled away down into
the city. Twelve times. Midnight. The whirring faded,
ending with a click.

'They're all safely back inside,' said Jez smugly.

'And *all* the figures whirred round – the happy children and the people working in the fields, the smiling mother and the musician. It wasn't only the miserable figures from the bad times.'

Before Jez could stop him, Luka pushed his way forwards and out of the small door on to the platform. The night wind pulled at his hair. He opened his arms wide and screamed, 'Hey, everybody. Look up here. The Midnight Clock is fixed.'

People were beginning to gather far below. Their faces were upturned so that Luka heard the murmur of their voices, but no shots were fired. Luka heard soft laughter. Someone began to sing.

Jez put his hands firmly on Luka's shoulders. 'It looks like we've started something now,' he said and Luka heard the smile in his voice.

In the echoing halls of the Red Castle, the general stood up and wandered, hands in pockets, to the open window. He stopped. He saw a crowd gathering to watch the procession of figures around the clock. Should he send an order to the soldiers to fire on the crowd? Was this more insurgency?

No. He relaxed, leaning on the window to watch

the last of the figures trundle away inside the clock until the next hour struck.

There was one last figure. It was small, and it jumped around, almost too near the edge of the platform, waved its arms and shouted in triumph. Then a taller one took charge.

The general smiled and went on smiling until he noticed and straightened up his face. The boy Luka was right. The people were affected by what they saw. But how did Luka know that the angry, ugly figures were stuck out there by the clock face? He was blind.

The general went to sit back down at the table. There was no point going to bed so late. As he sat there, a bat skimmed in through the window. It flew past him at the table to touch a bunch of keys on the wall with its wing tip and whizz back outside. In the blink of an eye it was back, flying arrow-straight to touch those keys.

They were the keys to the dungeons.

The general had known deep in his heart what he would do ever since Luka's visit. Luka had asked him why there were prisoners weeping in the dungeons. Most of them had been there for years and there was no evidence against them. Luka's question persisted in the general's mind. Should he take the keys, go down to the dungeons where the water slopped at the small windows, and release the frail prisoners up into the light? Now the bat made it clearer still that he must act on his conviction before too long.

He must let his masters across the sea know about it, and the warlords too.

He would tell them all, when it was done.

Tiredness settled on the two brothers and Ivan the blacksmith as if someone had let a thick blanket fall on them.

'You could stay the rest of the night here,' said a guard at the bottom of the stairway. 'Come back to the billet with us and sleep on the floor. And there are empty rooms in that castle. Rather you than me in there, mind.'

'We must go home, thank you,' said Jez. 'There's bread to bake.'

'And horses to shoe,' yawned Ivan.

'Come on, home with you lot,' the guard called to the waiting crowd. The people began to move away, some of them calling 'Thank you,' into the night.

Even though the three of them were so tired, they

sang all the way home, humming Dimitri's tunes and songs Imogen had taught Luka at the orphanage.

'There are more stars than I ever knew packed into that sky,' said Jez. 'That means a hard winter ahead.'

'We'll soon be home,' said Ivan. 'But what's that across the road? There are soldiers.'

'It's a road block,' said Jez. He slowed down the van and wound down his window.

'Who is it?' called Luka.

'I don't know their faces,' said Jez. 'Good evening. What's happened?'

The soldiers ignored Jez. One of them stuck his face into the van and said, 'Who's that boy in the back?'

'That's my brother.'

'Pull the other one, peasant,' snapped the soldier.

'Hey, I'm Luka and that's my big brother Jez,' protested Luka, confused by these unknown, angry voices.

The soldier said, 'A boy has gone missing from the village. We've been told to find him. His mother is distraught and she's raised the alarm. She said her son has stolen something of hers. He could be anywhere.'

'Well, it's not *this* boy. This is Luka. We've been

in the city on business for your general. You're the new detail, aren't you? Who's missing? It can't be anyone from the orphanage because they haven't got mothers to raise the alarm.'

The van door was pulled open.

'Come on. Out you get. Out!' they shouted, grabbing Luka's arm.

'Get off him,' cried Jez and Ivan said, 'You're making a mistake, you know.'

'Have you got the boy?' called a sugary voice Luka recognised.

'I think so, Captain Lazslo. That wise woman – what's her name – Vaskalia, will be pleased we've found her son.'

'*What?*' cried Jez. 'She's no wise woman, and this isn't her son. *You* know that, Captain Lazslo. He's my brother. And I think you owe me some money for some carving.'

'I'm afraid he's right about the boy,' said Captain Lazslo to the soldiers. 'That's not Simlin. That's Luka. Let him go.'

9

BIG FAT TUMMY

'One day soon, I'll draw those figures on the Midnight Clock so that you can see them,' said Imogen.

'All of them?' asked Aidan. 'Would you even draw the nasty scary ones with the scythes and guns, Imogen? The little ones would be terrified. But it would be good for us all to see the normal ones, wouldn't it?'

Wouldn't it, thought Luka. *They just take seeing things for granted.*

Maybe he was just too tired. Maybe the spirit shift to the wolf leader and then the journey to the city had exhausted him, so that he could not think properly. He had no sight now. But Aidan had no legs. Everything was just shadows for Luka but at least he could run around places he knew, like this bakery.

Imo and Eva had brought the children for breakfast so Luka had got up to greet them, when he

403

really wanted to stay in bed up in the attic and catch up on his sleep.

He sighed. He put down his bread, even though it was smothered in his favourite jam: black cherry. He did not feel hungry now.

'Just think, Imogen, the new homes are nearly finished,' said Jez. 'There'll be all that clean new wall space. You can hang your drawings and paintings all over it. I'll make some more frames for them and it will be like an art gallery full of pictures.'

Pictures for other people to look at, not for me. And Jez will be there with Imogen most of the time . . .

'Watch that tortoise, Lisa,' said Dimitri. 'He keeps heading for my greengage tree. Don't let him out of the door or he'll eat the little greengage on the bottom branch.'

'He'd have to jump to get it,' said Lisa, 'and I've never seen a leaping tortoise.'

'I'm looking forward to that greengage getting ripe and juicy,' said Dimitri, smacking his lips. 'I shall share it with someone special.'

Someone special . . . that's Big Katrin.

Luka was pleased that Dimitri loved Big Katrin. The baker deserved someone so special. He was pleased that Jez loved Imo, too. He wanted them to be happy, and yet he felt so alone. He wanted his mother and father back.

Luka was proud of his gift. He had used it to save the children from the traffickers, and to find the cave of sparkling blue rock so that Jez could carve it and earn money towards the new buildings. The man with the hair of frost, in the cloak of earth colours, could not call him reckless now. Luka had become the shaman boy.

He had shifted his spirit into a power creature four times now, and it was wonderful.

So why wasn't he happy? He felt so alone, so distant from everyone.

As Luka sat despondently at the bakery table, while the children chatted and laughed around him, the Cloud Cat eased herself into his mind. At once he was comforted. Of all creatures, his elusive, lonely snow leopard was the closest to him.

The dog pushed her nose into his hand, foffed into his palm. Luka patted her, absentmindedly. Then he slid off his chair and sat on the floor with her. The dog rolled on her back so that Luka could rub her tummy. She was a little overweight, especially since she had come to the bakery, but as his hand rested on her warm, full tummy, Luka knew there were other little hearts fluttering inside her. It reminded him of the Cloud Cat with the two tiny tabla hearts beating in her womb.

Luka thought: *The father is one of the young wolves* . . .

As he sat on the floor, stroking the dog, he heard sniffing. It wasn't the dog. It was someone on the other side of the door. Luka stood up. He felt for the handle and turned it quietly. He knew who was out there. He knew who was hungry and wanted to be inside. The boy's unwashed clothes smelled of fear, wood smoke, pee and acrid plants. Luka half expected him to turn and scoot away.

'Come on in, Simlin,' he said. 'There's plenty of bread.'

Everyone in the bakery stopped talking. Jez barged forward.

'Your mother had the soldiers out looking for you last night,' he cried.

Luka heard the yard gate slam shut. Simlin had lost his nerve and run away again. In his wistful mood he thought, *Simlin is lucky to have a mother.*

Then he could have kicked himself. What a stupid thought. Imagine having a mother who made a fool out of you like that!

'The skinny one has been hanging around the orphanage all the time, Luka,' shrilled Aidan. 'He wants to come in. He has this old glass ball tucked in his shirt but he won't share it. All he wants to do is play with the little ones' toys and spy on Imo.'

'Some of you weren't very welcoming to him,' said Imogen.

'It did come in once,' cried Lisa. 'I tried to show it the beans growing in the jar.'

'Didn't stay long, did he?' crowed Aidan.

'You called him a cranefly, Aidan,' said Imogen testily. 'And spitting at him didn't help, did it, Florin?'

'You can't blame the children for not being friendly to him,' said Dimitri.

'We have to give him the chance to change,' she said.

'I suppose so. But now he's run away from home, I don't think we'll hear much from Madame Vaskalia. She's got no son to make into a mighty shaman. She's sulking indoors. She won't bother us *any* more. Hear that, Luka?'

Luka heard it. He was not sure he believed it.

He sat quietly, sensing himself outside everything again. This room full of people seemed a foreign place. Somewhere he did not belong. The Cloud Cat crouched in the corner of his mind, waiting for him. He decided that the world of the shaman, the spirit-shifter, was the right place for him.

Early next morning it felt chilly with damp. Half-way down the staircase Luka held his breath, listening. Dimitri unbolted the door and stomped out to his wood store. Luka heard the click of the dog's nails as she padded out into the yard with him. Light as a sprite, carrying his drum, Luka slipped out and turned right across the bakery yard and felt his way to scramble over the stone wall. He felt something soft and sticky clinging to his cheek. It must be a spiderweb. He wiped it away. The air was heavy with melancholy. It was not thronging with life as it was in springtime, but sighing as it waited for winter to cut in.

'I'm not going anywhere near the Depths of Lumb and I'm not going to fall in the river,' he said as he climbed the hillside. 'I think I know a good place.'

When he ran with the wolves, Luka's mind and paws followed maps he could not see. Now those maps were still in his mind. He could sense the way to places. He remembered the thicket where Jez had picked bluebells for Imogen. There was a hillside nearby where he could settle down to play the drum and call the Cloud Cat.

There were no bluebells to smell now, but he felt the long grass full of late daisies, still closed for the night.

'This is the place,' he said and sat down. The grass was wet so that he jumped up again, fast. The seat of his trousers was soaked by the frost. Luka decided to keep on walking until the sun came up and dried all the frost away.

But he walked too far south.

10

UNDERGROUND SECRETS

Vaskalia woke from the turmoil of her dreams. She cursed and spat on to the floor when she saw that Simlin had not come home again. What was he doing? He had never asked her permission to stay out. She chuntered away to herself as she scrummaged among the pin-sticking dolls, around the floor, in her shoes, in the log pile, even in the cooking pot, but what she was searching for was not there.

The seeing ball was gone.

That was the one thing that Simlin *could* do. He had inherited the power to summon happenings from his father. The moment Vaskalia allowed that thought, the fiery spectre of Simlin's demonic father rose up in her memory, flames around his feet and craziness in his eyes. Black snakes twisted from his ears and nostrils and on his cheek burned a scorpion, its tail poised to flip and sting, as fast as a whiplash.

'Get away from me, wastrel of the rocks,' she cried. 'A she-scorpion carries her eggs for more than a year. But I feel as if I carried your scorplet son for even longer than *that*.'

At last the crazy, fire-headed man left her mind. Vaskalia put her head on one side and began to croon as she busied herself with her herbs, preparing a spell. A smile flitted around her lips. She turned and searched through the spell tokens she kept under her lumpy pillows. There were so many – a snip of hair bright yellow as a blackbird's beak from that cheeky cripple, a shaving of sparkling blue stone, a squashed tomato, snippets of hair ribbons, a broken string from a lyraki, a ball of dough, a mouldering piece of wet nellie and some white and grey fur.

Today it was the tendril of black hair she wanted.

Luka walked on, trusting the direction his feet took, until he felt the lukewarm rays of the sun touch his face.

'I want to stop now,' he said, but his feet just kept walking, as if drawn by a magnet.

Suddenly his legs gave way and he sat down on dry grass.

'All right, it's not the place I had in my mind, but it will do.'

He began to wish he had brought something to eat, although he knew he should not eat just before his shape-change. Food would slow him down, make him sleepy and blunt his senses. He pulled the drum from inside his jacket and focused on the image of the Cloud Cat in his mind. She was a long way away. He would have to work hard to summon her away from her two blue-eyed cubs. Dimitri had told Luka that the snow leopard father leaves when his cubs are born and so the mother must stay close.

Just as he was about to begin tapping his drum, Luka felt something touch his ankle.

'I've got socks on to stop these shoes rubbing. So whatever you are, you can't sting me.' But whatever it was wasn't trying to sting him. It was trying to drag him along. It had fastened around his ankle like a strong cord.

It tightened and began to dig in, so that Luka stuffed his drum back inside his jacket and struggled to his feet calling 'Hey, stop.' He hopped on the other foot as the cord pulled him along and then he was right up against a wide tree trunk. He put up his hand. The bark felt rough as tortoise skin. There were smooth, heart-shaped leaves. There was a tangle of branches all around the tree trunk, as tough as snakes. *Ivy.*

'No . . . get off me!' he shouted as it sneaked around his wrist in a tight circle and pulled. With his other hand, he tried to grab the tree trunk and hold on but it dissolved against him in a shower of sawdust and there was nothing below his feet.

Luka tumbled far down inside the tree and landed on hard, dry soil.

For a while he lay, winded. His back hurt. He tried to understand what had happened to him. He was in some kind of pit under the earth. He had been dragged down. Ivy could not do that by itself. Some power had made it catch him. He ran his hand over the tendrils and felt tiny suckers underneath, like the legs of a centipede. But who had any power over plants? *Vaskalia, that's who . . .*

He began to cough and splutter. All he could smell and taste was earth . . . earth, damp, ancient, choking earth all around, enclosing him. He spat it out and struggled to find something in his pocket he could blow his nose on, but there was nothing, so he wiped his nose on his sleeve and coughed. His throat was sore from the soil. In his head he heard Aidan's squeal of scorn: *You never went down to the darkest place, did you, Luka?* and he thought, *I am in the darkest place, the place that terrifies me.* He remembered what Imogen always told them: *The only way is up.*

Luka made himself stand. He put out his hand. He was in a little cave made by the tree roots. The cave led on into a tunnel. It was a tight fit and he had to stoop as he felt his way along, avoiding roots that might scratch his face or catch his foot and trip him up. Once he heard scuffling. He smelled a strong smell. He did not know which animal it was. Perhaps it had a burrow all the way down here and he had disturbed it.

Soon Luka could hardly stay upright because the tunnel was becoming full of energy. It knocked him off his feet again. The force underground was overpowering. Roots and shoots vaulted for their lives away from the depths where the earth moved and shifted, shaping itself and deciding what it would settle for. Luka knew that far, far below him, the earth was in turmoil. There, earthquakes and volcanoes began and giant masses of land shifted and fought.

He was so enclosed that he couldn't breathe deeply and the air was stale.

This is what it must be like in a grave.

A scene moved into Luka's head and sat there. It was one of the winding streets in his village, before it was ruined. He heard gunfire. Enemies were hiding on roofs, behind doors, round corners, sniping.

The gunfire stopped.

A man raced along the street, head down. He was carrying a child. He stopped close to the wall of a house, set the child down, and crouched, chest heaving as he struggled to breathe. The child cried, stepped away, and the guns cracked into life again, bullets bursting on the wall all around the child; the man threw himself over it to shelter it from the hailstorm of shots. The man sheltered the child so that not one bullet hit him.

The child was a little boy with curly hair.

The man's body stopped every shot that would have hit his son.

Further up the narrow street, in a doorway, cowered Luka's brother, Jez, much younger than he was now. Jez had his arms wrapped around himself. Luka heard again that dreadful sound of his brother howling, throwing back his head to cry his anguish.

The howl became a whimper, over and over again.

Now Luka heard the sounds of his mother's grief. He had shut them out of his mind, until now. Yet in the midst of this horror, he knew something that made his heart quicken: Luka's father had saved his son's life. He had given his own instead. He loved Luka that much.

Luka sat still under the earth. The shock held him still until he was left with a sense of calm. The underground did not terrify him as it had done before. There could be nothing worse than what he had just remembered.

'I can get out of here,' he said. 'At least I've still got my drum.' He tried to think of a creature which could live down here under the earth. A mole? A worm?

When he stood up he felt warmer, and put up his hand to the earthen ceiling. It felt warm. He patted his hand a little way to the left. Still warm. He patted along to the right. It was warm there, too. He began to hit up at the earth ceiling with his fists. Over and over again he hit it, but nothing happened so Luka began to scrabble, clawing away with his fingers. A few grains of soil landed on his face so he shut his eyes and mouth tight.

There were sounds from whatever was above.

'There's somebody up there, I know there is,' he said. The warmth must be from someone's fire. He had come quite a long way. It might be the bakery. Luka's heart leaped and he scrabbled and pawed harder, until a lump of earth fell on him, knocking him off his feet.

He sat there for a few moments, dazed. Then he stood, reached up and found the hole. If he could get his hands through and grip the edge, he could pull himself through. If only he had strong muscled arms like Jez.

Luka did not have to pull himself all the way up through the hole, because someone grabbed his hands and tugged hard. With a *whoosh* he was through and collapsed exhausted on an earthen floor. It smelled like an animal pen and it was hot. There was a fire. Waves of flame rolled their light over his eyelids.

Luka lay there, shivering and warm by turns. The floor was baked earth, the atmosphere choke-thick and sooty. His fingers found something near them. It was a small bone, picked clean.

Above him, something shifted from one foot to another. Wings stretched, creaking as if they were hinged. They flapped heavily. He heard a caw and a shriek from a large bird. Scents crept into his nostrils: bitter herbs, the musty aroma of dried flowers, sweat, the mousy smell of shoes worn thin, a dark stench of soggy mushrooms.

There was an explosion on his eyelids, and fierce crackling, from more wood on the fire. It roared up with such intense heat, Luka feared his body would scorch. He shuffled backwards and found his shoulders against a lumpy wall. He smelled olive wood burning.

'There. A roaring fire to keep you warm, Gabriel's son. That fool Peter stacked all those logs up in the square but he didn't bring me any. And they were logs from an olive tree that was my dowry tree. They cut it down, with not a thought for me.' Her peevish voice spiralled higher and ended in a wail. 'So I sent the donkey up there to bring back my tree. There were so many logs. So heavy that they made his legs buckle *tee hee*!'

Luka felt as if he was paralysed in her home. *Her*. His enemy. Vaskalia. All his courage and strength seemed to drain away, but he cried, 'That wood was for everyone to share this winter.'

'You've never learned when to keep your mouth

shut, have you?' she sneered. 'We'll be warm here together all winter long, warm and snug as bugs in a rug. Just you, my Bone Cracker and me. Simlin has gone. So you can be my son instead.'

Luka stood up and stumbled to where the door might be, clumsy in a space he did not know at all. He realised from the heat on his legs that her smoky fire was in the middle of this room so he backed away. The wall was wooden. He ran his hand along it as he edged around the room. Almost immediately he was at a corner, then another, and another, and one more, and still there was wall, but she grabbed his shoulders.

'There are five sides,' said Luka.

'Of course there are five sides. My house is built in the best shape there has ever been. A pentangle.'

She steered him away from the door, saying, 'You really shouldn't wander around, little boy. You might walk into the fire. Sit here.' She pushed him down on to a wobbly chair. Something was lashed around his arms and chest while Luka squirmed and cried to her to stop but she bound his ankles to the chair legs so that Luka felt something biting him between his trousers and his shoes.

'Is that ants nipping me?' he cried.

'No. It's the ivy cord. Ivy is so useful, isn't it?' she crowed. 'The suckers cling tight as leeches. You won't be out of *my* house in a hurry.'

11

FLAME BERRIES

Simlin hung from the branch of the oak tree by his long arms. He had lived up here for a few days now. Last night had been very cold, so he had broken off some branches and leaves from a chestnut tree nearby and woven them into a nest between two strong branches. He had hidden the seeing ball in a hole in the trunk.

The tree was beginning to shed its leaves, swirling like ashes. The wind snatched at his nest. At least Simlin had been warm in the five-sided house. He thought longingly of that smoky fire in the middle of the floor.

He had wondered if he should hide in the baker's woodshed but the big woman would chase him away with a rolling pin. Where would he really like to be? In the orphanage, colouring with the crayons and paints, and listening to stories from the women.

The only trouble with the orphanage was that it was full of children.

The other day, sad-faced Eva had called to him, 'Come in and have something to eat, love,' and pretty Imogen said, 'Don't mind if the children say silly things, Simlin. They're not used to you. That's all. It will take time.' Simlin *did* mind. Aidan called him Weaselnose, Cranefly and Fartface. Florin said he smelled like an old poo pot, *bang bang*. The girls were worse. He dare not pinch them back in case the women saw. Even Stefan with the big packed bottom scuttled away like a hedgehog if Simlin came anywhere near him.

Simlin pulled himself up and reached inside the hole for the seeing ball. The owl tried to peck him. Simlin peered into it.

Luka was in the ball. There was a shadow behind him. Simlin put his face up so that his breath clouded the ball and he had to rub it with his sleeve and look again. What creature was the boy becoming?

The shadow behind Luka was not a creature.

It was Mother.

Simlin saw that Luka was on that rickety chair. Simlin was never allowed to sit on that chair because it belonged just to Mother. He screwed up his eyes to see. Luka could not get off the chair. She must have tied his hands.

Serve him right, Yeehee yipyip snort. That would teach the blind boy to do tricks and have a big bully brother and friends and pretty women and live in a bakery with cakes and a dog and a cat with kittens instead of nasty messy Bone Cracker. Now he would have to stay in the five-sided house with Mother for ever and *ever*.

She wanted to keep the blind boy. Instead of him.

Simlin frowned. He did not want to go back and live there, *No*, but he did not want Mother to keep this other boy, either.

The boy was still on the chair. Simlin wondered if the boy felt as cross as Simlin was, kicking and growling and twisting with rage, when she stuffed him in that box with turnips and onions. That was when he was small like Stefan. The people in the orphanage were kind to Stefan. They looked out for him.

Nobody looked out for Simlin.

A sob swelled up in his throat and his nose began to dribble. He sniffed and wiped his nose on his sleeve but the more Simlin thought about his feelings the more his nose ran. *It's Mother's fault.* The sob changed as if molten metal was poured down his throat, along his spine and up into a curve at the end, a curve that could whip over and sting. The metal set into hard iron.

Air rushed past his face and ruffled his hair. A storm was coming. Simlin placed the seeing ball back inside the trunk as the wind gusted and began to tear away the last leaves from the creaking oak tree. The clouds exploded and rain lashed him right through his clothes, cold as knives. He swung his legs backwards and forwards and dropped to the ground.

As Simlin scarpered through the trees, leaping on acorns to pop them with his long feet, some tiny flames burst in the corner of his eye. Flames in a cage of silver-grey branches. Simlin stopped. Stared. They were not flames after all. They were firethorn berries, bright and translucent as the setting sun in winter.

Mother was wary of them. Powerful magic, she said. Birds did not eat them.

Simlin struggled to break off a twig. It was hard as iron and long silver thorns scratched his hands. The berries felt right in Simlin's hand. He liked fiery things.

The berries were round and hard as beads. Simlin ate one. It made him gasp, so sweet and so sour, *thvoo!* made him suck his cheeks full of spittle. He felt dizzy. His head spun around and his throat burned and then he did not want any more firethorn berries.

The drumming rain stopped as suddenly as it had started but Simlin did not return to his oak tree. He trotted on, his mouth closed for once, tight with purpose.

He would make a spell now. He was his mother's son, after all, and he had watched her many times, heard her incantations, listened to her call the old magic. All he needed was a vessel for his spell. Soon he found a flat stone and a smaller one to pound the berries to a powder. Wrapping the spell in a large leaf, Simlin ran back home.

12

WILD CHILDHOOD

'I should have had a son like you, shaman boy.'

Her voice sawed on and on. There was not one note of music in it anywhere. The chair creaked as Luka tried to flex his arms and legs, desperate to put his hands over his ears and keep out her insistent whine.

'But you have a son already,' he said. 'You have Simlin.'

He tensed, waiting to be hit, a blow to the head, a burn on the arm. This place simmered with violence. Luka watched the noises, waiting, dreading what she might do to him.

A stopper popped out of a bottle. There followed a gurgling sound and a smell of fruit and fermentation, swigging and glugging and volcanic belching that stank, making Luka queasy.

Her voice reeled. 'If I had a son like you, blind boy, I could be the queen mother of the old magic. Just think what my magic could do with you as its slave.

I'd rule this village. They'd not laugh at me again.'

'What would you do for the village? The gift is for everyone, not just for the shaman and his family.'

Either she was too rolling drunk to hear what Luka said, or she just ignored him.

'I was trapped into motherhood by that scorpion head. Think of it. A jewel of a lady such as myself, wasted on a fire fiend. Just as your father was trapped by Evangelina so that he had sons he did not want.'

'That's rubbish,' cried Luka. 'He wasn't trapped at all. He *did* want us. My father loved me, and he loved Jez. My father loved me enough to save my life and die for me.' Hot tears began to course down Luka's face. 'Your son has left *you*,' he said out loud, surprising himself.

'But I've got me someone *much* better,' she chortled. 'I can keep you here forever. We will resurrect the shaman's cloak.'

She waited. Luka heard her little intake of breath. Holding it, waiting for his reaction. *Sly.* He knew what had happened to the cloak, and she was guessing.

'You will be my new son,' she said. 'You will use that gift for *me* and make me queen of the village. Everything must change to put me in my rightful place.'

'Why must everything change?' asked Luka.

'I shall rule the village by the old magic. *My* magic. They will be sorry they ever scorned me and looked down on me, all of them. The fat bald baker, that mute giant Katrin with her dark eyes, soppy Imogen, droopy Eva and stick-in-the-mud Peter Bus, farmers and shoemakers and those drunkards who stagger to the inn . . . they'll be sorry!'

Luka heard her shuffling around the table, fussing with pots, snapping herb twigs, and grinding something with her pestle, something that smelled charred, like fire.

'Your gift will turn you into a trickster for me,' she said. 'You will fetch me money and jewels and drugs from the city. They'll all see that I am the most powerful woman this side of the mountains.'

'The people in the village have never hurt you,' said Luka. 'Why do you resent them so much?'

'Because I *do*. Tell me, if you are oh-so-clever, why are you on your own now? You've no mother, Luka, and no father, have you?'

'No but it's only because of the war, and I've got a big brother and the dog and Dimitri and Big

Katrin and all the children at the orphanage.'

'And what do you remember? When you were little, what can you remember?'

'Sitting on my mother's knee and hearing stories from a big blue book. Telling her stories, too. She said she liked my stories. And I remember riding on my father's shoulders and looking in people's windows. And eating bread and cherry jam.'

'Well, aren't you the lucky one! Shall I tell you my memories?'

'All right,' said Luka. He thought she might not hurt him if he agreed with her, and he was curious.

'I was born in this very house,' said Vaskalia. 'I fought on a mattress with too many other children, all kicking me in the face. My big brothers sold medicines. They took me deep into the woods and they *left* me there, Luka, left me with the wolves and wild boars, left me to gnaw on tree roots and toadstools. I lived as a wild child. A moth-eaten old bear took me to her den for the winter. After that, I had to fend for myself.'

'That must have been horrible,' said Luka. Something in him felt that she was not telling the whole truth. If he had been sighted, he would have seen that her eyes levelled while she spoke.

'So I taught myself the old magic, the tricks of the plants and fruits and fungi. I became an excellent sorceress. Then came *that* day. I was captured by rascals from the other side of the mountain and forced to join in their magic rituals. I begged to come home. At last they brought me back here but everyone had gone from this house. I was alone, except for the baby in my belly . . . and look what *that* turned into!'

Luka started to speak but she smacked his mouth and cried, 'The villagers shunned me if they met me in the street but they bought my spells and potions from the market. They wanted me to cure their spots and boils and squits and sprains. *Tee hee!* I had spelled them ill in the first place.' He heard her pour liquid into a cup and swig it down.

'So there I was,' she burped, 'a brave and lonely woman. *Your* mother had it lucky.'

But my *mother is not here*, thought Luka.

'I'm going to make a spell now,' she said. 'It will be the best I've ever made. The nasty power animals you love so much . . . the swallow . . . here's his feather . . . that foul big cat . . . some fur . . . and the wolf with the silver eyes . . . You won't be needing them when you work for me. So . . . here is everything on my table, ready. Everything I need,' she gloated. She yawned, sucking in the air. 'Everything ready . . . mix it up well.'

Vaskalia babbled on, pouring drinks and swigging it down, until her words meant nothing to him. Luka heard springs twang. She had gone to her bed. The five-sided house was restless. The wood in the fire shifted and charred, the vulture on the rafter shuffled and stretched, somewhere in the room tiny voices cried. Vaskalia snored and farted and smacked her lips in her dreams.

Luka was aware of a presence here. Malice. It clung over everything like grime.

Jez and Dimitri would come looking for him soon, wouldn't they?

The door eased open. A slight draught ran across the earthen floor and around his ankles. Luka tensed. He breathed in, wanting to catch Dimitri's smell of flour and spices, Big Katrin's scent of lavender, or Jez's smell of fresh sweat.

He did not know this person's scent.

It was one of old dirt and dry leaves and clothes that longed to be washed. He heard the whistling of his breathing and knew instinctively who was untying the ivy cords that bound his ankles to the chair. He heard the Whisperer slip away to find a blade. He tensed at the slicing of the ivy ropes at his ankles, and the cutting close to his wrists. Relief. He eased his arms round to the front, massaging them to get the circulation flowing again.

The Whisperer hovered by the chair. He took Luka's hand and drew him across to the unseen door and outside where the air was so much sweeter.

'Thank you,' said Luka. 'Does she bully you?'

There was a long pause. The voice said, 'Luka *not* an idiot.'

'And I'm not a saphead or a moonraker. And neither are you. I know who *you* really are. You're Simlin. You're the Whisperer. You hid up in the orphanage roof and called me all those names. I know that you have a scorpion mark on your forehead because you were watching when I came down the waterfall with the otter, and then –' Luka stopped himself. He did not want to remind poor Simlin what a fool his mother had made of him in front of everyone at the summer festival.

He said, 'I know Vaskalia is your mother, but who is your father?'

'From other side of mountain with head all on fire.'

'And what is up there on the rafter?'

432

'Bone Cracker. Loves Mother. Big bird. Bald head, doesn't get all stuck up with blood. Black feathers like a beard all round beak. Goes hunting when Mother asks him.'

'I know he does. He came after me in the Depths of Lumb and knocked me down the gorge.' Luka reached out for Simlin's arm. 'I must wait inside a little longer, Simlin.'

Simlin took his fingertips again and led him back to sit on the chair. Luka heard him meddling with the fire, laying more wood lightly on the top.

Then he was back near Luka, murmuring, 'I made more fire. Put something nice to roast on top. Mother will sleep more. She drinks too much purple potion. Making magic with spotty fur and feathers. I leaving now. You come too?'

'No. Not yet.'

'Luka must not stay here long. *Please* . . .'

'I won't,' whispered Luka. But he had to stay here, had to make his spirit change into the Cloud Cat and confront Vaskalia for the last time. He must not run away from facing his darkest fears, however dangerous it was to stay here.

Simlin stole away towards the door. He stopped to make an extraordinary sound: *Yipyipsnort.*

He's laughing like a piglet, thought Luka and he could not help but smile.

He reached inside his jacket. There was his little drum, almost calling out to him to be played. Luka placed it on his lap and began to drum softly with his fingertips, matching his heartbeat and the rhythm of his pulse.

'*I'll* show you magic, Vaskalia.'

Luka set his mind on the Cloud Cat.

At last his mind's eye found her high in the mountains, with her two cubs stretched sleeping in the pale curve of her body. The Cloud Cat twitched. She heard Luka's silent call and the soft beat of his drum. Her eyes flared open.

The cubs' eyes flickered wide blue and closed again as they went back to sleep.

The Cloud Cat eased herself up and stretched to the white tip of her tail. She picked her way across the rocks and down the mountain. Luka watched her coming to him across her vast territory, her body and limbs lithe and beautiful in her seamless, dappled fur.

She balanced high on a rock, and yowled to him, announcing that she was there.

'I'm here. I'm waiting for you,' whispered Luka.

The Cloud Cat leaped the chasm and raced down the mountain slopes. Soon Luka would run with her, in those open spaces, in the crystalline daylight of the mountains, and he would see through her eyes.

On top of her smelly, elephant bed Vaskalia stirred. She rolled over, spat on the floor, slid off the bed and stood up.

'Go on then, sorceress,' cried Luka. 'Let's see what can you do.'

13

BATTLE OF THE SPELLS

The noise that burst out of Vaskalia's mouth was not human. It buzzed and damned and made Luka clap his hands over his ears.

The one word he heard among this clamour of spell-making was his name, *Luka.*

The five-sided house shook with discord. The rafters rattled and the fire spat. Luka struggled to keep his mind fixed on the Cloud Cat and pull her towards him, as Vaskalia tried to tempt her away towards destruction. Never pausing in her incanting, Vaskalia piled more wood on to the fire. Luka heard it catch light, spark and sputter. The flames roared on his eyelids, threatening to keep out his snow leopard with a barrier of fire.

Still her tuneless chanting ground on and on, and the rasping of her pestle on the stone of the grinding mortar as she mixed the ingredients for the spell. Luka's body was beginning to feel hot, too hot, as if she had lit a fire inside him.

Panic fluttered in his heart. Just in time he heard the echoing voice of the man with the hair of frost.

Luka, listen to me: you have run over the earth with the Cloud Cat, flown through the skies with the swallow and swum in the river with the otter. This is the element of fire. You have always smelled fire when I am around, but this time, it is used against you. Now deal with it.

Luka put his mind to snow, the high sky and the rushing waterfall. These cooling spirit experiences would hold the heat of the fire at bay until he could make his change.

'Where are you, Cloud Cat? Come to me.' Luka summoned all his hidden strength and forced himself to breathe deeply, closing his mind to Vaskalia's toneless spell-singing. His fingertips found the drum and began to play, shutting out the feelings of heat that threatened to sizzle his muscles and sinews.

The door of the five-sided house burst open.

Luka felt that thick fur brush against him, and smelled the powerful, sour leopard scent. The unearthly cry echoed around the five-sided house and out across the village. For a moment Luka was lost, cast out, nowhere.

And then the shift was done. Luka's spirit was in the Cloud Cat.

For the first time Luka saw the woman who hated him so much.

When he was small he had played with a set of painted wooden dolls that fitted one inside the other. Their heads were bound tightly with scarves to hide their hair. On their cheeks were circles of pink paint and there were no pupils in the middle of their white, staring eyes. Vaskalia was the same squat shape as those dolls, but her face looked as if someone had grabbed her cheeks and twisted them so hard that her mouth turned forever downwards in resentment. Her eyes rolled, each its own way round, like striped gobstoppers left behind in a sweet shop.

Up on the rafters the vulture beat its wings in terror, flapped to the floor and shuffled fast out of the door, with one baleful backwards glance.

Vaskalia waved her cleaver above her head. The Cloud Cat bounded across the room. With one swipe of her huge front paw she sent Vaskalia spinning away so that she landed crumpled against the bed, her cleaver clattering on to the hearth. In the furnace heat its blade began to soften and bend.

The Cloud Cat turned, opened her jaws and picked up Luka's body by the back of the neck, in the same way as Syrup carried her kittens. With his last little strain of strength, and nudging help from the Cat, Luka's body struggled up to her back with his arms draped around her neck.

The Cloud Cat leaped through Vaskalia's door and loped up the road, her shoulder blades moving like pistons. Through her eyes, Luka looked at the broken houses of his village. He saw the geese and the chickens dashing away to hide among the rubble, the profusion of flowers outside the old orphanage and the little gardens set full of plants by the children, the cascades of nasturtium and pink geraniums.

The Cloud Cat turned along a narrow street. Luka saw the wall where his father had crouched, sheltering his son's body, before he was shot himself. Luka saw the chips the bullets had gouged in the stone. He saw the dark red stain.

That was where his father died.

They ran on up the street towards the bakery. The leaf hands of the horse chestnut tree were turning gold. The twigs were hung with round spiny green baubles, like medieval weapons.

The Cloud Cat ran on up to Dimitri's blue door. She stopped and eased the limp body off her shoulders and on to the worn step.

Then, with Luka's exultant spirit in her mind, she loped up out of the village and on to the mountain slopes.

14

FIRE BUS

The animals knew about it first.

In the bakery, the cats ran upstairs, bellies low to the floor.

The dog whimpered and trotted to press herself against Dimitri's legs.

The tortoise sat on the other side of the room with his head pulled into his shell. Big Katrin charged downstairs. She looked at Dimitri and sniffed loudly.

Dimitri sniffed too. Of course. *Fire*.

Big Katrin thought at once of the orphanage. She strode across to the door and opened it. In toppled Luka.

'But the children are back,' cried Dimitri, 'and the homes are nearly finished. *Now* where has he gone?'

Big Katrin shot Dimitri one of her soulful, brown-eyed looks that made him feel as if she saw things he could never imagine.

'I'll take him upstairs,' he said.

Now that the bakery door stood wide open, the smell of burning was strong and there was an awful sobbing sound. Little clouds of smoke, dense and round as the seed heads of wild woodbine, rolled through the air up the narrow street.

Dimitri pounded downstairs again and out into the street.

The smoke clouds turned purple-grey. They came from the southeast, bowling and rolling through the air like smoke signals from a warfire. People were hurrying out of their houses to find out where the fire was, and Jez came running from the orphanage. After him came Eva and some of the older children who would not stay at home.

'Imo is staying with the little ones,' cried Jez, 'but where's Luka?'

'Upstairs on my bed,' said Dimitri. 'But where's Peter? Please don't let him be asleep at the inn. We need buckets and a bus. If Peter isn't here to drive it, then I will.'

'No chance, baker,' grumbled Peter's voice. 'You may be Talking Man but you're not the bus driver. You get the water and I'll get me bus.'

Everyone who could brought buckets of water and loaded them on to the bus. Eva brought the old school bell and rang it as they chugged out of the village to find the fire.

The five-sided house was roaring. Every now and then there was a spurt of lime green among the orange flames, and puffballs of purple smoke as if from a steam train. The donkey was straining at the far end of his tether, sobbing in fear.

'It was 'er pinched all that wood from the square,' bawled Peter, braking as near to the house as he could. 'Let 'er fry, let 'er burn, let 'er barbecue, the greedy witch.'

'Stop it, Peter,' cried Eva, untying the donkey.

'We have to put this fire out, no matter who started it or whose house it is,' said Dimitri. 'Jez? You're the strongest. Get right to the front and we'll pass you the buckets.'

Up roared a jeep, with two soldiers and Captain Lazslo.

'We've got a hose,' he shouted. 'So find us a stream, baker.'

'Find it yourself,' snapped Dimitri, but soon he relented and showed them a stream on the other side of the road.

In the dusk, the flames burned dully, with noxious fumes that did not smell like woodsmoke at all. Eva began to retch, but suddenly cried, 'Where is Simlin? He's not in there, is he?'

'I saw him running up out of the village just now,' said Jez. 'Where's his mother?'

'Vaskalia? Vaskalia, are you in there?' cried Eva. '*Shhh, everyone . . .*'

They stopped passing buckets and listened.

All they could hear were timbers spitting and groaning before they collapsed in showers of dark red sparks, and berries bursting like small grenades.

'Dimitri, what shall we do?'

Dimitri's heart felt as if it was heading down into his boots. Did they really want him to rescue that woman?

He turned and looked into Big Katrin's eyes. He knew for sure that he would lose Katrin's respect if he did not try to rescue someone from a burning house, even someone as disliked and feared as the sorceress who would bring hurt to the village, who had told the traffickers where to find the children and who bad-wished all the people he loved.

Dimitri was not fast enough.

Jez was ahead of him, pushing his way into the burning five-sided house with his arms across his face. He went to the rescue, because he had remembered what had happened on the night of the festival, when Luka had begged him to be merciful to Simlin.

Now he heard Luka's voice in his memory, saying, *It might have been me.*

Horrified, Dimitri watched Jez's tall form flicker and disappear into the inferno. He thought, *That's the last time I'll see Jez alive. What'll I tell Luka when he wakes up?*

'Get that hose on this house,' Dimitri shouted at the soldiers and ran to direct the gush of water from the stream on to the flames. Still the buckets of water came, but every time the fire began to die down as it was quashed, there would be a burst of noxious orange and a loud popping noise, like a rebirth, and then a shape loomed in the red centre.

Dimitri wiped the sweat and soot from his face and blinked, trying to decide what it was. The shape staggered towards the jet of water and stood there, mouth open to catch the water. No. *Two* mouths were open.

Jez was carrying someone.

He set her down in her garden. The plants leaned towards her and one stretched out a tendril to her face but stopped short of touching.

Vaskalia sat hunched over her pestle and mortar. It was still packed full of something, that looked like a pounding of feathers with white fur. The dirt in the seams of her face could not disguise her scowl, even though Jez had saved her from burning to death.

Jez's face and arms were charred and sore, but he was back in the smouldering pile before anyone thought to stop him.

When he came out again he was carrying a small, blackened drum. He sat down on the grass and turned it over and over in his hands, staring at it, and began to cry until Dimitri bustled over to comfort him.

15

INTO THE UNKNOWN WORLD

Simlin roosted in his oak tree in the woods above the village. Leaves drifted down past his face as the tree wished them away. The year was changing fast and so the tree was saving its strength for winter. Simlin shivered in the chill that came with the dark, but also with elation.

Below him, beyond the village, the sky was stained with orange. Even up in his oak tree, he could smell the smoke from burning wood, and from the burning pyre of Mother's concoctions, messes, spells and poundings. *All of it*, thought Simlin, gleefully; her liquids thickening in jars, her bundles of leaves and pieces of animals stored in the corners, the hair-clippings, nail parings, shreds of material and traces of people she desired to harm. Even the pin-sticking dolls swaddled in their mummy bandages burned slowly and thoroughly. Simlin could hear them squeal. He turned the seeing ball lovingly in his hands, giggling because it was safe with him and not growing hot and bursting among the dolls.

He cocked his head to catch the tiny explosions of the firethorn berries he had tucked in among the logs. Simlin swelled with pride so that he thought the one button left on his shirt would burst. *He* had burned down the five-sided house. *He* had made the spell with the firethorn berries after all those years of listening to Mother's spell-chanting. He'd never tried before, never really wanted to practise the old magic. But tonight – yes!

The sounds and words had come so easily to his lips. They were already queuing up in his head, ready for incantation. They were noises he had known all his life.

Drowsily, he heard flapping and hooting around his roosting tree. Ragged rooks swarmed around his head, cawing and croaking, but Simlin was now so very tired that their rook party did not keep him awake. He wrapped his long arms around his knees with the seeing ball in the middle. He felt safe up here.

When he woke again, it was light and there was no cawing or croaking, just hooting all round his head. 'Go away, owls,' he hissed and spat up at them. The owls blinked and disappeared into the tree trunk, and Simlin realised it was daytime.

The sky was grey as the donkey. Simlin gazed out across the treetops. *Orange glow gone now.* A haze of smoke still hovered beyond the village. He polished the seeing ball with his sleeve.

Mother.

Mother sat in the seeing ball. She had a black face. Her eyes bulged with anger in the middle of the ashy grime. Simlin polished the seeing ball again. In his tummy those worms struggled with each other, the worm of disappointment and the worm of relief.

He put his face close to Mother in the seeing ball. Her two arms, two legs, gobstopper eyes were still all there. Her hair was singed on her forehead so that she looked a bit bald. Bald, and very, very, angry. With him. How did she escape? The blind boy wasn't with her. Simlin did not bother to search for him again in the seeing ball. He had decided that Luka would be safe with cakes and pretty women and little girls in the orphanage.

Mother glowered back at Simlin from the glass ball. She made up his mind for him.

Cannot stay near the village now. Take seeing ball and go.

So Simlin set off into a world he did not know.

16

THE LEOPARD LANDSCAPE

The snow leopard hurtled down the mountain-side from crag to icy crag. She was chasing a deer. She landed on a pointed rock, balanced to wait for the perfect moment and then leaped for the kill, clamping her jaws around its neck. She froze again, waiting, her mirrored eyes with no expression. When death was done, she carried the deer, back up to her blue-eyed cubs, who were crying like birds with hunger.

Luka did not know how long he had been here, in this landscape of rocks and snow. It was a leopard landscape. It echoed his Cloud Cat's fur so that in it she was almost invisible. Each day of this secret, remote life had its pattern of hiding, hunting, feeding, sleeping, keeping watch across the mountainside.

After feeding time, after the ripping and chomping and the scent of fresh blood, the Cloud Cat rested on her ledge. Luka could look out into a blue-white world of ice pearl and crystalline snow that gleamed over the mountains.

With full stomachs, the cubs slept in contentment. After this coming winter they would not need to be with their mother all the time, but at the moment she fed them, washed them and played with them too. The cubs reared up to her, meowing and chirruping like fledglings, holding her beautiful face between their enormous round paws. Eyes closed in affection, they butted their small heads against her. She would hold them down gently while she licked them clean. *Mother love*, thought Luka.

When the cubs were independent, she would be a solitary creature again. Except for a short time spent with the male leopard when she mated, she would be on her own, living her unseen life. Luka relished this solitude.

The silence in the mountaintops was overwhelming.

Up here, the world was spread before him. He saw it, with such a special joy. The snow hares were holding a festival of playing and chasing. In the sky the gold-rimmed eagle sailed on the air swells. The river was mercury-cold, edging down the slopes and on to the sea. Somewhere the otter was tumbling in its clear waters.

Luka felt the life force churning, on and on, under this deep hush. He felt it as an invincible current, flowing on, never halted by whatever people did to try to control it. The world could happily exist without people. He decided that he could exist without them, too. Certainly they could live without him now. He had found the shaman's way of helping his village and now it would go from strength to strength, and did not need Luka any more.

The snow leopards lay in their dry cave. A snowstorm began. Quickly, a door of solid grey-white closed over the cave mouth, cutting them off from the rest of the world and shutting out all light. The Cloud Cat would stay here with her cubs until the blizzard lessened. This weather was not strange to her and her perfect coat was made for freezing temperatures. She had buried a cache of goat under some juniper bushes a little way from the cave mouth, but that was only one more meal for the snow cat family. *How long would it take for them to starve?* wondered Luka.

The leopards shut their eyes determinedly and slept.

The blizzard relented. The Cloud Cat padded out to her cache and dragged back the goat meat, still fresh from its mountain fridge. She ripped off a leg for herself and the blue-eyed cubs tore up the rest. They ate, squabbled and slept.

Luka counted two more nights. They were imprisoned by snow. He began to remember often who he was in another life. He missed Aidan, Aidan with no legs and the hair that Imogen said was as yellow as a blackbird's beak. In his head Aidan's fat voice squealed, *Come on then, you with the empty eyes. What about the rest of your story? You have to tell us the end, you know. We're waiting . . .*

Down in the village they would have their midwinter celebrations soon. This year there would be music every night, in the bakery, orphanage or the inn, from Dimitri and Sith and Peter pounding the barrel just as his grandfather had. Big Katrin would be baking cakes every day. On New Year's Eve, the villagers would write their dearest secrets and wishes on paper, then fold them very, very small, and cast them into the fire.

Last New Year, Luka had written that he wanted to find his mother, and he wanted to find the Cloud Cat. He could not see what his pencil had actually written on the paper, but he knew what he hoped it had written there.

And Jez? What would his wish be this time? Luka wanted to know.

The cubs yowled. They scratched at their mother with their paws, wanting her to feed them again. Their ribs were beginning to show, even through their thick fur and although they slept most of the time, they mewed with hunger when they woke.

Luka felt distant from them, almost as if he was hallucinating. Once when he drifted awake, and gazed transfixed into the maelstrom of snowflakes, he had an urge to leave the cave. *Outside*, he begged the Cloud Cat, *Outside please*. Weak though she was, she slunk out of the cave and lay before its mouth. The snow spun as if it turned only around them. It stopped for a while as if it was thinking.

The blizzard rolled away across the mountains like a giant tumbleweed. Over in the east a pale yellow sun rose shimmering into the sky. The steep mountain opposite the snow leopards' cave was wrapped in mist. The sunlight reached out and tore this mist open.

Someone shouted, 'Luka.'

The shout dissolved the cloud and through the Cloud Cat's eyes he saw a man striding along the slope. He shouted out to Luka again, and waved his arm in greeting. Luka thought the tall man was wearing a cloak but the sunlight was so dazzling he could not see clearly.

Now the man swung back his arm and pointed down the mountainside.

'That is enough, reckless boy,' he shouted. 'Go back to your life.'

Then he turned his back on Luka and strode away. His voice echoed around the mountaintops and around Luka's mind.

It's the man with the hair of frost, the shaman from the past.

Yet as he watched the figure turn away, Luka thought it was his father.

The man disappeared. Luka stared across the roof of the world. The sky above them had ice clouds sailing across it so that it looked like another range of mountains and glaciers in the sky. In his head the words echoed: *Go back to your life . . .*

The Cloud Cat stretched and prowled out to hunt for food. Her ears pricked at a sound. She stopped and stood, motionless, her pointed ears flattened in concentration. Just one big front paw lifted oh-so slowly and hovered, ready to launch her forward.

Below them, a goat was scraping back the snow, searching for grass. The Cloud Cat hurtled headlong towards her prey. It took all her strength to drag it back to the cave. The leopards fell on it hungrily.

They slept again, but Luka did not. He kept thinking of his life in the village and of the people he loved: Jez and Imo, Dimitri, Aidan and the orphans, Big Katrin . . . He began to miss them, so much that it hurt. In the end, he was not the Cloud Cat's child.

When the leopards stirred and woke, Luka looked at the cubs for the last time. How beautiful they looked, as charming as if they were toys, with their long tails curled around their small round heads and their furry paws as big as cushions. He thought, *If I ever see them again, they won't be cubs any more, but full-grown snow leopards. Their tummies are full. They'll be safe hidden up here while the Cloud Cat takes me back.*

And off set the Cloud Cat, along the ledge past the juniper bushes and all the way down the mountainside, bounding from rock to ledge, and on again, above the river, dropping down to drink thirstily from the cold water. She slid down the scree, never losing her balance on the shifting moving pavement of stones, and raced across the lower slopes and on through the woods.

They saw no one. By the time the Cloud Cat ran past the bare fruit trees and through the hole in the wall around Luka and Jez's old house, the sky was speckled with stars. In the dark streets the snow leopard glimmered silvery-white. *Ghost cat.*

Through the silent village they padded, round outside the bakery yard. With one bound, the Cloud Cat leaped the wall. The back door stood wide open. Inside the warm bakery there was a rhythmic, rumbling sound from Dimitri, snoring away in his chair with three cats on his knee. The cats woke, bristled as big as porcupines, their green eyes stretched wide in terror, but they dare not move.

The Cloud Cat did not falter. She ran on, into the warm, cinnamon-scented room. She turned and padded up the stairs, as if she was an extraordinary dream. Up and up she ran, into the attic and there was Luka's body lying on the bed.

Luka saw *himself.* So white, his small face veined with mauve, face framed with black curls of hair. So *thin.*

The Cloud Cat stood by the bed. She rested her chin on it awhile. She took a deep breath and purred out towards Luka's body. His spirit left her and hovered between the two bodies, leopard and boy. In this moment, Luka had his last look into the Cloud Cat's wild, otherworld eyes before he lost her.

Now his spirit was back in his own body. Luka listened to the Cloud Cat pad out of the room, down the stairs and out into the yard to leap the wall.

A moment later she yowled to him twice from the fruit trees, calling her *Goodbye*.

17

A WAY OUT OF THE VILLAGE

Luka's body lay on his bed in the attic all the time his spirit had been away with the Cloud Cat.

Big Katrin fed him three times a day with warm broth and sieved jam, tipping drops into his mouth with a small spoon and holding his wrist to feel if his slow pulse changed.

And Jez? He was terrified. When he had rescued Vaskalia from the fire, she had been snarling, 'That fiend, that snow leopard, it leaped right over me into the night,' and Jez's heart sank for he was sure the leopard had taken Luka with it. Every spare minute, he sat by Luka's bedside.

The last morning as he sat there after the bread was in the oven, Luka sat up. He yawned, stretched up his arms and said, 'Oh, hello, Jez.'

'Hello YOU!' shouted Jez and threw himself forwards on to his brother, squeezing him so tightly that Luka cried, 'Hey, you're hurting me. *Geddoff.*'

'I've been here for the past three weeks, you little

horror,' cried Jez. 'I knew you were with the snow leopard. I knew that's where you'd gone. I wanted you *back*.'

'Sorry if I worried you,' mumbled Luka.

'I tramped *miles* in the snow, looking for that flippin' leopard, calling and calling. One day I even picked up Dimitri's shotgun. But I knew if I hit the leopard, I would hurt you too.'

Feet clopped and pounded up the stairs, and a second later Dimitri and Big Katrin joined in the cuddling. Big Katrin felt Luka's pulse. It was quicker again. She had been so frightened. She knew he was the gifted shaman boy, but even so, he was small and young and had risked his life and health too often. This time she had feared that he might stay forever with the Cloud Cat.

Dimitri gabbled all the news: 'Katrin fed you three times a day with broth and jam. She put it through a sieve first so you wouldn't choke on the cherries. Jez has been in a right state, wouldn't talk about you, even to Imogen. They've nearly finished building the new children's homes; Ribi has had a baby girl; we've planned a party to welcome you back, Luka, and to greet the baby too.'

Luka heard the dog's nails clicking on the

461

floorboards.

'Oh, and the dog is pregnant,' said Dimitri.

'Yes. It was the young grey wolf,' said Luka. 'But what happened to *her*?'

'Your brother rescued her.' Dimitri's voice was gruff, but Luka heard a note of pride in it. 'He's a fool, but he's a brave fool. He's a hero. Vaskalia's house burned down to a spill of ashes, but they built her a shelter for the winter. Imogen keeps taking trays of food and leaving them by the door – typical Imo.'

'And what about Simlin?'

'We haven't seen him for awhile,' said Jez. 'He's probably on a roof somewhere.'

'I don't know what Vaskalia will do without him to torment,' said Dimitri. 'Now then, my dear Luka, you are going to eat the best breakfast ever. Katrin has a new line in baking. I've named them her pastry nests. Some have apricots in the middle, some black cherries, some have marzipan. Will you sample them for us?'

'I'll just try the cherry one today,' said Luka. 'Maybe the others tomorrow.'

Jez said, 'When you're stronger we'll take you to see the children. They keep coming round to see if you're back.' Jez stood and stretched his arms above his head. Things were good. He no longer felt as if he was wearing that heavy belt with the leaden charms all around his middle, bringing him down. He had his Imogen, his carving, and now he had his brother back.

It was another three days before Big Katrin allowed Luka out of the bakery. This last long change had weakened him more than any of the other spirit shifts. He kept sweating and shivering. For those three hazy days he lounged around, daydreaming, luxuriating in the familiar sounds and smells all around him. The dog lay heavily across his feet and the cats darted on and off his knee.

'Have you still got Alfonso the tortoise?' he asked.

'He's fast asleep in a box of leaves,' said Dimitri. 'He got slower and slower and wouldn't come out of his shell at all. One evening I saw him eyeing up the oven . . . so it was into a box and into the woodshed for his winter sleep. Now, Luka . . . Katrin thinks you'll be well enough to see your friends tomorrow. She's given you the all clear.'

Luka woke early, washed and dressed and waited impatiently for Jez to finish baking.

'This isn't the way,' he complained as Jez steered

him right at the top of their street instead of left.

'It's the way to the new homes,' said Jez. 'Imogen has moved the children in just in time before the winter. If it's as bad as the last winter, the old orphanage just would not last. The roof would cave in as soon as it snowed.'

There was a warm tiled porch at the new home, not a draughty stone one. Jez took Luka into a room to the left. It smelled of fresh wood and polish, not blocked drains and damp.

'Hello?' shouted Luka and his voice echoed in an empty space. He heard a whisper, '*Hide it, NOW,*' and then back around him came their voices, shouting, 'Hello Luka, Hello.' Their feet drummed on the wooden floor as they charged towards him, and there was another sound that Luka did not know. A mixture of humming and swishing, almost too faint to hear.

'There's not very much furniture here yet,' said Lisa, grabbing his hand, 'that's why it echoes. But there's a big comfy chair just for you.' She pushed him back into it and Luka, nervous in this unknown space, was glad she had done so.

'Mmmm,' said Luka, stroking the chair's padded arm. 'Is this the story chair? It feels great.'

'It is. But you're too early, Luka,' rang out an imperious voice. 'We're not ready for you.'

'Aidan, if Luka wants to tell the story now, then let him,' said Imogen. 'Luka, we're all so glad you're back with us.'

'Oh go on then, tell it now,' huffed Aidan, 'and then I'll take you out.'

'Story. STORY. *STORY*,' they chanted, thumping the floor. So Luka told them about the ivy tree, and drumming up the Cloud Cat, travelling to the mountains, the blue-eyed cubs in the cave and of running upstairs while Dimitri slept. He missed out big parts of the story. He did not tell the children about being underground in the shifting earth, or about finding himself in Vaskalia's house, being tied to the chair and hearing her spell-making. It would frighten some of them too much.

Neither did he speak of his father.

At the end of the story, when Luka told of hearing the Cloud Cat call her goodbyes, his lip trembled and he burst into tears. His put his head down as he wept, but at once his hands were held and stroked.

'Don't cry, Luka,' said Lisa. 'You can go and see her again can't you?'

Luka raised his head to look at them and his eyes blazed. The children gasped and Lisa gave a little scream as Luka's eyes turned gold and burned with the wildness of the Cloud Cat's world.

Then she was gone. Luka's eyes were his own sightless ones again.

Lisa pleaded, 'Please stay with us for now, Luka.'

'Heeyo, Loooo-ka! Here is for you,' grunted a voice Luka did not recognise. Someone pushed a soft toy into his hands. Luka ran his hands over it and felt a teddy bear with a soggy ear.

'Is that you, Stefan? Are you up walking on two legs now?' he cried.

'YES! I not on the floor. I walking, VERY fast.'

'And so, Luka, am I.' Aidan's voice was quivering with pride. 'You others had better finish what you were doing while *I* give Luka a special guided tour.'

'Just you be careful with him now, Aidan,' warned Jez. 'Hadn't I better come with you?'

'No, Big Brother. Stop trying to control us. But, er – would you lift Luka on?'

'Move over, then, porker,' teased Jez. Luka felt himself lifted and put down on a seat next to Aidan.

'Luka. Welcome to my Ferrari. Ready, Steady ZOOM,' squealed Aidan and they were off, whizzing across the room and out down a ramp and into the street.

'It's my new toy,' screamed Aidan. 'The fastest wheelchair in the world. Imogen gets so worried because she can't catch up with me. Sit tight, Luka, and hold on.'

They rushed on, with Aidan roaring *Brrrm Brrrm* and the air whizzed past Luka's face and he giggled so much he thought he might wet himself. 'Stop, Aidan, stop,' he begged but they were trundling down a hilly street. The scent of baking was in the air, and the peppery damp of autumn.

'The wheelchair makes me free, Luka,' cried Aidan. 'Are you enjoying yourself?'

'Not half,' said Luka. 'We're out of the village now, aren't we? No buildings around. We could go all the way to the sea, Aidan. You didn't go there last time, did you?'

'No, but we'd have to take a picnic.'

'Aidan,' Luka squeezed his arm, tightly. 'Stop. I can hear . . .'

'What is it?' cried Aidan, braking.

'Let's wait . . . I feel sick . . . Vaskalia is near,' he whispered. 'I don't want any more struggles with her. I can smell old fire. I suppose that's the ashes

467

of the five-sided house. I can hear her snipping in her garden.'

'It's all right . . . we'll go behind this wall,' whispered Aidan. 'She's tearing up plants. Or what's left of them, and she's dropping berries and flowers into a bag. Hey . . . here's Captain Lazslo. He's leading a donkey. They're fighting.'

'Come . . . ON,' Captain Lazslo's sugary voice had a hard edge in it Luka had not heard before. There was scuffling and spitting, and shrieks of 'Untie me, get me off,' with swearing and curses so demonic that even Aidan gasped in shock.

The hooves of the donkey stamped on the road. Vaskalia's feet pounded his flanks so hard that he brayed his anguish. Captain Lazslo shouted, 'We must leave this cursed village, Vaskalia. We'll make a new life over the sea.'

'No. I've never been this way before,' she wailed. 'There is something in the way that keeps me in the village. Get me off this animal *now*.'

'Come on, Vaskalia,' wheedled Lazslo. 'You'll be a new-age healer, a magic woman, a plants woman, a celebrity. You'll get rich. Trust me . . .'

'Yes, get out you evil bag, we hate you,' said Aidan, but just not loud enough for anyone but Luka to hear.

There came a mighty *wallop*. The donkey brayed like a banshee and set off down the road at its fastest trot with Vaskalia's bottom smacking loudly up and down and her shrieking, 'Owwee.' Her scream stretched out behind her like a lurid scarlet scarf.

Luka perched by Aidan in the wheelchair, straining to hear those sounds go on down the road away from them, leaving at last a restless silence.

'Maybe we won't go to the sea today,' said Luka.

'Maybe we won't. Now . . . let me show you how I turn this thing around.'

18

THE SHAMAN'S CLOAK

When they arrived back, Eva was polishing a table with beeswax. Luka ran his palm over the cool, smooth wood.

'I bet I know who carved this,' he said. 'You'll be as good as great-grandfather, Jez.'

'We needed a really big table to meet around,' said Jez. 'Especially when Katrin brings us all these pastries . . .'

'Wait,' commanded Aidan. 'We must have the presentation before the golden flakies. Sit Luka in that chair again. No. On second thoughts, stand him in the middle of the room . . .'

'Have you quite finished bossing everyone around, Aidan?' cried Lisa.

'For now,' said Aidan. Luka felt Stefan's soggy little hand sneak into his and he let himself be led into the middle of the room. He waited. He heard fussing and giggling and then a breath taken in before a fanfare of children's voices *TA-DA!*

On his shoulders was set the softest cloak ever. It reached down to the floor. Luka stroked the different velvets, silks and wool of its diamond shapes. It felt as if he was wrapped in friendship.

'It's all the colours you could ever think of, Luka, all the colours of trees and birds and grass and fields.'

'And flowers and butterflies and earth . . .'

'And skies and clouds and water too. We chose the earth colours and sewed them together. Well, Eva did help a little bit.'

'It's the perfect cloak for our shaman boy,' said Dimitri. 'This one, here, is dappled dark and white, like your snow leopard.'

'Thank you,' said Luka the shaman boy.

'And now that's all over,' announced Aidan, 'let's get to the pastries,' and he whizzed towards the table to grab a flaky full of glazed apricots.

Those nights of late autumn were cold. Luka slept with his shaman's cloak over the top of his bed. Sometimes the dog was there too, sometimes the occasional cat, unless Katrin found them and chased them outside.

Luka sometimes woke abruptly, hearing Vaskalia screaming in his mind. There was rage in her scream, and pain too. Luka shivered until he persuaded himself that she really was gone from the village. Then he thought of the Cloud Cat, until he drifted back into sleep while the autumn gales began to rise and flow over the skylight in the roof.

From his perch halfway up a pine tree, further towards the mountains, Simlin muttered, 'Stop doing it, wind,' at the swaying branches. The gale made a sound in them that was like that metal-coloured water at the other end of the land and threw the little crossbill birds around in the branches.

Simlin could not sleep, even with plugs of moss in his ears, so he dropped down to the forest floor and sat with his back against the tree trunk and his thin legs stretched straight out. His toes were blue again. *Need shoes. Want boots like Jez.*

When the grey light of dawn seeped down to him, Simlin felt twitchy. A big spider ran out from the leaves on angled legs with little brown kneecaps. It looked at Simlin and abseiled up the tree trunk on a rope of silk. Simlin watched it disappear and wondered if he should have eaten it. No. A spider was rather like a scorpion, except for the stinging tail. Better find more brambles instead.

He sighed. Consulted the seeing ball.

Mother was in there.

But she wasn't in there now. It was a re-wind from earlier, Simlin could tell by the way the edges of the picture were wavy and melting. The man with the pink lollipop face was in there, too, tying mother up on to the donkey. He was saying 'Come *on*, Vaskalia. We have to catch that boat.'

The man fastened Mother's arms and legs to the saddle with orange onion string. He swung his arm back to wallop the donkey's bottom so that it brayed and bared its yellow teeth and off it rocked at a rickety donkey gallop down the road, with Mother lurching about like a sack of potatoes and the lollipop-faced man running after her, waving his arms to make the donkey go, all the way down to that metal-coloured sea.

The picture faded.

Another one took its place, much sharper. This picture was happening *now*.

Mother's face loomed huge and near, then far away, near and far again, with the black hole of her mouth in the middle. She was hollering. She was ill. And there was a crashing booming noise. *Water*. Big water. Mother was on a boat. Mother's face was green as a bean. And then – eee-ur-yuk! Mother was very very pukey sick.

Simlin saw a commotion up in the air. It was the Bone Cracker, clinging by its big feet on to a tall stick, a mast, high up there, swaying about in the wind and flapping. So Bone Cracker was going over the sea too.

Yipyipsnort. Bye bye. Mother has gone away without me.

Simlin laughed and chortled. He glanced into the seeing ball again. It was crashing and booming in there and the mast swung right across like a clock's pendulum, with Bone Cracker clinging on still. Then the mast was gone. The boat was gone too. Simlin blinked. The sea surged up and made a high sharp wall, jade green. It crashed down again. The waves flounced white. Simlin looked for the boat. He could not see it.

Simlin tried out a little gurgle of laughter. Then he wept. He wept on until a shaft of weak sunlight shone through the trees on to his leafy place. He shifted until the light was on his face. His face dried.

He stood up, brushed the leafy bits from his legs and set off through the forest back to the village.

Maybe that Eva lady would let him sit in a corner

of the new home, if he did not whisper names at people and run after the girls. Maybe he could help with the cooking now?

They might let him stay.

19

LUKA'S SONG

'There's going to be good music tonight,' announced Dimitri, spinning a plate on his index finger. 'We've plenty to be pleased about. Help me get this table back to the wall, Jez. Ah. Here's Sith, and Ribi too, with their beautiful daughter.'

Everyone wanted to hold the baby, especially Big Katrin and Luka.

'What's she called?' asked Luka, sniffing the baby's sweet-skinned forehead. He had never smelled anything like it before.

'She's called Kyria,' said Ribi. 'She's our wonderful baby girl. It's good to see you again, Luka. I know you needed your time alone, but everyone missed you so much. The village needs celebrations. It needs joy.'

When everyone had settled, Sith and Dimitri played. There was banging on the blue door, and Peter turned up with his knocking stones to drum for some dancing. Big Katrin would not let him drum on her big table. She made him play on a flour barrel instead. 'I'm going to play something just for you, Luka,' said Dimitri. 'It's Luka's Song.'

Luka's Song

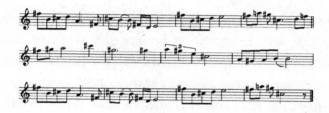

When he had finished playing this beautiful music, Dimitri put his fiddle and bow down on the table and said, 'I can't carve stone or paint pictures, but I can make music. And that music says what you mean to us all, Luka.'

'Go on, Dimitri,' cried Jez. 'Tell everyone what you told me this morning. Because if you don't, I will.'

Dimitri cleared his throat. Even so, his voice still had a catch in it when he said, 'Hold out your hand to show everyone your ring, please, Katrin. I am the happiest man alive because she has accepted this ring from me. The wedding will be on the first day of spring. Katrin wants to make the cake and ice it too.'

Winter began in earnest. Overnight snow fell and changed the world into an unknown place. Dimitri persuaded Jez to deliver the bread on foot because he feared that his van would get stuck in the drifts.

Big Katrin set herself to make jam. She filled armies of jars with apple and blackberry jam and cooked dark cherries and raspberries to try out a new flavour. She put a saucer of jam on the table to cool. Luka ran his finger lightly across it and felt it wrinkle as the jam set. He tasted it and cried, 'Delicious.'

He heard her washing more fruit and piling it into the jam pan to simmer.

'Wow, even more?' he said. 'I don't know the smell of this lot.'

Katrin put a fruit in his hand. It was small, smooth, with a stone in the middle and it had a plum scent.

'It's a damson. It's purpley-blue,' she said.

Luka sat for a while before he realised what he had just heard.

The next night, after an early supper, Luka lay around yawning but felt too sleepy to go upstairs to bed. The dog leaned heavy and warm against his legs. Dimitri put on his greatcoat and boots.

'Give me a hand to fetch in more wood, Jez,' he called.

Luka heard the door close behind the two men. They took time throwing logs into the wheelbarrow and then trundled it inside again, stamping the snow off their boots. Jez tipped up the barrow, spilling the wood on to the floor to dry by the ovens.

Dimitri puffed his way back to bolt the door. He warned, 'The sky is clear and crackling with stars. It will freeze hard tonight.'

He built up the fires in the oven.

Luka sat up straight, wide awake, convinced he had heard a footfall out in the yard. The dog staggered to her feet and padded to the door. Luka felt a draught. The dog was wagging her tail.

There was one faint knock on the door.

'Wait. You never know who's out there,' warned Dimitri.

'But the dog is happy, whoever it is,' cried Luka.

He heard Dimitri ease back the bolts. As the door swung slowly open, a ridge of snow fell in on to the floor.

The light from the bakery shone out on a small figure, hooded with scarves. As the figure lifted its face to look up at them, the hood fell back.

Jez gasped. The woman's face was translucent pale, just like Luka's, framed with tendrils of black hair. Her eyes were silver.

Jez took her hand and she stepped into the warmth of the bakery and Luka ran joyfully towards her with his arms outstretched.

He did not need his sight to know who had come back to them.

THE END

'Time to find out if you are a magician!'
said Gwyn's grandmother . . .
'Time to remember your ancestors:
Math, Lord of Gwynedd, Gwydion and Gilfaethwy!'

On his ninth birthday
Gwyn is given a brooch
and told to cast it into
the wind. High on the
mountainside, Gwyn
hurls the brooch into
the air and waits . . .
It is only later that
Gwyn discovers
the wind has sent
something back:
the snow spider.

So begins Jenny Nimmo's award-winning trilogy,
a story of Gwyn's extraordinary battle against evil,
of worlds glittering with snow and ice.

WINNER OF THE SMARTIES GRAND PRIX

www.jennynimmo.me.uk
www.egmont.co.uk

KENSUKE'S KINGDOM

WINNER OF THE CHILDREN'S BOOK AWARD.

I heard the wind above me in the sails. I remember thinking, this is silly, you haven't got your safety harness on, you haven't got your lifejacket on. You shouldn't be doing this . . . I was in the cold of the sea before I could even open my mouth to scream.

Washed up on an island in the Pacific, Michael struggles to survive on his own. With no food and no water, he curls up to die. When he wakes, there is a plate beside him of fish, of fruit, and a bowl of fresh water. He is not alone . . .

www.michaelmorpurgo.org
www.egmont.co.uk